Praise for IN TH

"This is a harrowing journey of s   ....o the indomitable spirit of one lone man as he spirals deeper and deeper within the Holocaust—while also recognizing what it takes, minute by minute and day by day, to survive decades into the future. This painful yet beautifully written novel adds to the necessary literature of the Holocaust. Hicks is determined to undo the erasures of time while revealing our humanity with a clear-eyed lens. This is what the art of the novel was invented to do."

—**Brian Turner,** author of *My Life as a Foreign Country* and *Here, Bullet*

"Patrick Hicks has managed to bring two of history's greatest events down to the molecular level in the extraordinary character of Eli Hessel, a survivor of the Holocaust and a member of the vast team of scientists that put a man on the moon. This story is gripping in its tragedy, thrilling in its detail, and unforgettable for its protagonist, whose will to not only survive, but thrive, live, and love is a testament to the human spirit. *In the Shadow of Dora* is tenacious, just like its hero. I'll never forget it."

—**Peter Geye**, author of *Northernmost* and *Wintering*

"In the Shadow of Dora is an astonishing novel. With a poet's eye and meticulously lyric prose, Patrick Hicks unspools a harrowing tale that begins in a Nazi concentration camp and ends on the Apollo 11 launch pad. It is between these two extremes—the most base of the basest of evils and the highest of all human achievements—that Eli's story unfolds. Hicks' novel is fundamentally a narrative of inquiry and self-interrogation: Is the past what defines us? Does the future redeem us? How can you know if you're dead? This is a profoundly moving book."

—**Jill Alexander Essbaum,** *New York Times* bestselling author of *Hausfrau*

"Spanning decades and continents, *In the Shadow of Dora* reveals in aching detail the heights of human ingenuity and the depths of human cruelty, and, most importantly, the ways those heights and depths are inextricably intertwined in the history of the twentieth century. This is a revelatory novel."

—**Joe Wilkins,** author of *Fall Back Down When I Die* and *The Mountain and the Fathers*

"In this compelling novel based on historical facts, Patrick Hicks places America's glittering quest to land on the moon squarely inside the dark shadow of the Holocaust. Few novels I have read so effectively and disturbingly question the relationship between the triumph of technological achievement and our willingness to ignore injustice."

—**Kent Meyers,** author of *The Work of Wolves* and *Twisted Tree*

Previous Praise for Patrick Hicks

"This is a vividly detailed, terrifying, convincing, and completely spell-binding story rooted in those murderous events we now call the Holocaust. [...] Patrick Hicks has accomplished a very difficult literary task. He has given a believable and fresh and original face to barbarism. What a fine book this is."

—Tim O'Brien, author of *The Things They Carried,*
Winner of the National Book Award

"In *The Commandant of Lubizec,* Patrick Hicks imagines the unimaginable and thus gives us a glimpse into the terrible complexity of the human heart. This is a fascinating and important book."

—Robert Olen Butler
Winner of the Pulitzer Prize

"Hicks' prose is clear and unflinching [...] Thought-provoking and gut-wrenchingly powerful."

—*Kirkus Reviews*

"The fictional presentation in *The Commandant of Lubizec* measures up to any factual account of the Holocaust this reviewer has ever read. Highly recommended, especially for general readers who wish to know more about this unspeakable chapter of human history. Even specialists will be taken in by its human-interest dimension."

—*Library Journal*

"The stories in *The Collector of Names* haunt me the way that Joyce's 'The Dead' haunts me. And for the same reason: the precision of the evocation of our mortality, set against the different music of our lives."

—Bruce Weigl, author of *Song of Napalm,*
Winner of the Lanan Literary Award

OTHER BOOKS BY PATRICK HICKS

Fiction
The Collector of Names
The Commandant of Lubizec

Poetry
Library of the Mind
Adoptable
This London
A Harvest of Words (editor)
Finding the Gossamer
The Kiss That Saved My Life
Draglines
Traveling Through History

IN THE SHADOW OF DORA

A Novel of the Holocaust and the Apollo Program

PATRICK HICKS

STEPHEN F. AUSTIN STATE UNIVERSITY PRESS

Please address correspondence to
Permissions: Stephen F. Austin State University Press
sfapress@sfasu.edu

Portions of this novel were published in slightly different forms in *Guernica* and *The Wrath-Bearing Tree*. Chapter four, "The Vengeance Weapon," was a finalist for the Steinberg Essay Prize with *Fourth Genre*.

ISBN: 978-1-62288-907-5
Cover art: Tristan Brewster
Managing Editor: Kimberly Verhines
Editorial Assistant: Jerri Bourrous

for the victims

PART I

"The rocket will free man from his remaining chains,
the chains of gravity which still tie him to this planet.
It will open to him the gates of heaven."

—Wernher von Braun

INTO THE TUNNEL

He was tired and cold when he arrived from Auschwitz. The moon hung above him, battered and beaten, as he trudged down a long concrete road with thousands of other men. The train that had carried him across Germany huffed in the night. A whistle pierced the frosty air—it was a single note, strangled into silence. The huffing engine took on water as he licked his dry lips. He tried to swallow. Searchlights paced the dark as dogs strained against their leashes, their front paws wheeling the air. Guards stood along the road and yelled at the prisoners to move faster, faster. Behind him, bodies were tossed from the railcars. They hit the pebbly ground in sickening hard thuds. Stones skittered away.

Eli glanced at the moon. It looked like it had been pistol-whipped. It hung in the sky, wounded.

"Move it, you pieces of SHIT!"

Another voice chimed in. "March in unison! Your left…your left…your left."

He had no idea where he was or where he was going. The shadowy bulk of a hill was on his right and, in the bright moonlight, he could see a haze of pine trees lining its ridge. To his left were strange metal cylinders with nozzles on them. They were stacked on flatbed rail cars.

The men kept moving, trudging, schlepping. Their wooden clogs clacked against the concrete road. Dogs continued to snap and bark. There was the smell of wet fur, and there was something else too, a smell he couldn't quite place. It was a mixture of coal and creosote. There was also—he breathed deeply—the smell of decaying bodies. Yes, he noticed it crawling down his throat now. The stink of rotting meat and grapefruit, that's what a corpse smelled like. Over the past few months he had grown familiar with that smell, that reek.

But where was he?

The journey from Auschwitz had been hard. They'd been stuffed into wooden cattle cars and, as they rocked and clattered over hundreds of miles of tracks, men had to relieve themselves where they stood. They were crammed in cheek by jowl, and the weakest often slipped to the floor. There, in pools of urine and excrement, they rarely stood up again.

Eli stumbled. He was woozy, his lips were chapped, and his tongue was a leather strap. It hurt to swallow. Worst of all, on his lower back, at that place where the spine meets the pelvic girdle, he had a large bruise. A hobnail boot had kicked him into the cattle car a few days ago when they left Auschwitz, and although he couldn't see it, he knew it must look like a horseshoe with studded dots. Whenever he twisted at the waist, a sharp firework of pain sizzled up his spine. He worried one of his vertebrae had been shattered, but there was nothing he could do about it. He had to walk faster. Faster. He wobbled, and willed himself forward. He squinted in concentration and tried to stay at the front of the line because, behind him, prisoners were being beaten with metal rods. The concrete road beneath his clogs was splashed with oil. Or maybe it was blood? It was hard to tell at night.

"You rags, you pieces of SHIT! Your left…your left…your left. March in unison!"

He ignored the nipping pain in his stomach and watched his feet move beneath him. The blue and white stripes of his trouser legs swung in and out of view. He wondered where they were being taken. A gas chamber maybe? He'd seen such things happen at Auschwitz many times before. He'd seen whole families walk down a gravel path and he'd seen the black tar of their burning bodies rumble up from the crematoria. Flames shot out from the chimney and the whole sky above Auschwitz was stained a dull orange during the night. The heat from thousands and thousands of bodies made the moon shimmer as if it were underwater.

He focused on his swinging legs and didn't think about his mother or father, his younger brother, his grandparents. They were gone. They had been turned into ash long ago. And yet, somehow, he was still alive.

"Faster, you sons of bitches!" a guard yelled. He used a cigarette lighter to look at his wristwatch. "We don't have all night."

A dog attacked a prisoner behind Eli. He didn't stop to help the man, not even when he heard the powerful jaws sink into the man's buttock.

The prisoner cried out in pain but the growling dog refused to let go. It was dragged behind as the man continued to march forward, forward, ever forward. The dog's nails scratched against the road. An SS officer—tall, lean, a pinched face—pushed Eli out of the way and began hitting the man with a metal rod. It sounded like a rug being smacked clean of dirt. As they marched on, the cries from the man were like little waves washing out to sea. Soon, all Eli could hear was the sound of wooden clogs clomping against the road.

Maybe he could run away?

Barbed wire was on either side of him and there was a guard tower illuminated beneath a searchlight up ahead. No doubt the fence was electrified. And no doubt plenty of machine guns bristled all around. To run would mean—what, exactly? All of Germany was a concentration camp.

"Move it you useless eaters, you pieces of *SHIT!*"

The guard was from Berlin. Eli could tell from his accent. How could he be so angry and so full of venom? What filled the Nazis with so much hate? While he was thinking this, something surprising and alarming appeared up ahead.

The rail tracks gently curved into a mountain. There was a tunnel. Two massive sodium lights sparkled overhead like twin stars and they cast long eerie shadows on the ground. A cloud of moths jittered in the lights and for several long moments he wondered what they might taste like. Dusty, he thought. He imagined a bit of wing stuck between his molars.

When it became obvious they were going into the tunnel, Eli looked around in wild terror for a chimney or a vent. Were the gas chambers inside this underground place? Where were they being taken? And why? His muscles tensed and he almost stopped walking. He had to will his legs to keep on moving even though he was afraid of what waited ahead.

Calm down, he told himself. Calm yourself. It didn't make sense to ship everyone halfway across Germany only to kill them all. The Nazis could have done that easily enough in Auschwitz.

"All is well," he whispered to himself. "All is well."

But the claws of fear continued to scratch the inside of his skull. His asshole tightened and his eyes darted to the left, to the right, to the left again, looking for clues. If this *was* a work camp, where were the other prisoners? Where were their barracks and huts?

The moon was swallowed by a cloud and this made the dark beyond the searchlights absolute. The moon had been snuffed out, choked. Two enormous iron gates on either side of the tunnel were wide open, and camouflage netting was strung above the entrance like an awning. A white wooden sign was suspended from the ceiling and someone had taken the time to get the calligraphy just right.

Alles für den Krieg
Alles für den Sieg

ELI LOOKED AROUND. It was understood that German was the only language that mattered in the Reich. If a prisoner was confused or didn't understand something that was shouted at him, well then, he would learn soon enough how to speak the language of the master race.

When they entered the tunnel, a dampness fell over his skin. It was like a wet cloak had been placed over his shoulders. He began to shiver. And somewhere up ahead, metal banged against metal—it was deep and rhythmic—double-syllabled—*bah-wung—bah-wung—bah-wung*. A floodlight cast grotesque shadows against the wall and there was the low hum of a generator somewhere in the distance. He looked around and realized that everything must have been hewn out of the rock by hand. The floor. The walls. The curved ceiling. How many prisoners had died making this cave? Is *this* why he was here? To dig? To die?

They passed a cluster of SS guards who stood around laughing at some joke. They smoked and paid no attention to the column of prisoners who shuffled past. Bright balls of orange glowed at the ends of their cigarettes and, as they pushed each other playfully, they talked about roasting a wild boar. For a delicious moment, Eli allowed himself to imagine what it might taste like. The fibrous meat, the juices, the sucking of marrow from bone.

"Keep moving!" someone shouted from the rear. It was a French accent, which surprised him.

Steel pipes were bolted to the wall and he wondered what they were for. Vents for a gas chamber maybe? No, no, that made no sense. What if there was a leak? When he looked up at the rounded ceiling he felt claustrophobia run though his chest like spiders. What if the ceiling collapsed? How many thousands of tons of rock were above him? Eli looked for support columns or beams but didn't see any. The air around him was thick and oppressive. It crowded his lungs.

He looked down at his wooden clogs. They were badly stained from the mud of Auschwitz and he counted his steps in order to control his fear.

One…two…three…four…

All is well, he told himself. Yes, all is well.

When he looked up, he saw a winch and two long dangling chains. The rhythmic banging got louder. *Bah-WUNG. Bah-WUNG. Bah-WUNG.* There were hundreds of prisoners working in the tunnel up ahead. They were dressed in blue and white striped uniforms, just like him. The light was weak and this made the underground world feel sunken and submerged. What were they doing? Mining for gold?

As he got closer, he realized they were hunched over tables and assembling gearboxes. Others worked on metal tanks. Down a side tunnel, a group of prisoners carried a huge nozzle the size of a church bell.

"Drop it and you get twenty lashes!" a voice roared out.

It was a kapo. He was a man, usually a criminal, who was given extra food if he agreed to do the dirty work of the Nazis. In exchange for beating his fellow prisoners, he got a good night's sleep and a full belly. Sometimes, he was even given chocolate or fruit.

What happened next happened very fast. The nozzle suddenly teetered sideways, the metal cone slipped, and when it bounced onto the ground— sending out a low ringing sound—the kapo immediately began hammering a prisoner with a stick. The blows rained down hard, and bloody stains formed on the man's back.

"Be gentle with that!" the kapo shouted. "Gentle! Gentle! Gentle!"

An SS officer watched all of this in bored curiosity. He had a long face and, in the weeks to come, he would turn out to be a source of strange new pain for Eli. On this particular occasion though, he simply lit a cigarette and stood back with crossed arms. A deep inhale. Cherry glow. Smoke vented from his nose. Eli studied this man's clean face, his manicured hands, his trim build, and he couldn't help but notice the high polish of the man's jackboots. They twinkled in a perfection of night. He had probably showered recently and he was no doubt well fed. Eli turned away from this guard and looked once again at his clogs. He knew better than to look the SS in the eye. The rules of Auschwitz must surely apply in this place too.

"Fresh rags," another SS guard yelled out. "Welcome."

As they marched deeper into the tunnel, Eli saw that many of the prisoners didn't have shoes at all. Their feet were bloody and caked with grime. He also became aware of the overpowering smells around him: diesel, the sulfurous burn of arc welding, and there was something else, something he recognized from the factory at Auschwitz. Beneath his clogs were little pools of water and he wondered if he could bend down and cup some into his hands. Could he do it quickly? Would he be noticed?

All around him were the scrapping of spades against wet rubble. The floodlights of the tunnel gave way to carbide lamps. Soon everything flickered and it was hard to see. He stumbled over a thick cable and tripped. Others were having trouble too.

When they rounded a corner, he decided to chance it. Eli bent down for a handful of water. It was beautiful and wet and primal against his skin, but when it passed over the dry seal of his lips he spat it out. It tasted of urine.

A moment later, they were ordered to a halt.

The sound of hundreds of clogs coming to a stop filled up the tunnel. It was like horses clattering to a standstill. At first, Eli couldn't tell what he was looking at. He squinted and waited for his eyes to adjust. A skirt of light fanned onto—he wasn't sure. There, in a long line, were giant metal tubes that looked like torpedoes. Each one was two stories high and they had a nozzle on the end. Maybe these torpedoes had been built for some kind of secret submarine? Maybe they could be loaded onto a massive U-Boat and sent across the Atlantic to attack New York or Boston? Maybe Hitler was taking the fight directly to the Americans?

A voice yelled out from the edge of the light.

"*Mützen…ab!*"

Eli and the others immediately took off their caps and slapped them against the seam of their trousers. They stood at stiff attention.

There was a long pause and, during this silence, Eli felt a sneeze coming on. He wriggled his nose in the hopes of fighting it off. He once saw a prisoner get hit in the face with a crowbar just for sneezing. It killed the man instantly, and he fell to the ground like a sack of wheat. The tingling continued, so Eli held his breath. He willed the bright itch in his nasal cavity to go away, he curled his toes inside his clogs—he focused on that part of his body—and, slowly, the sneeze evaporated into memory.

A man in a business suit appeared. He wore a white smock and, even from this distance, Eli could see the spark of a Nazi pin on his lapel. Off to the side was the SS officer with a long face, the one he'd seen a few minutes before, the one with perfectly shined jackboots. He smoked a fresh cigarette with one hand and held a pistol in the other.

"You're in it now," a kapo yelled. He opened his arms like a friendly entertainer and his voice brightened. "Welcome to Takt Strasse."

Eli had grown up in Berlin and he knew that a *takt* was a little baton used by orchestra conductors. The kapo, who had the green triangle of a criminal stitched onto his striped uniform, pulled out a wooden club from behind a metal cabinet. He lifted it into the air and said, "On Takt Strasse, I keep time on your heads if you do not move quickly enough. Do you understand, my assholes?"

With both hands, he brought the club down onto an imaginary head. A pause and then, "In this place we build *rockets*. Yes, we create machines the Americans and the British cannot even imagine. You are looking at the future, my assholes. Our superior technology is going to win this war."

Eli looked at the torpedoes and nodded. Ah, he nearly said aloud. He understood now. These things weren't designed to fly through water; they were designed to fly through air. He blinked at the realization of what surrounded him. Each one of these rockets could kill...how many?

"You are enemies of the Reich, and in this kingdom beneath the mountain you *will* work to destroy your own countries. Do you understand?" There was a smile on the fat face of the kapo. "In this place you will build wonder weapons the likes of which the world has never seen." He paced and moved the club like a scythe. "This is your last home, my assholes. The only way out of this camp is through the chimney."

Eli nodded at his new reality. In Auschwitz, after his family had been sent into the sky, he had come to understand what such speeches meant. In this place called Dora, death would be a way of life. There would be death in the morning. Death in the afternoon. Death in the evening. Death would be everywhere, like oxygen. Death. Death. Death.

"Listen up," came a deeper voice. "Approach this table in groups of five. We need to process you."

And so it was that hundreds of starving men entered one of the most secret concentration camps in the Nazi empire. When it was Eli's turn, he held his cap with both hands. But he thought this made him look too much like a beggar, so he stood at attention. He stiffened and felt the hobnail bruise on the small of his back.

"Age?"

"21."

"Do you speak German?"

"Yes."

"Occupation?"

The Nazis believed one simple and ironclad rule: only valuable workers were allowed to stay among the living. All others were wheeled into the darkness. Eli knew he needed to make himself useful. He knew what he needed to say.

"I'm…an electrician," he lied.

The prisoner behind the desk stamped a green work order and handed it to Eli without looking up. There was an inky swastika and a number: *41199*.

Eli Hessel, a Jew from Berlin who hoped for many more decades of life, turned away and let his mind focus on clear, clean water. Yes, he thought, he'd love a tall glass. There would be ice cubes, big ones, big enough to sting your upper lip when you took in the cool wetness. The water would flow down his throat, wet and pure.

And with this pleasant image hovering on his tongue, he stepped into a sub-tunnel.

He went to work.

A PRISONER ONLY CARED about what was immediately in front of them. This is what Eli would tell people years later. It was tunnel vision, both literally and figuratively. To survive, you needed to focus on the minutes before you and move through them with caution. To exist in a concentration camp was to stare down a poorly lit passageway and know that demons hid somewhere up ahead, their teeth razor sharp, their eyes ready to flare open at any moment. Dora was wickedness made flesh; it was hell brought to life.

In many ways this subterranean concentration camp fits our image of the underworld almost perfectly. Our very earliest stories about descending into the earth are also about entering a realm of death. It is dark and cold. Our eyes cannot see through the hazy murk and the sun has been snuffed out. There is also the fear of the rocky ceiling above cracking, fissuring, splitting apart, and it is easy to imagine the suspended weight above crushing down upon us. To be inside the pit of the earth is to be buried alive and it is this primal fear—this fear of being entombed—that still hides in the dark recesses of our modern imaginations. In ancient mythology the underworld was home to nightfall and gloom. It was a place of labyrinths, crypts, and hidden waterways. It remains the dwelling place of our nightmares. To go underground is to enter the realm of monsters. And so it was for the prisoners of Dora.

But it wasn't always like this.

First, the place had to be created. It had to be built.

DORA

THE OFFICIAL NAME OF THE CAMP was KZ Dora-Mittelbau. The KZ stood for *Konzentrationslager* and work began on the tunnels on August 28, 1943, when over one hundred prisoners from the nearby camp of Buchenwald were ordered to dig into the hardened rock of an abandoned gypsum mine. By Christmas of that same year, more than 10,000 prisoners were hammering their way through a stubby mountain called the Kohnstein.

Perhaps "mountain" is too grand of a term though. It was a ridge that lifted up from lush farmland, jack pines sprouted up from its hump, and it was home to a rich variety of wildlife. Beneath the soil was a tough rock called anhydrite. It was so hard, in fact, that the tunnels wouldn't need supporting beams, which is precisely why the Nazis decided to create a factory deep inside its heart. Huge internal spaces could be chiseled into the center of this mountain and this meant American planes would never be able to spy the assembly line of rockets hidden inside. The Nazis knew the enemy would fly on, seeing nothing, suspecting nothing, and even if they found out what was happening in the cool depths of the earth, no bomb could ever punch its way down to the factory floor. It was a natural fortress. The war could never touch it.

In the early days of the camp's existence, the growing cavity of rock was a place of constant noise and dust. Prisoners blasted holes into anhydrite around the clock. They hunched against walls before each explosion and, as they crouched there with hearts racing inside bony cages, they must have wondered if the ceiling would collapse. Would the tonnage of rock suspended above continue to hold? While they imagined a waterfall of rocks tumbling down, that's when the cracking detonation of TNT happened up ahead. A rolling white cloud covered them, submerged them. Dust particles filled up their lungs. And, whenever they spit, their saliva was like paste.

Once the dust settled, they were ordered to clear away the largest chunks of rock. The prisoners tossed huge jagged pieces into rail carts called *grubenhunten*. And then, by sheer force of will, these men muscled the carts down to a narrow-gauge locomotive that pulled the stones out into the glare of the sun. These men—these expendable tools, these ghosts in waiting—were beaten if they moved too slowly or if the *grubenhuten* got derailed. No plumbing or toilets existed and this meant prisoners had to walk through streams of excrement. Not surprisingly, tuberculosis, typhoid, and pneumonia spread at fearsome rates. Withered men fell to the ground in unrelenting numbers. Still, the work continued.

The Nazis didn't care who lived and who died. This was slave labor and the bodies of these men were considered to be property of the Reich. To this day, it's unclear how many prisoners died building the tunnels, although the numbers are thought to be in the thousands. Naked bodies were hauled away to Buchenwald where they were burnt in a crematorium. As more prisoners were fed into the tunnels, the SS at Dora-Mittelbau felt this was too inefficient—all those trucks traveling back and forth, wasting gasoline—so they requested an oven of their own. This wish was granted by Berlin. Once the oven was fitted into place and fired to roaring life, it didn't take long before human ashes were tipped into a ravine that acted as a garbage dump.

By early 1944, two huge tunnels were finished, along with rail tracks that curved out from their gaping mouths. Some 35 million cubic feet of space had been gouged out of the Kohnstein to make way for rocket assembly. Each tunnel was a mile long and two stories high. If we think of Tunnel A and Tunnel B running parallel to each other—with a gentle S curve to both—a number of smaller tunnels connected them. The world's largest underground factory was finally ready for use, and the idea of the rocket was about to move from the realm of science fiction into the realm of science fact. What would soon roll out from the tunnels would not only change the twentieth-century, it would rumble down the decades to come.

ELI DIDN'T KNOW ANY OF THIS when he arrived because the prisoners who built the tunnels were all dead by the summer of 1944. But even if he *did* know how Dora-Mittelbau had been brought into existence would it really matter? No, not to Eli. He only cared about the narrow path between life and death that appeared before him. Such was the tunnel vision that existed in the underground camp. Most of the prisoners felt this way. For them, the present and the future were all that mattered. The past? That was a place of pain and loss, it was a place that held images of happier times and of family members who had not yet been murdered. And so, Eli didn't think about the past. He made it cease to exist. He put it in a box, and buried it.

He was housed in Barrack 118 along with 400 other men. It was a clapboard shack with thin windows and a dirt floor. It was one of many barracks that had been set up outside the tunnels, and the whole outdoor complex was ringed by electrified wire. Searchlights roamed the night. In the distance, dogs barked and he sometimes heard classical music drifting out from the SS camp. Occasionally, laughter sliced the night air and, once or twice, he heard the sound of popping gunfire. The SS at Dora consisted of men who had long careers at other concentration camps. They knew what they were doing. They were stone faced and cold.

Triple layered bunks had been shoved into the barracks and it was here that shivering men nuzzled into each other for warmth. As the curfew siren wailed, Eli searched for sleep. After sixteen hours of ruinous work, during which time he had seen five men collapse from hunger and one get beaten to death, getting a good night's sleep took on existential importance. A good night of sleep might repair the damage that had been done to his joints and ligaments, it might help clot wounds, and it might allow blackened eyes to heal. He rarely dreamed when he was in Dora. He usually just slipped into the void. If he *did* dream though, it was always of food.

His uniform was infested with lice and whenever he tried to sleep he could feel them walking across the landscape of his body, nibbling here, nibbling there. It felt like his skin was on fire and that he had already entered the oven.

He scratched his eyebrow and felt a white speck moving beneath his fingernail. The man next to him twitched in his sleep. His breath stank, and the smell of shit was on the man's uniform—he obviously had dysentery and hadn't made it to the barrel in time. While the man snored on, Eli studied his skeletal face, how the eyes darted back and forth beneath papery lids. Maybe this man, this stranger with a homosexual's pink triangle, would transform into a corpse in the next few hours? Such things happened all the time. Just yesterday, the kapos woke up Barrack 118 for morning roll call and found seven men dead. One had hanged himself with a belt.

Eli glanced out the window. The moon was pock-marked and brilliant. He saw that it was bleached white, like the walls of the tunnels of Dora, and in the drowsy chambers of imagination, he wondered if the moon and the tunnels were made from the same rock. He saw himself quarrying into the moon, digging down, down, down, deeper into its belly where he could sleep in glowing warmth. Sleep, he thought. To drift away...

A gust of wind rattled the window.

He adjusted his wooden clogs beneath his head. He'd made a pillow of them so they couldn't be stolen. This hurt the base of his skull, but that was better than waking up to find that he would have to walk around the camp barefoot. Imagine walking into the tunnels like that, he thought. He could almost feel the cold against his toes.

When he was kid in Berlin he loved running through grassy parks and seeing July sunshine trickle down through oak leaves. The warmth was delicious. Trams rattled by. Maybe he'd stop at a café on Kurfürstendamm and get a huge slab of chocolate cake. Maybe he'd sink a finely polished fork into frosting and lift the crumbling goodness up to his lips where—

His eyes fluttered open and he felt hundreds of mouths on his body. Stop, he counseled himself. Go to sleep. Go to sleep so you may live.

And with that, he drifted into the abyss.

The lice, meanwhile, continued to feed.

DORA DIDN'T HAVE A GRAND GATEHOUSE that prisoners had to march through. And unlike Auschwitz, Sachsenhausen, and Dachau, the phrase *Arbeit Macht Frei* wasn't emblazoned over the entrance. Instead, the gate at Dora was simple, artless, and there was no such phrase. There was, however, an unofficial camp slogan that everyone knew. It hung silently in the air. *Vernichtung durch arbeit.* Extermination through work. This was the essential element of Dora and it's worth noting that between 1943 and 1945, one in three prisoners died there. Put another way, a gas chamber wasn't necessary at Dora. Prisoners were simply worked to death and, in so doing, the Nazis could extract as much useful labor as possible from their bodies.

Eli came to know the camp well in his first week. There were the tunnels, of course, where he and thousands of others were forced to work. This industrial area of camp was called Mittelbau—this is where the V-1 and

V-2s were assembled. The V-1 was a small "flying bomb" with wings and a rudimentary jet engine. It was launched from a long ramp and, when it ran out of fuel, it fell. It usually caused more terror than damage. Although these flying bombs were produced in the tunnels, Eli never personally worked on them. He would come to know the more advanced, accurate, and destructive V-2. The world's first rocket.

To the west of the tunnels rested the SS camp. This was off limits to prisoners and yet, whenever he marched past it, he could see fine little homes, a fancy pub, dog kennels, a stone walking path, and a vegetable garden. To the south of the SS camp was the rail yard where the V-1s and V-2s were loaded onto trains. Further to the west was the gatehouse and the inmate's camp. Aside from the stench of death and unwashed bodies, the first thing a visitor might notice would be the guard towers and the searchlights. If we imagine a shallow valley with hills rising on three sides, this was the topography of the inmates' camp. Entering through the nondescript gate, a visitor couldn't help but notice the massive roll call square and, fanning out from this, a shantytown of wooden barracks.

The prisoners were woken at four in the morning by the kapos. They entered the barracks with rubber truncheons and flayed away until everyone was assembled in the *Appellplatz* for roll call. Thousands of striped uniforms had to stand at attention while the SS strolled among them. Dogs strained against leashes. They barked and bared their yellow teeth. Men in guard towers yawned and smoked cigarettes. They cradled their machine guns while a swastika on a flagpole snapped and flapped.

Roll call often lasted for hours in the drizzling rain. The prisoners stood at attention with their caps off while a kapo shouted their numbers. A soft breeze moved through Eli's hair. He shivered and listened for his new name. He was no longer Eli Hessel. He was 41199.

"*VIER EINS EINS NEUN NEUN!*"

"*Jawohl!*" he said, raising his hand. And in this way, he was counted among the living.

As the count went on, crows circled overhead. They wheeled around and landed on barrack rooftops, cawing. Sometimes, if the wind was right, Eli could hear church bells bonging in the valley below. Wisps of smoke lifted up from unseen distant chimneys. He wondered what they were eating for breakfast in the nearby city. Eggs? He liked to imagine eggs. Boiled. Poached. Fried. Scrambled. Baked. Thick with butter.

When they were dismissed, everyone rushed for a breakfast of rutabaga soup, a slice of moldy bread, and coffee that tasted of acorns. The first time Eli drank the soup he saw blobs of oil floating on top. The soup arrived in fifty-five gallon drums—they probably once held petroleum—but he didn't care about this. He poured the soup down his throat and tore at the green bread. The coffee disappeared, too. And when it was all over, he looked at his dirty hands and ached for more food. Many of the prisoners went over to the empty metal drums and began to lick them clean. One of the cooks, a burly man with thick forearms, hit them with a ladle.

"Stand back. That's all for today!"

Eli saw some of the men eat lice off their shirt. Others ate snails they found on fence posts. One man tried to eat tufts of grass. Eli watched all of this and wondered if he, too, might do the same thing in a few weeks. Yes, he had to conclude. Yes.

The loudspeaker crackled and a voice rang out. "Attention—" There was a shriek of feedback. "Attention…return to the roll call square. Attention… return in the roll call square."

They moved back as a brass band started up. French horns. Trumpets. A lively tune. Moments later, thousands of men marched out of Dora towards the tunnels. The work day had begun.

The prisoners came from all over Nazi Europe and each man in a blue and white "zebra suit" had a letter stitched over his left breast pocket. B was for Belgians. P was for Poles. I for Italians. N for Czechs. R for Russians. F for French. There were a lot of French in the camp, Eli noted. Many of them had fought in *La Résistance* and it was common to hear their language flutter up from workbenches. To Eli, it sounded like birdsong.

As they marched for the tunnels, he glanced at the sooty rail yards. A steam engine huffed on a side track as coal clattered noisily into its bin. A puff of black lifted up. Near the SS camp, two prisoners were changing a tire on a Mercedes—another buffed the chrome headlamps. It must be good to be outside, Eli thought. The wind picked up and the trees began to rustle and sway. The sky was a brilliant morning blue. Birds soared overhead, riding the currents until they disappeared, free.

His arms were heavy and he shuffled to keep his clogs from falling off.

"Move it, you pieces of shit! March in unison. Your left…your left… your left."

They turned for Tunnel A. It was a gigantic black opening, a wide mouth. Soon, the long column of starving men were swallowed by the mountain. Eaten.

LATER THAT NIGHT, when he was ordered back to the barracks, Eli adjusted his oil-stained clogs beneath his head. A man in the bunk above began to cough and it rattled the whole wooden structure. At the far end of the barracks someone pissed into a metal pot.

Water, he thought.

It made him think about evening roll call yesterday (or was it the day before?) when a man was paraded in front of them. One of the SS guards announced that he had jumped into the concrete fire pond in order to get a drink. This was strictly forbidden, and the man knew it. Now, he must pay for his crime. This man, a fellow Jew, stood before them and looked down at his bare feet. He wobbled slightly and there was a bruise on his jaw. An SS guard picked up a bucket of ice water and doused the prisoner. His mouth opened in mute shock and he began to shiver violently. Another bucket of freezing water was poured over his head and seconds later the man dropped to the ground like a wet rag. To the surprise of everyone—including the SS—the man was dead. Apparently the cold was so shocking, so striking to his weak body, that it killed him instantly. Eli had seen many deaths, but this one seemed particularly cruel.

Yes, Eli had to admit, Dora was shocking, but there was more to it than that. The entire camp was built upon a foundation of malice and spite. It was for this reason the SS had a soccer field and a cinema built for the prisoners. It would never be used of course, but these amenities were always there, right in sight of everyone, and they existed purely to taunt the inmates with what they could see, yet never enjoy. "Work harder," the SS smiled. "Maybe you can watch *Snow White* next week?"

There were also young women that had been forced into prostitution. Eli had walked by the brothel many times, he had seen long lines of inmates who waited patiently to paw at their milky bodies and, as far as he knew, they were the only women in the whole camp. If a prisoner did especially good work, an SS guard might hand over a voucher. This piece of pink paper could then be handed over for fifteen minutes of sex. Of all the suffering at Dora, we have no accounts of what happened behind the closed doors of the *Bordell*. If any of these women did survive the war, they likely faded back into society and never uttered a syllable of what had been done to them. And no wonder they didn't tell about their experiences: they were raped ten or fifteen times a night. For months. Such places like this also existed at Auschwitz, Buchenwald, and Sachsenhausen. It is rarely talked about today, but it happened.

As the man at the end of the barrack finished peeing, the music of his final few splashes tinked against the side of the bucket. Eli looked at the bunk above and felt the whole structure vibrate as the coughing man continued to hack out phlegm. He might be dead tomorrow, Eli thought, but another will take his place.

BEFORE WE SHIFT OUR ATTENTION to the tunnels and all that happened there, a few final words need to be said about the camp's name, Dora. Most of the other Nazi camps were named after the town or district where they were situated—Mauthausen, Auschwitz, Dachau—but this wasn't the case for Dora. No, this secret camp got its name from an alphabetical code, much like how we name our tropical storms today.

Dora. Just a hush of air. Dora. The tongue taps the upper flesh of the palate and then curls back until there is only an escaping breath, an exhale.

"Dora."

So simple to say, and yet so hard to put into words.

HORSE HEAD AND OHM'S LAW

HIS JOB WAS TO FUSE CIRCUITS. He was given a soldering gun, a pair of needle-nose pliers, and a thin rope of pewter. With a nod of his head, he made the welder's mask fall down over his eyes and he torched metal into bubbling lines of superheated liquid. A moment later, the glowing light was extinguished and he lifted the mask to inspect his work. The seam was smooth and shiny. Perfect.

Eli reached for a sticker.

He wrote his identity number on it—41199—and stuck it next to his work. This was done so the SS could trace any shoddy work directly back to him. Civilian workers with technological expertise were always conducting spot inspections and, whenever they found an error, the worker was hunted down and beaten. Sometimes they were hanged at evening roll call. Eli triple-checked his work and shifted his weight on the wobbly wooden stool. Lights hummed above and from somewhere down the enormous tunnel there was banging and yelling. A pistol went off and the sound echoed down the ceiling like a crashing wave. No one dared to look up.

His stomach grumbled for rutabaga soup and he was overcome by a strange desire to brush his teeth. It had been—how long now?—at least six months since he'd found a box of baking soda at Auschwitz and used his finger to clean his mouth.

He lifted his cap and scratched behind an ear. His shadow on the stone wall across from him did the same thing. The air around him, he noticed, smelled exactly like the U-Bahn back in Berlin. Scorched electricity and urine.

Things could be worse, he told himself. At least he had a job that didn't demand heavy lifting. At Dora, prisoners with technical skills worked in the tunnels. Others were forced to dig ditches, haul rocks, and build barracks for the ever-expanding camp population. If you got weak, you were forced to do work that was all the harder. "*Vernichtung durch arbeit,*" Eli whispered to himself.

He moved quickly when he heard approaching footsteps. He had gotten very good at knowing the subtle differences between the jackboots of the SS and the wooden clogged gait of an exhausted prisoner. The kapo in charge of this section of the tunnel was a lumbering mule of a man named Erich Kempf. He was well fed, he wore a handsome smile, and he carried a thick cane as he paced his little kingdom. It was easy to tell when Kempf was approaching because his clogs on the floor were accompanied by the *tap*, *tap* of his hickory cane. As he moved through the tunnel, he usually whistled Tchaikovsky's "1812 Overture."

As dangerous as Kempf was though, the real terror was a guard named Horse Head. He was six feet six and he walked around the underground factory with his hands cupped behind his back. He was an SS officer and he always seemed bored until something unusual caught his eye. That's when a smile brightened his face and he turned toward the problem, slowly. His head was so elongated that prisoners called him *Pferdekopf*. Horse Head. His real name was Erwin Busta and he was from a small Austrian town. No one knew when Horse Head slept because he always seemed to be on the prowl with a heavy rubber stick. He beat men randomly, savagely, striking here, striking there, and he had a sawtooth tongue. He yelled out insults as he brought his stick down onto skulls and ribs. When he finished terrorizing one section, he walked on, happy to fill another section with panic. His hobnail boots clicked against the floor and he had a teenage boy run ahead of him to warn everyone that he was coming. He enjoyed the power of fear and he knew how to make the horizon of his arrival all the more terrifying. "Horse Head is coming!" the boy shouted. "Horse Head is coming!"

Eli blew into his cupped hands. Even though warm machinery hummed around him, and even though he worked in tight quarters with other prisoners, the cold of the tunnel leeched into his skin. It made him shiver. A sudden memory of his mother wrapping a blanket around him on a cold night drifted into his imagination. The potbelly stove crackled and spat as she placed a bowl of oatmeal in front of him. Her lips touched the top of this head.

"Where's Paul?"

It was his work station partner who asked the question. Eli raised both eyebrows as if to say, *What? Didn't hear you.*

"Paul. Where is he?"

Eli glanced at the empty stool to his right and shrugged a shoulder.

Moshe Rozner, his work partner, reached into a yellow metal box and pulled out a fuse. He twisted it into place and put on a sticker. He spun open a vice that was clamped to his table, threaded in a copper tube, and his fingers moved quickly. He spoke without looking up. "Was he taken to the ovens?"

Eli also didn't look up. It was dangerous to talk. "Don't know. He had plenty of energy yesterday."

It was true. Although Paul Delacroix was thin, he had wide shoulders that made him look stronger than he really was and this saved him during a number of selections. He was also resourceful and somehow managed to get several more portions of bread than anyone else. He had been arrested in Normandy for loosening a section of rail line that made a supply train tumble off the tracks. He was caught, tortured, and sent to Dora. Now he built rockets that would thunder towards Paris.

Eli whispered, "Maybe he's on a new work detail?"

Moshe opened his mouth as if to say something but at that moment a group of prisoners marched by with a huge rocket fin. It was badly dented, like it had fallen from a great height, and they clacked by, clearly struggling under the weight. One of them had a swollen purple eye and he had to cock his head in order to see where he was going.

Eli studied his dirty hands and felt an SS guard move past their table. There was the smell of cologne. His entire body tensed until the work detail—and that smell—passed.

Moshe spun his vice shut and continued whispering. "I saw him at roll call. He wasn't a corpse this morning. Where *is* he?"

Eli grunted in the hopes that Moshe would shut up. The silence between them grew thicker as the rhythm of work swallowed them both. They moved quickly. Their hands flashed and moved. The wooden table was stained with grease, and the sides were smooth from the endless rubbing of arms against it. Eli saw flecks of salt moving on the table. Lice. Maybe his lice. It made him wonder: do you own a parasite if you're the host? Are they "his lice" or just lice?

Overhead lamps cast double-shadows on the wall and a generator thrummed in one of the side tunnels. Wooden crates were stacked next to the table and a slender green tank of acetylene was propped next to him. Its chemical symbol was painted in yellow. C_2H_2. Behind them was an elaborate wardrobe that had obviously been stolen from a country house and brought into the tunnel. It was full of mallets, crimps, extension cords, and rasps.

Eli looked at his fingernails, which were gritty and black. His knuckles were stained with soot. What on earth did the rest of him look like? It had been months, maybe even a year, since he last looked into a mirror.

He snapped down his welding mask and liquefied a strip of pewter in a bright flash of starlight. He tested the voltage with a needle, applied a sticker, and placed the fuse into a cart. Someone would come along in the next thirty minutes and take the fuses away to be bolted onto fuel tanks and then, sometime in the future, a spark would travel through his work and ignite a fury of flame. A rocket would curve into the crisp undiscovered blue and travel at supersonic speed towards someone's house, someone's school, someone's life.

He glanced at Delacroix's empty stool.

In spite of what Moshe thought, maybe Delacroix *had* been taken to the ovens? Just fifty meters away was a service tunnel that was used as a morgue. Maybe he was there? It was a large jumble of bodies that had been flung into an ugly heap, and they all looked the same—opened mouthed, cloudy eyed, limp, almost rubbery. They would soon be carted away for burning. Prisoners who acted as undertakers would come along in their own good time with wheelbarrows. All these men had to do was haul corpses and they made a game of it by racing along the tunnel to see who could reach the sunshine first. Sometimes, if they hit a cable, the whole wheelbarrow would flip over and corpses would tumble out. The SS laughed at these so-called "Chariot Races" and the winner often got a pack of cigarettes, which could be traded for a hunk of sausage.

Eli heard whistling.

"Kempf," Moshe hissed. "Pass that copper tubing to me, and that thing there. No, no, *that* thing." He snapped his fingers a few times. "Hurry… hurry!"

The whistling got louder until, finally, a shadow fell across their table. A moment later an enormous hand reached for a fuse. The knuckles were pale stones; the nails were neatly clipped. Eli felt his body pucker and, almost against his will, he looked up.

Kempf had sharp blue eyes and freckles. His striped uniform was clean and he wore an armband with the word *KAPO* stitched onto it. He pulled out a chunk of bread from his trousers and began to eat. The bread looked fresh. Sunflower seeds were on the top.

"How are we doing, my assholes?" he asked while chewing noisily. He used his pinky finger to pick a bit of bread out from his molars. He studied Moshe for a long time. "Tell me…what were you before Dora? A lawyer? A teacher? A banker? Do you see my green triangle here? I've got six convictions on my record. Two for manslaughter and four for robbery. The world has turned upside down on you, my asshole. I'm in charge here. Understand? If you need a translator for what I'm saying, here it is."

At this, he placed his hickory stick on the work table.

"Now, now, now…how many fuses have you done this morning?"

Moshe stammered. "I-I've been working as fast as I can, Herr Kempf. We're missing Delacroix." He nodded to the empty stool. "This slowed me down. Actually, it's slowed *both* of us down."

Anger flared inside Eli. He didn't need to be brought into this.

Kempf clucked his tongue and let out a little groan. "Oh dear, oh dear."

"So you see, Herr Kempf, I have to do *his* job before I can do *my* job," Moshe added.

"You've done…? Only fifteen?"

"Yes, but—"

"But nothing. There should be thirty fuses by now." Kempf's eyes narrowed and his whole face curdled with rage. In one swift blinding movement he swung his walking stick down onto Moshe's head. There was a sickening crack as Moshe slumped to floor. His cap rolled away.

Kempf brought down the stick again, this time onto Moshe's back.

"Please!" Moshe shouted as he tried to scramble away.

Eli snapped down his welding mask and flared the acetylene torch to life. A spark of light illuminated the darkness and he went about the business of melting a bead of pewter. It flowed like blood.

"You," Kempf said, turning to Eli. The man was green and shadowy in the underworld of the welder's mask.

"Yes, sir?" Eli asked. He kept the acetylene torch lit. He liked having the protective talisman of fire in his fist.

Kempf leaned in, his face glowing like a green ghost. "I want fifty fuses when I return." There was a long pause before he added, "Turn that damn torch off. Look at me, 41199."

Eli snuffed out the hissing flame and lifted his welder's mask.

"When I return, I'm going to count how many fuses you've done. For each fuse that's missing, you'll get a rap on the cap." He snapped his uniform against his large belly and took a step back. He offered a toothy smile as if nothing had happened and his whole face was suddenly warm and pleasant again. He began to whistle, turned neatly on his heels, and dragged his shadow away.

Eli immediately grabbed a rag and began daubing the side of his friend's head. The stream of blood was as wide as his thumb and he couldn't make it stop. Under normal circumstances a wound like this would need stitches. He kept daubing and dabbing. He applied pressure.

"You okay? How do you feel?"

Moshe sucked in air through gritted teeth. "Ach. My God that hurts." He blinked and touched the side of his head. "Pass that rag to me, would you?"

Eli reached for an oily cloth and watched Moshe stuff it into his cap.

"Come," Eli said, helping his friend back onto the stool. "Kempf'll be back soon." There was a moment of silence before he made his voice deep and mocking. "You must work faster, my asshole."

Moshe grunted a laugh and, together, they set about making fuses as fast as their fingers could move.

AT DORA, PUNISHMENT WASN'T JUST a form of intimidation; it was a way to keep prisoners from thinking too much about escape. With the threat of physical violence always hanging over them, prisoners were constantly on edge. They could be whipped or kicked or have a dog set upon them at any moment. The guards often tried to outdo each other with their sadistic creativity and, in fact, Eli once saw a man who was forced to stare into the glaring lights of the tunnel. An SS guard held a gun to his head and said he'd pull the trigger if the man looked away. After five minutes, the prisoner was blinded. Yet another prisoner, an older man who was a Jehovah's Witness, was forced to swear at God. He had to yell a river of obscenities to the sky while a gun was cocked at the base of his skull. During all of this, the SS strutted around. They smirked and laughed. They asked him why Jehovah didn't come down and save him. "Where is your God? Tell me."

Such moments of spectacle were a reminder to the prisoners that they were powerless, helpless. The SS, the kapos, and even the civilian workers who handled the more technological aspects of the rockets, all had the ability to make prisoners feel vulnerable. Everything in Dora was designed to unweave any strand of independence a prisoner might still carry. It wasn't just a question of losing freedom—it was much larger than that. In fact, Eli often felt like he was becoming a child again. He couldn't drink when he wanted to. He couldn't wash when he wanted to. He had to ask permission to use the latrine, and he had to eat whatever was placed in front of him. He went to bed when someone else dictated and he was subjected to a brutal system that controlled every waking moment of his life. He was even given a new name—41199—and he had to do whatever he was told. Prisoners were broken down. They lost vital parts of themselves. They were made to be less than they once were.

Eli clicked the acetylene torch and frowned behind his mask. No, he decided. They weren't being treated like children—that would imply they were still human beings—they were being treated more like machines. A machine was replaceable. A machine had no past and no future. A machine couldn't make decisions for itself. And a machine didn't have a mind of its own.

He looked at the glowing spark in his gloved hand and felt as if he were drowning. The world around him was dark and crushing. He felt like he was at the bottom of the sea, rusting away like the *Titanic* or the *Lusitania*. Bits of himself were floating away.

When he raised his mask, he took in a lungful of air. "How many fuses to go?" he asked.

Moshe counted. "Seventeen."

A teenage prisoner ran into their section and stood beneath a huge iron winch. He cupped his soiled hands around his mouth and yelled out a phrase that filled Eli with tingling fear.

"Horse Head is coming! Horse Head is coming!"

He looked around frantically to make sure everything was in order. He straightened tools and lined up fuse boxes. The story of Passover floated through his mind and, as he glanced at streaks of blood on Moshe's side of the table, he hoped that Horse Head—the angel of death—might keep on moving, might pass over them both. Words from his youth filled his ears. *Pesach. Malach Hamavet. Zeman Cheruteinu.*

His fingers quickly braided wire and he reached for an Ohmmeter to make sure the needle fanned to the right. Good, he thought. All is well.

"Horse Head is coming!" the boy yelled further down the tunnel. Stones skittered away from his clogs. "Prepare yourself. Horse Head is coming!"

Eli closed his eyes and counted his breathes. He thought of a calm lake and sunshine. He thought of harmless butterflies floating past him on a July day.

Jackboots clacked slowly against the stone floor.

He reached for a sticker and, as he did so, he wondered if he should be in the process of welding when Horse Head arrived. Would the bright spark of light and the zapping hum of a torch attract more or less attention? Which was better? What should he do?

When SS-*Hauptscharführer* Erwin Busta entered their section of the tunnel, he tapped cigarette ash onto the ground. Smoke threaded up as he stood there open-mouthed, breathing. He said nothing at first. But after a long minute, he chewed on a fingernail and spit the jagged bit onto the floor. Eli kept working and smelled the man's cologne. Most of the SS wore cologne because it helped to keep the smell of the prisoners in check.

Horse Head dropped his cigarette on the ground and twisted the tip of his polished boot over it.

Eli snapped his welding mask down and flicked a flint spark. The world around him was dark, opaque, and only a shimmering ember of green could be seen between his hands. He hoped the blinding star he'd just created might make Horse Head back off.

"Halt." The voice was dark and heavy. A long time passed before he continued. "You claim to be…an electrician? Is that right?"

"Yes, sir."

"I do not believe you."

Eli felt small looking up, up, up at the great height of Horse Head. The man had an unusually large brow and his cheeks were flushed red. Eli looked at the man's sledgehammer fists.

"Sir, I was an apprentice in Poland, sir."

"Where?"

"Kraków, sir."

"Your German is very good. Why is that, I wonder?"

"I was born in Berlin, *Hauptscharführer*."

Horse Head studied the yellow star on Eli's uniform and seemed interested, as if he had just learned an unusual new fact. "A Jew from Berlin? I thought you were all gone."

Eli didn't know what to do, so he stared at the table. Should he go back to work? Should he remain quiet?

Horse Head pointed at one of the tools on the table. "Tell me, my Jewish electrician, what is this called?"

Eli's mind went blank.

Horse Head yelled out, "WHAT IS THIS CALLED?"

"It's...it's a voltmeter."

There was a long pause before Horse Head shook his head. "No. It's a comparator."

The towering SS officer with a swastika on his arm pulled out his rubber truncheon. He rapped Eli on the head—not hard—but it stung.

"And this? What's this called?"

"A connector."

"No. That is a fork terminal."

Eli closed his eyes and waited for the blow. It didn't come.

"And this? What's this?"

He looked at what Horse Head was pointing to and couldn't believe his luck. The answer spilled out of him.

"That's an Ohmmeter." He reached for a scrap of paper and scribbled out a mathematical formula. "It measures this...V equals I times R. That's Ohm's Law. V is for voltage, I is for current, and R is for resistance."

Horse Head raised an eyebrow.

Eli kept talking, his words bumping into each other. "Ohm's Law states that electrical current passing through two points of a conductor is equal to the potential difference across two points. It's named after Georg Ohm, a brilliant German who discovered the formula."

"You are an educated Jew."

Eli worried about this. "No, no, no, *Hauptscharführer*. I am not educated. I am just a simple electrician."

Horse Head pointed to the empty stool. "Who sits there?"

"His name is Delacroix."

Horse Head rolled his eyes extravagantly. "His number. What is his *number?*"

"I...I can't remember."

Moshe spoke for the first time. "401679, *Hauptscharführer.*"

Horse Head swung his full attention to the other side of the table and brought his truncheon down hard onto the table. Tools bounced into the air. The Ohmmeter clattered to the floor.

"I. Didn't. Ask you." His neck muscles bulged and his whole face seemed impossibly longer. His eyes flared with dark fire. "What's in there?" he asked, pointing to the wardrobe behind them.

"Tools."

"Open it."

Eli jumped up, threw open the ornate doors, and there, curled in a corner, was Delacroix. Eli froze in shock and turned to Horse Head. "Herr *Hauptscharführer*, I swear I didn't know anything about this. I didn't know he was—"

"Shut up. You there, get out."

Delacroix clambered out and stood at attention. He clicked his heels together and snapped off his cap in a single fluid motion.

"What's the meaning of this?" Horse Head asked. "What were you doing in there?"

"I...I was for the tools looking," Delacroix said. His accent was heavy and he spoke German with difficulty.

Horse Head stepped closer to the Frenchman, only a few inches separated them now, and he spoke very slowly. "You were...sleeping...in there. Weren't you?"

"No, *Hauptscharführer.* I was for the tools looking." Delacroix's eyes were wide with terror. "I am hard worker. I was not for the sleeping."

Horse Head struck him under the nose with the palm of his hand and this dropped Delacroix to the ground. He held his bleeding nose with both hands and his eyes watered as he spoke. "I was not for the sleepings, *Hauptscharführer!* I was for the tools looking."

Horse Head kicked him in the chest and this made Delacroix curl into a tight protective ball. The gigantic man in black jodhpurs and a peaked officer's cap began hitting him with a truncheon. The rubber stick came down, blow after blow. Shoulders. Chest. Groin. Thigh. Head. The cracks were loud and awful. It sounded like a tree being chopped down.

After many long seconds of rage, Delacroix stopped moving. Horse Head kicked the man's skull, he waited a moment, and then kicked again. He pulled out a perfectly ironed handkerchief and daubed sweat from his brow. All that could be heard was the hum of a generator. Oily blood leaked from Delacroix's head.

Horsehead turned to Eli and pointed an accusing finger. "You *knew* he was in there, didn't you, 41199? I bet you take turns sleeping in that wardrobe. I'll teach you to lie to me."

Eli put up his hands. "No! I'm telling the—"

He didn't get a chance to finish. Horse Head brought the truncheon down onto Eli's forehead with unworldly force. The tunnel instantly became blurry and he wobbled around on legs made of taffy. Even as he was hit again, he told himself that he must not fall down, he must not fall down, *he must not fall down*. Another blow came, and another, and Eli turned his back. Horse Head kicked him in the buttock and this sent him flying into the acetylene tank. It clanked and rolled away.

"Do you think this is a holiday resort? Do you think you can take a snooze on my watch?" Horse Head flinched as if he was going to strike again but, instead, he picked up a rag. Slowly, purposefully, he wiped blood from his truncheon. He tossed the rag onto Delacroix's still body.

"That rag is ready for the chimney. Take it away."

Horse Head shoved past Eli. He paused, half-turned, and added, "Take the doors off that wardrobe right away. If I catch either of you sleeping on the job again, I will destroy you."

He snapped his fingers for the waiting boy to run on ahead. Eli had completely forgotten the child was still standing beneath the winch, but now he ran down the tunnel. "Horse Head is coming! Horse Head is coming! Prepare yourself!"

After calm had once again settled into their section of the tunnel, Eli allowed himself to sink to his knees. His head throbbed and something warm trickled down his right cheek. He closed an eye and noticed that he had double-vision. There were two tables, two torches, two Moshes. He tried to stand but kept slipping. The world seemed to tilt.

"Easy," Moshe said, lifting him onto a stool. "I've got you." His work station partner dabbed his temple. "Can you work?"

Eli groaned. All he wanted to do was lay down and place an ice pack on his head.

"You must work," Moshe said, rubbing Eli's back. "We have seventeen more fuses to make before Kempf returns." He smiled and added, in a deep voice, "You must work faster, my asshole."

Eli nodded in understanding. The spool of pewter in front of him spun in and out of view. He coughed, squared his shoulders, and put the welding mask down over his face. The world fell back into darkness. No matter what happened, he told himself, he must never give up. He must fight to the death to live.

A bright arrow of flame roared out from his acetylene torch and it looked like he was holding a miniature rocket. As he focused on the light he thought of Ohm's Law. He thought of powerful currents traveling through systems. He thought of resistance.

"Yes," he said under his breath. "Resistance."

THE VENGEANCE WEAPON

THE WORLD'S FIRST LONG-RANGE ROCKET weighed almost 28,000 pounds and it was so technologically advanced that Nazi Germany became the first country to put an object made by human hands into space. The "Kármán Line" marks the boundary between our world and the starry black that lies beyond. Thus, at least according to this measure, space begins 100 kilometers above sea level, which is roughly sixty-two miles straight up. During one particular test in the summer of 1944, launching from an island on the Baltic Coast called Greifswalder Oie, the V-2 soared past the Kármán Line by almost fifty miles. The Nazis, however, weren't interested in setting altitude records. They only cared about height so that the V-2 could arc over the top of a deadly parabola and then scream its way back down toward earth, where it would punch holes into cities hundreds of miles away. The V-2 was never designed to stay up in the heavens. It was designed to fall.

The rocket was essentially an enormous projectile that didn't require a cannon. A button was pushed, fuel ignited in blinding fury, and off it went into the clouds. Although Eli had no way of knowing it at the time, he and the other prisoners at Dora were building the world's first ballistic missile. He later came to understand its terrible destructive power and that the V stood for *Vergeltungswaffe*. Vengeance weapon. For its victims, it blew open the door to the next world.

The V-2 was the brainchild of a young man named Wernher von Braun. Quick with a smile, he made parties sparkle with laughter and was known as something of a ladies' man. Though only in his twenties, von Braun knew how to organize, how to charm, and—most importantly—how to turn blueprints into realities. He was the center of gravity for the V-2 program at Peenemünde: all major decisions orbited around him, and he made sure his rockets hit their intended targets. Von Braun joined the Nazi party in 1937 and, three years later, Heinrich Himmler personally invited him to join the SS.

Although von Braun accepted this commission, he would spend the rest of his life bending attention away from the fact that he was involved with the same organization that ran Dachau, Treblinka, and Auschwitz.

At first, Hitler was totally unimpressed with the V-2. He saw it as simply a massive artillery shell with an extremely long range. But as Germany began to lose the war, he slowly warmed to the idea. He wanted to punish the Allies by turning their pretty little cities into smoldering wastelands. On a July evening in 1943, von Braun dimmed the lights in an underground bunker and showed the Führer a silent movie of a V-2 taking off. As the color film splashed life against a concrete reinforced wall, Hitler sat slumped in a wooden chair, a black cape draped over his shoulders. He watched a rocket shoot into the sky on a mute flame, then it arced away at three times the speed of sound. Hitler beamed and jumped to his feet. He wanted to know what the "annihilating effect" of the warhead might be and apologized that he hadn't believed in the project sooner. Clapping his hands together, he made the young SS officer a professor on the spot. It was a rare honor. Within days, an order was given for thousands of V-2s to be built. The goal was to launch them like locusts towards New York and Washington, D.C. In time, maybe they could even hit Chicago.

After the war, when fame tapped von Braun on the shoulder and he became the smiling face of America's fledgling space program, he downplayed his involvement with Dora-Mittelbau and tried to keep it in the shadows. Whenever he *was* forced to talk about it, he made it clear that he never visited the actual concentration camp. He said that he only saw the tunnels. While this may have been true, there was little difference between the two places. Brutality and wickedness happened in both. And so, if von Braun did have any private reservations about the massive number of deaths that occurred inside the mountain where his rockets were being built, he kept such thoughts to himself. He turned instead to blueprints. He focused on gyroscopes, propellant, and lift.

The idea for moving the rocket assembly underground happened shortly after waves of American and British bombers pulverized the existing plant at Peenemünde. Rather than rebuild a factory that could be hit again, the Nazis decided that everything should be hidden beneath a mountain. And so it was that they created a secret underground concentration camp. They marched skeletal prisoners into an old gypsum mine and ordered them to plug dynamite into rock, they ordered them to dig. SS-*Sturmbannführer* Wernher von Braun visited the underground factory several times—he worked in an office just eleven miles away—and although he would later say the working conditions were "hellish" in the tunnels, he apparently had no qualms about using slave labor to advance his career. Few Nazis did.

Dora-Mittelbau was built less than five miles from the city of Nordhausen. Resting in the north of the Thuringia district, Nordhausen was graced with medieval architecture, a fine cathedral and, before the war changed so many things, it was a proud city that had stood for over a thousand years. It was home to distilleries, breweries, and factories that made transportation equipment. At night, people gathered in restaurants to drink a popular beverage called *korn*, which is made from fermented rye. Swastika banners hung in the streets and the radio delivered good news about the future that Hitler was bringing to the nation. At first, the good news seemed unending: the annexation of the Sudetenland, the *Anschluss* of Austria, the conquest of Poland, and through it all, mighty England seemed powerless. And then the Führer truly outdid himself; he conquered France in less than two months. It seemed impossible. Something that years of bloody trench warfare had failed to accomplish between 1914 and 1918 had been achieved in just six short phases of the moon. After the invasion of the Soviet Union, however, the good news didn't seem quite so frequent. If anything, the war seemed to be turning. Broadcasting from Berlin's *Sportpalast* in February 1943, the Reich Minister of Propaganda, Dr. Joseph Goebbels, called for total war and promised that new "secret weapons" would soon be unleashed against the enemy.

THE VENGEANCE WEAPON HAD THREE different sections: the nosecone, which was packed with explosives and the navigation system; the center section, which held the propulsion system; and the engine, which had four tail fins around a nozzle to aid guidance and provide stability. The V-2s were assembled the same way that Henry Ford made his cars: each rocket moved down the tunnel and prisoners quickly added parts as it inched for the exit. Near the end, the V-2s were painted olive green, laid down onto rail cars, and moved off to different locations across Germany. From there, maps were taken out. Coordinates were set. Countdowns began—five, four, three, two—and each one rumbled up into the blue. A towering column of smoke was all that remained as rockets curved for London, Brussels, Antwerp, and Paris.

However, vexing problems remained that prevented the V-2 from being successfully mass-produced. In particular, Nazi scientists struggled with gyroscopes, turbo pump generators, and servomotors that moved the air vanes. These vanes proved especially tricky because attempts at controlling something that was going several times the speed of sound were virtually unprecedented. How do you steer a bullet? And although the missile could be launched from just about anywhere, the men in charge of these sleek messengers of death favored roads that ran through dense forests. After the rocket was placed on a mobile launcher known as a *Meillerwagen*, it could then be towed into a clearing where it was propped upright and fired. Shortly after takeoff, the double-crack of a sonic boom could be heard for miles around. *Bah-boom!*

The V-2 entered English airspace at blistering speed. No one knew it was coming.

And because the V-2 moved at nearly five times the speed of sound near the end of its flight, air raid sirens all across London were suddenly useless. The rocket came down like a hammer. Upon impact, the warhead blasted a crater into the earth that was sometimes as wide as a football field. Soil, brick, glass, and other debris fountained up. Moments later, ambulances and fire trucks whined awake. Smoke twisted up into the sky like a ghostly exclamation point.

The rocket was no longer something of fantasy or the movies. It was now a weapon of mass murder. Many in London thought it was only a matter of time before the nosecones were fitted with anthrax.

A CAREER SOLDIER WHO HAD SEEN ACTION in the Great War of 1914-1918, Walter Dornberger was a brilliant designer who held four patents in rocket development as well as an engineering degree from the Institute of Technology in Berlin. He was appointed to the Mittelbau Advisory Council in late 1943, where he thought up the mobile launch platforms that allowed individual V-2s to be moved around the countryside and therefore avoid detection from Allied bombers. After pacing the tunnels of Dora-Mittelbau himself, and after being involved in crimes against humanity, Dornberger would go on to design high-performance aircraft for the United States. He would also play a significant role in the early development of the Space Shuttle. But before that, he and von Braun were honored at one of the most unusual award ceremonies of the twentieth-century.

It happened on December 9, 1944, at a place called Castle Varlar. This ancient monastery had been turned into a grand estate and, on this particular evening, the banquet hall was decorated with swastika flags, fine china, and silverware. Ivy was wrapped around a podium. A number of V-2s waited to be launched from the snowy gardens outside. Von Braun, Dornberger, and two other scientists were to be honored with the prestigious "Knight's Cross" and they wore tuxedos for the occasion. In between gourmet courses, the lights in the hall were shut off, a tall curtain at the end was pulled aside, and a V-2 was launched. Thunderous reverberations filled up the room as orange light from the exhaust flickered on the faces of the smiling men. The evening proceeded like this, alternating between food and firings.

Another important personality at Dora-Mittelbau was a man named Arthur Rudolph, who was in charge of production. Short and balding, he was von Braun's right-hand man, making sure the V-2s were constructed properly and were rolling out of the tunnel at a steady clip. He didn't care about prisoners dropping dead under his command; he only cared about quality control. He strolled through the tunnels to solve thorny engineering problems and, on at least one occasion, he ordered production of the V-2s stopped so that all prisoners could watch a mass hanging. This was meant as a warning for anyone who might be thinking about sabotage.

As an enthusiastic Nazi, it was Rudolph's job to make sure there was a constant supply of prisoners at Dora. His indifference to life is perhaps best exemplified by his reaction to being taken away from a lively New Year's Eve party to solve a problem at the underground factory. With 1945 looming, a strap used to hold down the rockets wasn't fitting properly. When he arrived at the tunnels, he realized there was nothing he could do until the morning. He didn't notice the starving prisoners working around him at a fever pitch, nor did he care about the greasy black smoke that curled out of the crematorium. It's possible that Arthur Rudolph stood outside Tunnel A on that evening, looked up at the moon, and wondered what the New Year would bring to him. Maybe, as he studied its bright celestial glow, he took long pulls from a bottle of champagne. A *Château Lafite Rothschild*, perhaps.

While we don't know what Rudolph was thinking on that particular night, we do know that in the decades to come he, von Braun, and Dornberger would all become indispensable to America's aerospace program. They would receive awards, honors, and ticker-tape parades. Their new country would welcome them. They would be showered with riches.

WHEN THE AMERICANS DISCOVERED what was hidden at Dora-Mittelbau in April 1945, they packed up everything they could lay their hands on. Some 300 rail cars were loaded down with fuel tanks, fins, nosecones, servomotors, and engines. These pieces of the future were sent across the Atlantic to another secret camp: The White Sands Proving Grounds in New Mexico.

The V-2 was studied, examined, copied, and made better. On October 24, 1946, a camera was bolted to the side of the rocket and it snapped a photo every other second as it roared up into the sky. The camera and rocket climbed to sixty-five miles (three miles above the Kármán Line) and took the very first photograph from space. The V-2 tumbled back to Earth and smashed into the ground at a blazing 500 feet per second. Although the camera was destroyed, the film encased in a heavy steel box was not. The photo taken that day was grainy, yet the curvature of the earth can be seen clearly, along with a smudge of cloud. Scientists called it a "Rocket-Eye View" of the world. Nothing quite like it had ever been seen before.

ELI HESSEL CARED ABOUT NONE of this, at least not at first.

During his time at Dora he was far more interested in survival—he stared down the long tunnel of each terrifying day—and he didn't care what happened to the V-2s when they moved beyond the barbed wire of the camp. What did these rockets mean beyond his workbench, his welding mask, and his little spool of pewter?

After the war though, when he was trying to follow the telemetry of a new life, he began to think about what he had built. No one seemed to care about the huge number of bodies that had been stacked up around the rockets. It was if it had never happened. And as the years ticked by, he began to realize that technology had a secret history. The crimes against humanity that occurred at Dora remained classified by the U.S. Army because they didn't want the world to know about the technological wonders that had been found there. The need for military secrecy was greater than the horrors that were committed. Propellant and sheet metal were given priority over blood and bone. Certain numbers were given priority over other numbers.

Design Specifications of the V-2:
Length: 45 feet, 11 inches
Diameter: 5 feet, 5 inches
Weight: 13.8 tons
Propellant: ethanol/water mixture and liquid oxygen
Propellant Weight: 8,400 lbs.
Range: 200 miles
Speed: 3,580 miles per hour
Warhead: 2,200 lbs. of amatol

Number of Attacks:
1,696 on Belgium
1,403 on the United Kingdom
76 on France
19 on Holland

Number of Deaths:
5,500 (estimated)

Number of Deaths at Dora-Mittelbau:
20,000 (estimated)

NUMBERS

"42003."

A soiled hand went up.

"37982."

There was another hand, with dirty fingernails.

"43679."

The thin leaf of a hand was raised. It shook.

"41199."

Eli raised his own hand as Kempf scribbled onto his clipboard. He looked well fed, relaxed, and his uniform was obviously brand new. "33—" he yawned lazily, "…721."

Silence.

Kempf said the number again, this time more clearly. "33721. Where are you?" A ribbon of breath streamed from his mouth. As he took a step forward, pea gravel crunched beneath his clogs. "33721!"

After a long loitering moment, he reached for a colored pencil lodged behind his ear and circled something on the clipboard. "45001."

Snow fluttered down in thick fat flakes. It melted on the heads in front of Eli. Water dripped down the shaved head immediately in front of him and he felt a flake get caught in his eyelashes. He blinked and listened to the continuing drone of numbers. Life after life was recorded as either present or absent, living or dead, flesh or ash. Now that his own numerical name had been called out he could relax, he could stare ahead and let his mind go numb. Maybe he was already dead and in hell? Surely this is what *Gehinnom* would be like. Maybe he *was* dead? Maybe he was cut off from God? Eli squinted at the thought. It made sense. If God was love, there was no love here, and therefore no God.

Several months had passed since he'd come to Dora and winter was finally giving way to spring. He shifted his weight and felt the cold porridge of mud beneath his wooden clogs. For a second, he worried about losing his balance and bringing Kempf over with his hickory stick. What was it the rabbis had told him? After twelve months in *Gehinnom*, a soul would either be destroyed or ascend to *Olam Ha-Ba*. How many months had he been in this place of demons? What was the total number of days?

"37812."

A hand went up. It was a Frenchman—Laurent?—was that right?—Eli couldn't remember the man's pre-camp name.

"42661."

As Moshe's hand went up, Eli felt a flutter of relief. Good. Yes. His friend was still among the living and this made the pain a little less terrible, a little less lonely.

On and on the count went.

Snow continued to fall.

The leaden clouds darkened and spilled down freezing sleet.

Eli let his mind wander from questions about the afterlife to huge meals at a restaurant to crawling into a bed with a goose down comforter.

After another half an hour he couldn't feel his fingertips and he wondered how he'd make fuses for the torpedoes. Funny, he thought. Everyone called them "torpedoes" in Dora. Maybe it was easier to imagine this? Building something for a submarine seemed more believable than building something that hurtled through the sky like lightning. "A torpedo for the air," Moshe once called it.

Lice jiggled in the stitching of his uniform and, although he desperately wanted to scratch, he knew it would bring Kempf or another kapo stomping over. He was powerless and paralyzed during roll call. No, he counseled himself, only humans could create this place. God has nothing to do with Dora. Perhaps it terrifies even him? Maybe he has looked away, ashamed at what his creation has created?

He looked beyond the heads in front of him. Tall jack pines were beyond the perimeter of the camp and, in looking at them, he almost felt free. But when his eyes moved to the guard towers and the searchlights and the snouts of machine guns he felt himself get small again. He could hear the humming pop of electrified fencing and imagined lice getting zapped. He imagined vegetable beef soup. He imagined a cozy fire and a mug of hot cocoa. He imagined his skin, clean.

"30329."

When the prisoner in front of him shifted his weight, Eli couldn't help but notice how filthy the man's uniform was. He had soiled himself with diarrhea sometime over the last few days and, in that moment, Eli dreamed of taking a hot bath and scrubbing away the raw odor of his own body. The water would turn a dark nut brown as he slipped into its cleansing warmth. And yes, after this bath he would purify himself with another bath, a *mikvah*. Under Jewish law this ritual washing would cleanse his spirit, his pores would open up, and the core of himself would drift away, spotless and clean. *Halachah*, he heard dreamily in his mind's ear. *Halachah*.

He wobbled on his feet and bolted awake. No one had noticed that he'd almost crumpled to the ground. He bit his tongue to stay awake. He bit harder.

"39920."

A pause. The pine trees stood at stiff attention in the distance.

"39920?"

A prisoner from somewhere on the left yelled out in a high voice, "He died during the night, sir."

Kempf nodded, lit a cigarette, and continued to call out numbers. It was a perverse version of attendance at primary school, Eli thought. Time passed. The clouds got darker. A body dropped to his right and it was hauled by its arms to a messy pile at the front. Another half hour passed and yet another body dropped. It too was dragged to the pile. And so it went: minutes passed, lives stopped.

During all of this, the rockets lay sleeping in the distance. He could see them beneath tarps on rail cars. A steam engine let out a trumpeting blast that echoed down the valley and, as water was poured into its sooty iron body, Eli licked his lips. He sucked on his front teeth to make some spit. When the engine's belly was finally full of water, it reversed down the tracks and banged into a long line of covered V-2s. The noise echoed through the trees. There was a two-toned whistle as the train panted out of camp. It chuffed hard, its wheels spun, and it *chunk-chunked* down the tracks. A huge plume of black smoke vented up.

Dogs barked at the noise, and it occurred to Eli that even if he managed to slip under the deadly voltage of the fence, and even if he managed to avoid a hailstorm of bullets, and even if he ran into the woods, the dogs would sniff him down and he'd be ripped to pieces. He nodded at the additional fact that he had no idea where he was. No clue at all. There were steeples beyond the rail yard—he could see them in the distance—but even if he reached them, he'd still be in his camp uniform. Maybe he could steal a suit? Maybe he could wander into a restaurant and order a plate of schnitzel and mashed potatoes. He would be given clean silverware and a fine linen napkin. There would be a pitcher of water with a slice of lemon. A waiter would approach and ask, *What can I get for you, sir? What do you need?*

Kempf quit calling out numbers and this made Eli's eyes refocus. Kempf stood next to Horse Head and they were laughing about something.

Another kapo appeared. He stood in front of the prisoners, took in a deep breath, and shouted out, "Caaaaps…*ON!*"

In one fluid motion, thousands of men replaced their cap onto their heads.

As they continued to stand at attention, Eli felt a niggling pain in his lower back. If one of his vertebrae had been cracked with that kick he received back in Auschwitz, it seems to have healed. At least that was something, he told himself. He shivered harder as the sleet picked up. It came down as knifing rainfall. They were sopping wet. Cold. Frozen. The breath of a thousand men lifted up and it made Eli think of steam engines. They each had a number bolted to their chests and, soon, they would roll into a tunnel.

Horse Head tucked his truncheon under his arm and began to study the clipboard that Kempf had handed to him. His black leather coat was buttoned up and he wore his SS officers cap at an angle.

"Prisoners of Dora," he finally yelled out. "Let me be perfectly clear about something…if I catch any of you damaging *my* rockets, you will be hanged. Do you understand me?" There was a pause. "You will be hanged slowly. It will not be a quick death. If you find yourself thinking about sabotage, I want you to think about your throat."

Other guards appeared and this could only mean it was time to march. But what about breakfast? Eli wondered. They hadn't eaten yet. Weren't they going to get a cup of cabbage soup?

"Someone," Horse Head yelled, "someone has *deliberately* clipped the wires on ten servomotors. TEN! That's ten rockets we can't use. Because of this crime, NONE of you are getting soup this morning."

Eli felt worry sizzle in his veins. No soup? But soup was life, soup was as necessary for the stomach as blood was for the heart.

"If we have no errors today, you might, maybe, get a portion of bread." There was another sneering pause. "Work hard, and we shall see." He shoved the clipboard back to Kempf and snapped his fingers as if he had suddenly remembering something. "Ah yes, we *do* have a little surprise for you at the entrance of Tunnel A."

The prisoners looked sideways at each other with worry. Surprises in Dora-Mittelbau were rarely good.

"Ten-shun!" Kempf screamed, bringing himself to rigid attention.

The sleet was beginning to slow and the brass band started up behind them.

"Aaaaand…march!"

The fleshy skeletons of the men stepped forward on bony knees and weak ankles. They shambled out through the iron entrance gate and moved towards the concrete road.

"March in unison! Your left…your left…your left."

A kapo sang out a cadence as Horse Head walked next to the clottering column. He held his truncheon at his thigh and barked out insults. "Pieces of shit! Useless eaters! Don't you dare damage my rockets!"

A black Mercedes drove towards them and rolled to a stop. Two small swastika flags sprouted up from the headlamps. The fenders were flecked with mud and the license plate had the double lightning bolts of the SS. Whoever was inside the chauffeured car was obviously important. The windshield wipers fanned left and right—squeaking because sleet was no longer coming down—and one of the guards rushed over to open the door. The man who got out was portly and had a wide smile. The guard clicked his heels together and offered a Hitler salute.

"Welcome back, sir."

The man waved his hand and put on leather gloves. He pointed at the rail yard and asked in a voice of calm authority, "How many today?"

The prisoners were ordered to a halt as the man in a leather trench coat studied the rockets in the rail yard. He had an easy smile and leaned towards the guard that had just saluted him. There was a bit of good-natured elbowing and the two men laughed at something. Cigarettes were brought out from a silver case. The engine of the Mercedes was turned off and this made the windshield wipers stop in mid swipe.

Another man—Eli had seen him many times in the tunnels before—hurried over. He was a civilian engineer and he had a wide nose with penetrating eyes. Instead of saluting, he shook the larger man's hand and they began slapping each other on the shoulder. It was clear they had known each other for many years and enjoyed each other's company.

Other SS officers gathered around this man who had a thousand-watt smile. He offered them all cigarettes. A packet of chocolate was brought out and it too was passed around—each SS officer snapped off a piece.

"Who's that?" a prisoner next to Eli asked.

"No idea."

"He's in charge of the torpedo program," whispered a voice behind them.

"QUIET!" Horse Head roared. His face turned beet red and a vein bulged on his forehead. It looked like an earthworm.

The important man glanced over at the shout and looked at the prisoners. It was a look that someone might give to a tool bench. He adjusted his hat with both hands and began to ask more questions. Eli couldn't hear exactly what was said, but he did catch words and phrases. "Oxygen Filling Points... Servomotors...Amatol...the Führer...London." The man strolled towards a rail car and climbed up onto it. The SS circled around him. Whoever he was, this visitor in a leather coat was a star they all seemed to orbit around.

The Mercedes growled back to life—its tailpipe rattled and the windshield wipers started up again—it did a Y-turn in the middle of the road and drove off at high speed, its wheels sizzling on wet concrete. To Eli, it sounded like hamburger being fried in a pan.

Horse Head took off a glove and put two fingers in his mouth. He whistled a sharp double-note. "Move out!"

Clogs clacked down a shallow hill as guards in their towers lazily held their machine guns. A gust of wind picked up and Eli felt a breeze move through his stiff frozen uniform. His penis was a shriveled prawn as he moved forward. He glanced back at the important man in the leather trench coat. Whoever he was, he stood on a rail car now and looked inside the bell of a rocket engine. He took out a camera and began taking pictures of the metal tubing that fed into the combustion chamber. He stood back and must have made a joke because the guards broke into laughter.

Horse Head stood in the middle of the road and pointed to Tunnel A. He hit random prisoners as they passed. He said, "There's a surprise waiting up ahead for you rags. Take a good look at it."

A portable gallows had been set up next to the yawning mouth of the tunnel. It was constructed of rough wood and looked vaguely like a wishing well. Suspended from the metal crossbar was a prisoner. He kicked the air softly—one of his clogs had fallen off—and his eyes were bulging, full of terror. Both hands were knotted behind his back and his face looked like plum wine. Spittle came from the side of his mouth.

"Have a good look," Horse Head called out. "That's a rag hung out to dry."

Eli's gaze slithered to the sodium light mounted on the side of the tunnel. It was a bar of luminous white. Look at that, he told himself. Don't look at the rope. Look at the light.

"If you break our rockets," Horse Head shouted, "we will break your fucking neck!"

As Eli marched past the dangling kicking shape, he heard the horrible wheeze of the man's windpipe cinching shut.

Curiosity got the better of him. He couldn't help but look.

The man had a red triangle and he was staring up, as if searching for proof of God. The dying man twitched and danced—he wiggled in the air—and the rope creaked. Eli told himself that in a few minutes this man would climb out of his body, he would slap dust from his uniform, and he would breath in fresh air. Soon, his ghost would stroll out of the camp. Soon, this man would get an answer to all that lies beyond.

Today it is you, Eli thought entering the tunnel. Tomorrow it will be me.

WHAT CAME FROM BERLIN

HIS FEET WERE SWOLLEN because evening count had taken over two hours. There was no need for roll call to last that long, but it amused the SS to walk among them. Bright searchlights slashed across the parade ground while, at the other end of camp, the sound of rockets being loaded onto rail cars could be heard. The wind rolled down from the Kohnstein and brought with it the smell of death. The crematorium was working overtime and the sooty remains of what used to be human beings billowed up into the sky before they were dragged back down to earth on a river of wind. Eli felt grainy particles in his nose. He held his breath and tried not to think about the ghosts that swirled around him, how they tried to enter his lungs.

The camp commandant paced with his arms crossed over his chest. Tall and lean, his name was Otto Förschner. He had a scar that ran like a snake across the bridge of his nose. Eli stood in the middle of the roll call square and hoped that the moat of flesh between himself and the Nazis might offer some kind of protection. Those on the edges were beaten—those in the middle were harder to reach.

His feet throbbed as he swayed from exhaustion. The SS shouted out words about purging Germany of evil, about how their new order was sweeping away the rotten garbage of Europe, and how the prisoners were just useless bodies that sponged off the state. It was right and just to create a more beautiful land. If this meant pulling up a few weeds, so be it.

Finally, at last, a voice crackled over the loud speaker. "Dismissed!"

Thousands of prisoners scattered. Their neat rows dissolved and those who were strong enough hustled away to get prime spots in the triple-layered bunks. Sleep wasn't just a temporary escape from the camp, it was a matter of survival. If you didn't get a good night of sleep it meant that you were more worn-out the next day, which might muddle your thoughts and cause mistakes, which could be deadly. Sleep was as necessary as food. Everyone knew this, so the middle layers of the triple bunks were preferred. The bottom wasn't any good because you might get leaked on from diarrhea, and the top wasn't good because you were too close to the roof and the cold. The middle was the Goldilocks area. It was warm and lifesaving.

Eli scratched the bony hollow of his armpit and then his scrotum. His skin was a type of grey paper that had been stretched over the rigging of his skeleton. He considered the open sores on his shins and began to worry. An infection?

None of this mattered right now, though. All that mattered was getting to Barrack 118 and climbing into a middle bunk.

Snow tumbled down in thick fat flakes. His clogs clattered on the concrete path as he passed the fire pond—the water was only frozen in the very middle—it would be so easy to go over to the edge and take a long slow drink. As snow hit the dark shore of the fire pond, it looked like the stars themselves were being pulled down from the heavens. Eli glanced up the hill and saw orange flames shooting up from the chimney of the crematorium. It roared and rumbled.

Up the steep path he climbed until he reached Barrack 118. A searchlight sniffed across the camp, hunting for prisoners who weren't moving fast enough. The door was already open when he got there and a few men were pissing in a lone metal bucket. A drumming ringing sound could be heard. One of the men farted.

Eli passed through to the sleeping area and stepped onto the dirt floor. It was caked hard, smooth. A coal stove was in the center but since they weren't allowed to burn anything, it was just a nuisance, it was just something to stub your toe on in the middle of the night. A searchlight fanned across the window and this sent spidery shadows scurrying across the wall.

With a heave as though he were getting out of a swimming pool, he pulled himself up into a middle bunk. Other men crowded in and fights broke out over sleeping arrangements. Eli laid flat, his clogs beneath his head, his hands over his heart, and he felt others climb into the bunk on either side of him. They were packed in tight. Like sardines, Eli thought.

He tried not to sink into the warm waters of his past—it was dangerous to remember life before Dora—but there was his mother sitting on a sofa as she sewed. His father was reading a book. His brother was there too, scooting a zeppelin across the carpet. The traffic of Berlin grumbled beneath the window of their flat. Photos were on the wall and he knew the story behind every aunt, every uncle, every cousin. He was unusually close to his extended family. They were as tight as a chain.

They lived on Sophienstrasse and attended the New Synagogue, which had a grand Arabian dome that rose high above the street. It was a hub for all the progressive Jews of Berlin. Libraries, schools, and a dizzying array of shops spooled around it, and when he was a boy, Eli liked to watch men and women rush into the telegram office just across the street. He liked to listen to their conversations. After Hitler came to power in 1933 he noticed that people were sending more telegrams. They looked worried and didn't talk quite so much. He wondered why.

His father was a professor of mathematics at Humboldt University and even though Eli didn't care about this when he was a boy he would later come to appreciate that his father worked alongside Erwin Schrodinger, Max Planck, and Albert Einstein. Whenever he visited his father's office, he saw books stuffed into cases and there was a huge blackboard on wheels that was always covered with equations. Chalk dust matted the carpet. He liked how his father's office was musked with the scent of pipe tobacco and aftershave.

During the summer, before so many things changed, he watched trams rumble by their flat and he secretly smoked cigarettes in the park with his friends. At night, they would sneak into Clärchens Ballhaus in order to watch women in low cut dresses whirl around. Smoke hung from the rafters and trumpets blasted out the bright fireworks of jazz. The fast beat of a bass made everyone shake and shimmy. Eli wasn't an elegant dancer, but he was energetic. His friends called him "Fish Bones" because he was so skinny and he flopped around the dance floor.

"Don't care," he shouted with both hands in the air.

At first, Eli didn't pay much attention to Nazism. It was background noise, it was some kind of political fuss, and sure there was a lot of street corner shouting, but who cared? He saw the swastikaed posters around Berlin of course, and he sometimes paused to consider the scowling man that looked out from them, *der Führer*, who looked like an angrier version of Charlie Chaplin. They both had that silly moustache—a toothbrush moustache, his mother called it—and they both waved their hands comically in front of audiences. Eli actually saw Hitler one afternoon. It happened on

Unter den Linden when an open-topped Mercedes rolled down the street not more than ten meters away. Hitler was in the back and he looked out at the city as if seeing something else. His eyes were cold blue, Eli remembered. Two motorcycles with sidecars followed the Führer's car, and they each had machine guns. One of the guns pointed at Eli before the motorcade growled down the street and off into the future. For reasons he couldn't quite understand, Eli thought of Elijah and his mighty chariot of fire rising up in a whirlwind. It was the story of a prophet who had come to change the world. Hitler, however, was far from the goodness of Elijah. The man preached a scripture of hate. Why did people like him so much? What was it about this man that made him popular?

Soon the brown shirts were marching through the streets at night singing anti-Semitic songs, and if you didn't salute as they passed you'd get punched in the face with brass knuckles. Signs went up saying that Jews could no longer use parks, drinking fountains, or sidewalks. Windows were smashed. The Nazis painted yellow stars onto businesses. They stood outside with crossed arms, and if someone tried to enter, they were shoved away.

"Move along," they barked. "Jew store."

Eli and his family began to stay indoors. They didn't go to the grocer, nor did they stroll around at dusk to watch the gas lamps flare to life, and he was forbidden to visit Clärchens Ballhaus ever again.

"It's too dangerous," his mother said, tussling his hair. "I know you're bored, but better bored than hurt. These brown shirts…they're thugs. Just two days ago they beat Shimon Eberhard so badly that he's still in the hospital." She scrunched up her face. "And this newspaper of theirs? *Der Stürmer.* Have you seen it? How can they print such lies about us and get away with it?"

At night, when the brown shirts marched down the street, his father drew the curtains and put on the radio to drown them out.

"This will pass," he said, smoking his pipe. "Our people have survived worse."

They sat around the table and played backgammon and pinochle. Soft music flowed from the speaker and the front door was now always double-bolted. Eli went to his bedroom and read books by H.G. Wells. He liked his stories about space travel and invisible men. "All is well," his parents said before clicking off his lamp and tucking him in. Yes, he nodded. All is well.

And then one evening, it wasn't.

It started when they heard shouting down the street, and whenever the wind changed direction they could smell burning. His father leaned out of the front window and said he could see an orange glow from the university area.

"Something's on fire."

He grabbed his overcoat and hat.

His father reluctantly went back to leaning out the apartment window and groaning occasionally. He stared at the glowing skyline and smoked cigarette after cigarette. The moon skittered behind clouds and his father turned on the radio for clues. Nothing. He tuned into the BBC and hunched over the speaker. Still nothing.

"You're not going *anywhere*," Eli's mother said grabbing his shoulder. She peeled off his coat and hung it on a peg. "Stay inside…please. Think of what happened to Shimon. Please…darling…stay inside."

"Why aren't we hearing fire engines?" he asked. "Something's wrong near the university."

He left early the next morning. In fact, he left so early that the world was still full of dark blue shadow and the only traffic on the roads were delivery vans full of bread. Eli's father would later say he worried that his office had been torched and that the dissertations of his postgraduate students might have gone up in flame. What if their work had been destroyed? How would they get their degrees? They had worked so hard—what if they hadn't made copies of their mathematical proofs? His own books could be bought again from publishers, and surely the university would cover that, but what of his students' work? As he approached the cream-colored buildings of the university, he saw that everything seemed to be in order. There was, however, something odd across the street in Bebelplatz.

He dodged a clanging tram and hustled over. In spite of the early hour, a crowd had gathered. There, in front of him, was an enormous pile of ash. At first he couldn't tell what he was looking at but, gradually, he realized it was thousands of burnt books. His knees weakened as he watched smoke thread up into the sky. The Nazis had raided the university library and pulled out everything they found offensive, which appeared to be most of the shelves. They doused these books and pamphlets and folios with gasoline and torched them. They made a bonfire out of ideas.

Eli's father bent low. The ash was still warm, still smoking, and when he touched it, his fingertips were dusted with grey powder. A few of the spines could still be read and he reached in to pull them out. Bertolt Brecht. Erich Maria Remarque. James Joyce. Tolstoy. Kafka. H.G. Wells. He gathered up these spines and put them in his satchel. It was foolish and wrong to think that he was saving them, and yet he couldn't just leave them there. He walked around the smoldering pile and plucked out books with his thumb and forefinger. He cried as he did this.

A gust of wind picked up and this sent ash spiraling into the morning air. It drifted like gloomy snow across Bebelplatz.

Later that evening, Eli's father, this same man who loved books, this man who had devoted himself to knowledge and wisdom, this man who did not drink, poured himself a large tumbler of whiskey and drank it in one pull. It was the first time Eli had seen his father with a bottle. And as he continued to down the numbing liquid, he gave a sour shudder and pointed at the window. His speech was slurred.

"All day, I've been thinking about Heinrich Heine."

"Who?" Eli asked.

"A Jew. Like us. One of his books was on that…that pile."

Eli waited for his father to continue.

"Heine wrote something that has been buzzing in my ear all day. He wrote, 'When they burn books, men are next.'" There was a pause. His father tipped back his glass and pointed at his son. "D'you know when he wrote that?"

Eli played with a lump of candlewax. He shrugged a shoulder.

"A hundred years ago." His father poured himself another whiskey and looked at his black shoes. "A hundred years ago." The beaten down professor shook his head, and when he looked up he said something expected and startling. "We must leave Germany." His voice was soft, but determined. He said it again, "We must leave our country."

They were on a train the next day with as many suitcases as they could carry, and as it rolled away from Berlin—moving faster and faster—Eli looked out the third class window and fumed at his father. He made a stone of his face. He refused to cry that he had to leave everything behind except for a few books, and he didn't look at his father. The man was a coward. He was overreacting. So what if a few books got burnt? Did this mean he had to leave his home, his friends, his life? He didn't hate the Nazis. He hated his father.

Professor Hessel took a job at Jagiellonian University in Kraków later that summer. It was a magnificent Polish city—even an eleven-year-old boy could see that—but it wasn't friendly to newcomers. Their flat was far from the Jewish quarter and Eli's parents told him that under no circumstance should he or his brother talk about the past.

"We're not Jews," they whispered. "Not here. Not anymore."

As Eli's father started the academic year of 1933-1934 at a new institution, his mother went about the business of making their three-bedroom flat as cozy as possible. She cooked familiar meals and, behind the privacy of a locked door, they honored the Sabbath. To the rest of the apartment block they were Catholics who weren't particularly pious. No matter. With the world changing so fast, more and more people were avoiding church on Sunday. The Hessel Family was no different.

They settled into their new life surprisingly fast and this suited Eli's father just fine. His mother, Eli's grandmother, was originally from Prussia and this meant he grew up speaking Polish as a child. Eli's mother, on the other hand, had an unusual gift for acquiring languages. She absorbed words and phrases like a plant in sunlight. She already knew French and Italian, and she enjoyed the challenge of Polish.

"When it is a matter of survival, you can learn anything fast," she told her children while boiling a leg of mutton. "We will speak Polish at home so that you can learn. If we're going to live here, if we're going to hide among these people, we must speak their language."

Eli struggled with the strange new words and grammar. It frustrated him that he couldn't get the thoughts that were swimming around in his head to leap across the bridge of his tongue. He pouted and kicked chairs.

"Stupid language."

"Stop," his mother warned with a raised finger. "Say that in Polish. How do you say 'stupid language' in Polish?" She crossed her arms. "Well...I'm waiting."

"*Gloppi jez?*"

She shook her head. "No. *Głupi język.*"

AT NIGHT, HIS FATHER LISTENED to German radio. He smoked a pipe and pretended to read but Eli could tell his father was really stewing about the news coming out of Nazi Germany. The announcer talked about how the Jews were destroying their nation and how Hitler would smash Bolshevism. Eli's parents held hands when they heard this. Their knuckles interlocked and looked like the spine of a hinge.

Weeks turned into months, months into years. Soon, to the surprise of the whole family, they had lived in Kraków for five years. It was 1938. His father had risen up the ranks at Jagiellonian University and become a full professor. He came home at six o'clock each night and whenever invitations to parties were offered he politely said no. Eli asked about this once, and his father said he was afraid that he might let his guard down.

"I might say something that I'd regret," he said, tamping tobacco into his pipe. "When the liquor's in, the truth's out."

Hardly anyone was allowed to visit their flat. They hid all trace of their Judaism in a wardrobe and only pulled out their heritage when it was absolutely safe. Their background was covered. Hidden. A secret.

And then one evening, Eli found his father listening to the radio and drinking a cup of milky tea. His hair was peppery grey and he held a sheet of paper. It looked like a list.

"What's that?" Eli asked, dropping onto the sofa.

His father handed over the yellow sheet. "These are things a Jew can no longer do in Germany. I've been keeping track."

Eli read his father's neat handwriting. Jews had been removed from government. They could no longer be lawyers. They were prohibited from attending university. They could no longer be editors or enlist in the army or become teachers. They were forbidden to change their names. They had to report all property in excess of 5,000 Reich Marks. They couldn't own a passport or travel between cities. Jews couldn't own carrier pigeons, use streetcars, go to the movies, or use public swimming pools. After dark, it was forbidden for Jews and dogs to walk the streets. And lastly, at the very bottom, all Jewish children could no longer attend school.

"Hitler has already marched into Czechoslovakia and Austria," his father said, leaning back in his chair. "What's next?"

"But he won't come here."

His father put a hand on Eli's shoulder and looked at him with a warm smile. "No. We'll be fine. I have made plans."

Eli tried not to think about politics and focused on being a good student. His parents reminded him that education was a precious right and over dinner each night they asked him about his classes. There were some subjects that soared over his head—literature, for example—all those novels, written in Polish—but he loved the elegance of mathematics. It was a powerful language of numbers. It was numerical poetry. He loved hunching over his desk at night and solving problems that dealt with flight. He began to imagine vectors lifting up metal wings and taking him somewhere else. He read books about rockets and space travel. When the lights were out, he lay in bed and wondered about the numbers that kept the Earth tethered to the sun.

His parents wanted him to become a doctor because it was portable work. "Knowledge doesn't need to be packed in a suitcase," his mother had said. "Doctors are needed anywhere you can imagine to go." His father talked to the biology department and it was decided that Eli would begin his studies at Jagiellonian University in the fall of 1939. He was eighteen years old.

The world, however, had different plans.

The Nazis invaded Poland on the same day that classes started, September 1, and they reached the gates of Kraków without much of a fight. Long columns of black helmeted SS stamped through the streets and swastika banners were unfurled from windows. Polish street signs were taken down with crowbars and German signs were put up. Everything was renamed. Kraków became Krakau. Jerusalem Street became SS Strasse. The market square of Rynek Główny became Adolf Hitler Platz. Suddenly, speaking German was an asset, and the Hessel family hunkered down in their flat to talk about the future. The air was electrified with danger.

Professor Hessel decided to get fake papers saying they were Aryan. It was easier to blend in now that German was the official language and he got documents on the black market saying they were Catholics from Berlin. In this way, they might survive life in Poland. However, to call Poland a country during this period of time would be incorrect because it had ceased to exist as a political entity. Poland was now called the "General Government" and it was nothing more than a colony of the Third Reich. All of the laws the Hessels thought they had escaped now surrounded them and this meant they had to lay low. If they had any doubts about their decision to camouflage their background, such reservations were quickly put to rest when all of the Jews of Kraków were ordered across the Vistula River and imprisoned in a rundown area of the city called Podgórze. Signs were pasted onto shop windows saying that any Jew found outside the gates of the ghetto would be shot. The Hessels locked their door and said nothing. They continued to hide in plain sight.

When university professors were declared enemies of the state, Dr. Hessel took a job as a janitor. He said nothing as his outspoken colleagues were sent away to concentration camps. He lowered his head and was glad that he hadn't said anything derogatory about Hitler. His quiet in the years before insulated him from the Nazi purge of the faculty at Jagiellonian University. He wasn't seen as a troublemaker. To local Nazi officials, he was simply a mousy college professor who loved math. Only the loudmouths were taken off to Buchenwald and Sachsenhausen.

Eli and his brother went into hiding and didn't venture out of their flat except when it was raining heavily. His mother also stayed indoors. Meals were cooked as quietly as possible, they rarely turned the radio up beyond a whisper, and Eli's father taught his boys math and physics. His father always seemed beaten down from his exhausting work but glimmers of his old self flared to the surface whenever he talked about coefficients, derivatives, and subtypes. He spoke in the poetry of numbers.

"$G\mu\nu = 8\pi G\ (T\mu\nu + p\Lambda\ g\mu\nu)$."

Books were smuggled into their flat and Eli read each one of them in bed. His favorite was Jules Verne's *From the Earth to the Moon*. When he asked his father to get more books on rocketry, the old man managed to do so. And whenever Eli gazed out of his window, he didn't look at the Nazis strutting around, he looked at a night sky that had been machine-gunned with stars.

Life in hiding continued and his father made good use of the black market. As a janitor, he was able to move from building to building. He hid chocolate bars, whiskey, and packs of cigarettes in garbage cans. For a while, it looked like the Hessels might ride out the war and emerge into the warm sunlight of peace as an unbroken family. This dream, however, came crashing down in the summer of 1944.

It happened when a neighbor began to wonder why two boys—now men—were living in the flat across from her and they never went to work.

This large woman with a happy face told the Gestapo that the family next door might be Jews. If these suspicions were correct, would she get their flat like the rumors said? It was so spacious and nice. Maybe they *weren't* Jews but surely it would be worth everyone's time if *someone* went over and asked a few questions. And she would get their flat, right? As well as the furniture? That was the deal, right?

Their door was kicked in a few nights later and soldiers with machine guns hit Eli's father in the head with their weapons.

"Papers!"

"Where are your papers!"

When he produced them—dazed and bleeding—they threw them on the carpet and began to dump out drawers. Silverware clattered to the floor. Dresses were thrown about in wild colorful arcs. Eli's mother clutched her boys and kept saying they were from Berlin.

"A mistake has been made," she pleaded. "We're Catholics, from Berlin. See what our papers say? See? Look."

The search continued until they came to a large wardrobe at the back of the flat. A tefillin was found. It had belonged to Eli's great-grandfather and even though it was dangerous to keep such an item, Eli's father couldn't bring himself to throw it away. A brass mezuzah was also found, along with an old Haggadah. When these items were shown to the family, there was silence.

The mousy professor squared his shoulders, stood up, and said, in a tone of fearlessness, "My people will outlast you. I'm proud of who I am."

The Gestapo officer took off his fedora and put it on the table. His leather coat creaked as he moved. A slow smile crossed his face. "We've built a special place in the woods for you." He turned to the soldiers and waved a hand as if he were batting away a fly. "Show them."

Eli, his mother, his brother, and his father were thrown into the back of a truck. Bits of dried mud and manure were on the wooden floorboards. Other men were tossed in and they were all taken to a warehouse where they waited for days without food, water, or lighting. More families were pushed into the dark. At last, after nearly a week, they were taken to a train station where they were loaded onto a cattle car. They had no idea where they were going or how long it would take to get there. They clattered through the night until they arrived at a huge rail yard. Shouting could be heard. A searchlight flashed into the car, temporarily blinding them. They passed through a short tunnel and the train came to a grinding hissing stop. After the door rolled open, guards shouted. Dogs snapped. They were ordered to jump down onto a gravel path, and as they did so, men lost their hats. Women lost their purses.

"Faster!" a guard screamed directly into Eli's face.

It was late at night and something strange hung in the air. At the end of the tracks were two huge bakeries that spewed out black smoke. Fire danced and sparked at the tops of the chimneys. Eli looked around and felt his mother put her arm protectively around him. Searchlights cut the night.

"We've got showers waiting up ahead," a guard said. "Hurry so you don't miss the warm water."

Men in blue and white stripped uniforms told them to line up—men on one side; women on the other— and Eli did as he was told. He looked for his mother in the crowd. Where was she? What was happening? Why were the bakeries burning bread?

He reached for his father's hand but—

HE OPENED HIS EYES. A searchlight roved across the cracked window of Barrack 118 and his stomach grumbled. He allowed his mind to conjure up an image of beet soup and moldy bread. The searchlight continued to sniff through the dark and, as Eli drifted off to sleep, a clear voice echoed in his ears.

My people will outlast you.

THE SHOWERS

HE WAS JOLTED AWAKE WHEN the SS ran into the barrack and began beating the bunks with rubber truncheons.

"Get up, get up!"

"Move it, you ass lickers!"

"You fuckers of dogs!"

"Wake up!"

They kicked and hit as they marched back and forth. Their flashlights slashed the dark. Eli scooted to the edge of the bunk, jumped down, and put on his clogs. Everyone stood in a tight line, breathing hard. Was this a selection? Would he have to run around and do squats in front of a doctor to prove that he was fit? The last time this happened, he was sent to the right, which meant he'd lived to see the tunnels another day. As for the left? He had no idea what happened to the men sent there. There were rumors they'd been sent to the infirmary, the *Revier*. It was a place for starving men. They waited for death on a dirt floor and they were given no food or water. No wonder the Nazis put the *Revier* so close to the crematorium. The wheelbarrows wouldn't need to travel far.

The SS continued to use their truncheons and they yelled whenever a prisoner's cap tumbled off.

"Put that on," they screamed, inches from a prisoner's face.

One of the guards, SS-*Hauptscharführer* Otto Brinkmann, had a face like a shovel. Bourbon was on his breath and he had a habit of biting his fingernails. In the dark, his head turned on a swivel and he cracked his truncheon down onto wooden frames.

"Faster, you cunts. Move it!"

Eli tried to look out the window. Were other barracks being emptied? And if so, would that be good or bad?

"Listen up!" Brinkmann roared. His voice was surprisingly high and he had a Bavarian accent. "We're going to be orderly and calm. Move out. Go, go go!"

As they shuffled into the night, Eli heard Moshe whisper behind him, "But where are we going?"

A man named André hissed. "Shhh! Horse Head is here."

Sure enough, the bulk of SS-*Hauptscharführer* Erwin Busta was standing at the doorway. He slapped a rubber truncheon against the palm of his hand.

"Good evening," he said as they passed. "We're going to have fun tonight."

"Oh yes, lots of fun," Brinkmann added.

One of the French prisoners whispered, just loud enough for Eli to hear, "*Surcroît de malheur.*"

The snow had finally stopped tumbling down and this meant the moonglow ground was unspoiled with footprints. Everything was clean and innocent as they moved for the roll call square. It seemed like they were the only barrack on the move, and this made fear firework inside Eli's chest. He felt dizzy. He couldn't spit. They walked past the roll call square, past the kitchen, past the unused soccer field, past the southern barracks, and they turned towards the back of camp—where were they going?

They marched in unison, their clogs squeaking on the fresh snow. Eli recognized the heads of André, Moshe, and Zev just in front of him. He couldn't exactly call them friends, but they did work together and they watched out for each other whenever possible. Friendship in Dora was rare. You never knew when someone might vanish, so why take the time to get attached? Friendship also required generosity and kindness. Eli had seen so-called friends gobble up bread that didn't belong to them. He had seen friends steal wooden clogs. He had seen friends accept camp money from the SS in exchange for information that got another man beaten or shot. Whenever Eli thought about helping another man, he often paused and wondered what he would get in return.

He looked at the heads in front of him and wondered if they were going to die in the next ten minutes. It could happen. Maybe they were being marched into the woods where a firing squad was already waiting? Maybe their guns were already oiled and loaded. He felt an odd sense of calm about this. It was almost like sliding into warm water. He reached for Moshe's shoulder.

"We'll be fine," he said.

The man in front of him half-turned his head. "We will, yes."

Horse Head ran ahead and stood at the entrance of a brick building that Eli had never seen before. A parallelogram of light spilled out onto the snow. Several guards stood at the edge of the concrete path and they held machine guns loosely at their hips. A truck idled in the distance.

Eli looked up, down, to the left, to the right—he tried to absorb the reality of what stood before him. Was this the gas chamber? He hadn't seen one at Dora yet. Surely one existed though.

They were pushed into a large room, one that had eight dangling lightbulbs overhead. There was the sound of hundreds of clogs scrapping against the wet brick floor. There were so many men around him that he couldn't move his arms and he couldn't turn around. Fear pumped through his veins and he wondered how many minutes of life he still owned. Would he be in this world at sunrise?

Horse Head's voice sounded behind them. "Shirts on the right, trousers on the left."

Another voice piped up. It was Brinkmann. He climbed onto something, a box perhaps, and he said, "Shirts on the right. Trousers on the left. Leave your caps by the door. I repeat…leave your caps by the door. Hurry now, the water's getting cold." He cupped his hands around his mouth. "MOVE IT! The water's getting cold."

A record player started up, a hissing skip-skip-skip of the needle at first, and then Frédéric Chopin's *Andante Spianato, Opus 22* was soon dancing around the room. The piano was spritely, it twinkled and waterfalled as frightened men unbuttoned their blue and white striped uniforms. Music flowed around them as they dropped their trousers.

Eli touched the pfennig-size buttons on his shirt and made himself naked. He cupped his penis with both hands.

"Leave your clogs behind," Horse Head bellowed. "Let's go, let's go."

Music fell like rain, and there was the dull crack of truncheons hitting skulls. "MOVE!"

He'd had his clogs since Auschwitz and his feet had made the insides nice and smooth. His toes were calloused in just the right places and his heels were no longer full of bloody sores. If he lost his clogs now it would mean weeks of bleeding into a new pair. That meant infection, and that might mean the

Revier. His clogs were the last of his riches. If he were to give them up…? He would then have nothing of value. Nothing at all.

As the naked men pushed forward, he felt someone's penis against his buttock.

"Hurry," Brinkmann yelled. "The water's getting cold."

"Into the showers," Horse Head hollered from the back. A crack of what sounded like a whip could be heard.

He couldn't raise his arms, he couldn't turn around, and all he could do was ride the crowd into the next room. Filthy bodies caked with dirt, sweat, and dried blood were all around him. Every cell in his body screamed for him to *do* something. But what could he do?

He shuffled forward and realized that his precious clogs were lost. Gone. Vanished. He wanted to weep. Maybe he already was weeping?

He thought of the showers at Auschwitz-Birkenau. He hadn't seen the inside himself—no living soul had—but he'd heard rumors. He had heard about large rooms with fake showerheads bolted into the ceiling. He'd heard how the lights stayed on and how gas pellets were dropped down a pipe. Apparently this pipe had a spiral channel in the middle to make sure the poison distributed equally into the gas chamber. Those closest to the pipe died instantly; those against the wall took longer. There were stories of fingernail marks in the concrete as victims tried to climb over each other for the last of the good air.

Terror boiled in his chest. He began to shake, and even though that old feeling of running away filled up his muscles and made him tense, there was no place to go. He was pinned into place. He was as helpless as a butterfly in a kill jar.

"Faster, faster," Horse Head yelled. The sound of a truncheon coming down on shoulders could be heard from the back.

A strange and unexpected calm filled him up. Perhaps it was a type of surrendering to reality? His heart began to swell with kindness for the prisoners around him. They were good men. All of them. Every foible and mistake and little sin they had each committed seemed to flutter up from their shoulders. They were rich with glowing, radiant life. And regardless of what they had done before Dora, every one of them deserved tenderness for all the days still ahead. They breathed, and blood pumped through their veins, and memories rode the delicate tangle of neurons that made them who they were.

They deserved better than this. Why wasn't the universe stopping what was about to happen?

Horse Head beat and punched his way to the middle. "Make five lines."

André, a dentist from Dieppe, and Zev, a plumber from Prague, stood near Eli. Moshe was lost somewhere to the right. The room was cold—two huge windows were cantilevered open—and the breath of hundreds of men spilled up to the rafters.

"Make five lines," Horse Head said again, wiping sweat from his brow with a handkerchief. "Let's be done with this."

At first, Eli didn't know what was going on, but it didn't take long for him to figure it out. It had been three months since his arrival at Dora and his black hair was laced with lice. The Nazis worried about this because lice carried typhus, and under the right circumstances an entire barrack could be struck dead in less than twenty-four hours. This would hurt productivity, of course, but it also meant the SS themselves might be exposed to the disease. The prisoners often speculated what the Nazis might do if an outbreak did happen, and there was a persistent and popular rumor about a whole barrack being sent to the *Revier* all because one case of typhus had been discovered. The rumor went on to say that the barracks on either side of the infected barrack were also sent away. In total—the story went—over 1,000 men were sent to the infirmary and in less than a week they were taken up the hill. All of this happened because of one case of typhus. Just one.

Horse Head stood with a plaid handkerchief tied over his mouth, bandit-style.

Eli stepped towards a barber. He was a thin man with close set eyes. His nose looked as if it had been broken and he was missing a front tooth. He snapped his scissors and spoke without looking up. "Next."

Eli sat on a wobbly metal stool and felt the dull scissors rip at his scalp. His hair was pulled out more than cut. Blood dripped down his forehead as clumps of black floated to the floor. He held his penis and scrotum in fear. He winced and counted to ten. His right leg jiggled up and down, nervously.

"Next."

He stood up and followed a thin line of others to another room. His scalp was bleeding—he touched it with his fingertips to see how badly—and he saw blood smeared on his palm along with strands of hair. Why didn't they use electric clippers? It would be faster, he thought. Cleaner too. But maybe faster and cleaner wasn't the point.

He looked for showerheads in the room he'd just entered, but didn't see any. There were, however, four large cement bathtubs against a wall. They were a meter tall and a line of naked men were stepping into them one after the other. They dunked themselves in and came up, spluttering and shivering. They wiped their faces with both hands.

"Rags, come and get washed," Brinkmann laughed.

Eli took a step closer and smelled disinfectant. Of course, he almost shouted. It's to kill the lice! Joy fizzed in his chest when he realized he wasn't going to die after all. It wouldn't make sense for the Nazis to remove lice and nits only to gas everyone a few minutes later. Why get them clean if—? No, that wouldn't make sense. No sense at all. Eli held onto this pearl of realization and shuffled towards one of the concrete baths. The floor was wet and he wiggled his toes. Maybe he would see another sunrise after all.

When it was his turn, he threw a leg over the side and fell in. Disinfectant washed into his nose and he gasped for air. The water was grey from the other bodies that had gone before him, and a kapo stood next to the tub with a heavy pole. There was a look on the man's face that said, *Dunk yourself or I'll do it for you.*

Eli closed his eyes, took a deep breath, and lowered himself in. The ashen water stung his scalp. His balls shriveled. A million little knives lanced his skin. When he came up, his whole body stung. It was like bathing in bleach. Maybe he was bathing in bleach?

"Out," the kapo said. He knocked his pole against the tub. "Next."

Eli slipped on the tiled floor. His whole body was goose-pimpled and he couldn't stop his teeth from chattering. Horse Head stood directly in front of him. The man towered up in a black uniform, but he wasn't wearing his thick leather coat. He also wasn't wearing his officer's cap. Maybe he didn't want them splashed with disinfectant?

A prisoner behind Eli stood before the concrete baths and didn't move. Horse Head pushed Eli aside with his truncheon and walked over to the man. He roared for the prisoner to get in. "Next!"

The man held both hands to his mouth. He said something in a foreign language and pointed at the water. Horse Head threw his truncheon on the floor and picked up the man as if he were a sack of wheat. In a mighty heave, Horse Head tossed the prisoner into the chemical bath. The prisoner surfaced once, twice, and there was violent spray of splashing. Horse Head grabbed the kapo's heavy pole and began stabbing the water. Whenever the man surfaced for air, Horse Head cracked him on the skull. This went on for several minutes until, at last, the man floated face-down in the soup.

"Get that thing out," Horse Head said, calmly. He looked at the water splashed onto his uniform and made a face. He untied the plaid handkerchief from over his mouth and used it to dab at wet spots. "Look at this. It's ruined."

"That'll stain," Brinkmann nodded.

The prisoner's body was fished out of the tub and dropped onto the floor—wet, limp, and bleeding.

When Eli saw this, he hurried into the next room. He moved to the center and stood among the other men, shivering. They rubbed their backs together for warmth. They blew into their hands. Eli looked at the swaying light bulbs above and searched the ceiling for vents. The windows were open and that calmed him. If they were closed, well then…that would be something to worry about. The room itself was painted pale white and a network of copper pipes were overhead. There were twelve showerheads and he could feel a drain beneath his feet. All of this was reassuring. It's just a shower, he told himself. It's just a shower. It's just a shower.

"All is well," he whispered.

The room filled up with other prisoners, and once everyone was disinfected the SS and the kapos stood in the doorway. Brinkmann passed a cigarette to Horse Head, who was still dabbing at his uniform and tut-tutting. "Maybe it's for the best," he shrugged. "I need a new one anyway."

A screeching groan came from overhead and water began to fall from the steel showerheads. It was freezing but it felt so good to scrub his face. Eli closed his eyes and enjoyed the icy wet. Grime from the tunnels flowed down the drain. He looked at his feet and saw streaks of brown among the white tiles. His toenails were crusted with black and he wanted to reach down to clean them, he wanted to scrub his armpits and remove grease from beneath his fingernails, he wanted to run his hands all over his living body.

"Be quick," Brinkmann yelled. "This isn't a spa."

Eli stood with his mouth open and drank in the water. Others did the same. Hundreds of men stood like baby birds waiting to be fed. He rubbed his face, slowly, and smiled.

When the water thwanked off, he felt it trickle through his leg hair.

"Move it," came a voice. "Back to the baths. Faster, faster!"

They returned to the tall concrete baths and saw their clothes heaped into three separate piles—caps, shirts, trousers. He wondered when the sorting had happened. Maybe a team of prisoners had done it while they were showering? Were they even *their* clothes or had they come from somewhere else in camp? They looked wet, like they had been freshly dunked into the chemicals.

"Rags, find your rags!" Horse Head shouted.

The prisoners pushed forward in a dash to find trousers that fit. Everything was damp and there were more holes and rips in the clothing than ever before. The lice had been bleached dead but the fabric was now threadbare and tattered. Eli picked up a pair of blue-and-white striped trousers and saw a long tear down one of the legs. He reached for another pair and slid into them before they could be taken. The soggy warmth stuck to his legs and he realized the waist was too big. He needed a belt or some rope. Maybe he could find something in the tunnels? In the meantime, he would have to hold them up with one hand and keep searching the pile. He rooted around but the best trousers were already gone. Maybe he could trade with someone later?

Three kapos began to yell out the numbers that were printed across the front pocket of the wet shirts. It was like roll call.

"41023."

"37681."

"39082."

Eli listened for his number and hurried over to get his shirt when it was called. It was still soiled with dirt, and there were sweat stains in the armpits as well as the rusty splotch of blood where Horse Head had hit him, but at least the lice were dead. The fabric was warm and it kissed his skin when he put it on. He twisted the front of his shirt and watched water dribble onto the tile floor. Others did the same. He did up the pfennig sized buttons and continued to squeeze bleach water onto the floor.

"42022."

"38181."

"39967."

When the piles were gone, they were ordered back into the large room where they had first undressed. Hundreds of wooden clogs were strewn about and Eli immediately started looking for his pair. He held up his trousers with one hand and moved to the spot where he'd kicked them off. Where were his? They all looked the same.

Kempf, that beefy kapo who whistled the "1812 Overture," stood near the door and held his hickory stick as if it were a sword. "Grab two and be done with it."

His stick came down onto the head of a French prisoner and Kempf stood next to the unconscious body. "We're not shopping at Wertheim's. Grab two and stand at attention."

Eli got down on his hands and knees. Where were they? He scuttled around, sliding in the wet. There! There! He reached for one clog and started looking for its partner—he read the floor, left to right—where was it? Others were snapping up clogs and he reached for one at random to make sure he had *something* for his left foot. He kept searching. His eyes skidded across the floor.

He was so busy looking down that he didn't notice Kempf walking over. Without warning, the stick came down on the man next to Eli. The man, who was standing at attention, dropped, and his wet clothes made a splatting sound against the tiles.

As Kempf raised the stick again, the fallen man held out a hand to protect himself. "Please…I am sick. You don't need to hit me."

Kempf raised an eyebrow and took in a lungful of air. A moment passed before his whole face soured. "IN THIS CAMP THERE ARE ONLY HEALTHY PEOPLE AND DEAD PEOPLE." There was a long pause. "Which are you?"

The man stood up dizzily and fell sideways into the wall. He hunched into a ball and began to weep. "My family…" he said. "My family…"

Kempf grabbed a fistful of the man's uniform and dragged him across the floor. The prisoner kicked and flailed as he tried to stand up. The two of them went out into the night and a moment later there was screaming.

"I think," Horse Head said, tossing his cigarette onto the wet tiles, "I think our fun is over."

They were pushed outside and searchlights followed them down the snowy concrete road until they came to Barrack 118. The electrified fencing popped and crackled in the distance. Eli looked for Moshe, André, and Zev, but couldn't see them.

When they were all inside, a padlock was snapped onto the door. Everyone lay in the dark, shivering. The warm damp of his uniform quickly turned cold and Eli's sleeve began to stiffen with ice. He imagined a bonfire. He saw dancing flames and thought about holding out his outstretched palms for warmth.

Two men in the bunk below began to talk. Their voices were loud.

"No, listen to me, it *could* be done," one of them said. He spoke German with a French accent. "If we attack Horse Head, someone could get his pistol."

"Yes."

"And then we attack Kempf."

"And then we attack Kempf?"

"Obviously. It will be easy, if there are enough of us."

They spoke loudly, as if they wanted to be heard. "It's better to die once than be afraid of death all the time."

Eli nodded. This may be true, he wanted to say aloud, but it's also true that once you die you stay dead a long time.

Another man started talking about huge bowls of mashed potatoes and pots of green beans and lamb roasted with sprigs of thyme. His voice drifted into Eli's mind and he began to see thick loaves of warm bread, plates of herring, wedges of cheese, and jugs of water. A fire would be crackling in a hearth and he'd curl up next to it with a wool blanket. His belly would be full and he'd fall asleep in a room that had a heavy door—an oak door with many locks and bolts on it.

He smiled, and paddled away into the dream.

HE SOUND OF THE FUTURE

ALTHOUGH DORA WAS RULED BY routine, the Nazis often switched inmates on the production line to remind them that no one was indispensable. As far as the SS were concerned, fighting the war was clearly important but reminding the *untermenschen*, the sub-humans, of their proper place in the universe was more important. Even though rockets were rolling out of the tunnels, and even though these rockets were clearly a marvel of technology, the SS had the unwelcome realization that Germany was slowly losing the war. Everyone was going down the drain with Hitler and this meant that no prisoner should be allowed to survive. Everything must fall. Everything must burn. Put as many bodies into the furnace as possible, and stroll away. As far as the SS were concerned, a prisoner that lived might rat you out later. It was for this reason that bullets were placed into chambers and ropes were tossed over I-beams. In the last few months of the war, the work of death was everywhere. It was a frenzy of murder.

When Eli arrived at his work station, he sat on a stool and picked up a welding mask. His twelve-hour shift had begun. The table was a complete mess. Whoever had soldered fuses before him had left the tools jumbled in a pile and he couldn't find pewter anywhere. He stood up and went to the wardrobe behind him. The doors had been taken off months ago thanks to what Delacroix had done, and he could see that this, too, was untidy. In order to do his job, he first needed to clean things up, but this meant he'd run behind on the quota of fuses he had to make.

What to do?

He put his hands on his hips.

His stomach grumbled and he thought about the cooks who sloshed out breakfast. They were well fed and they smoked cigarettes. Eli had tipped his portion of beetroot soup down his throat and used his finger to wipe the enamel bowl clean. There was a beet chunk in his bowl and he saved it for last. It was earthy, it tasted of dirt, and there was something else too—the aftertaste of gasoline. His portion of bread was spotted with green fuzz but he didn't care about this. He wolfed it down. As soon as he had nothing left, he wished that he'd put a nubbin of bread in his pocket for later. It was a gamble to do such a thing, though. Someone might steal it or you might not be alive to enjoy it later. No, he shook his head. It's better to have food in your stomach than in your pocket.

He took off his cap and touched his scalp. He was free of lice for the first time in months, his clogs fit, and he had bread in his belly. He had even managed to find a length of rope to hold up his trousers. It was turning out to be a good day.

He replaced his cap and crossed his arms. Were those men serious about attacking Horse Head and Kempf? Maybe something would happen later this morning?

Someone cleared their throat behind him.

He snapped off his cap, spun around, and came to attention. The lamp from his desk made it hard to see who was in front of him. The shadowy man stepped closer.

"You're not working, 41199. How come?"

It was SS-*Obersturmführer* Hans Möser. Like Horse Head, he was feared by the inmates for his random acts of brutality and for how he wrote up reports to get them into further trouble with other guards on other shifts. Eli clicked his heels together and looked at the stone wall. "Sir, I regret to inform you that I cannot find pewter for soldering."

There was a grunt. He'd seen Möser strutting down Tunnel A but he'd never interacted with him before. He had a hawk nose and large ears that stuck out from the edges of his officer's peaked hat. His right eyelid sagged half-way down, which made him look like he was forever in the process of winking. Such an obvious physical deformity was surprising for an SS officer and Eli wondered if it was a war wound. Shrapnel maybe? His hands were pale and hairy. Eli found his eyes flicking to those hands. Möser was known for his cruelty and, during hangings, he often stood there with a smile on his face. After a minute or two, he would order the inmate cut down so the poor soul could get air back into their lungs. Then the man was hanged again. When Möser finally got bored, he snapped his fingers and left the man to dangle.

Obersturmführer Möser picked up a pair of needle-nose pliers and used them as a pointer. "Follow me."

"But sir, I'm supposed to work here. Once I find the pewter I'm sure that—"

"Follow me."

Eli stepped around his work table and walked behind Möser. There were hundreds of prisoners working at benches and these men in stripped uniforms moved quickly, they didn't stop to look up. Hammers clanked and there was the whine of pneumatic wrenches. Blue sparks from arc welding cast eerie shapes on the ceiling. Eli's shadow floated and shook against the wall.

Möser collected men as he moved. He used the needle-nose pliers as a pointer. "You...follow me," he said. "You, too."

By the time they reached the end of the production line, they were standing next to fully assembled V-2s. The engines were shiny and the nosecones— not yet fitted with explosives—were ready to lance the sky. A greasy electrical smell filled the air and it was hard to believe these weapons could ever get airborne. They looked so heavy, so chained to the ground. How would they ever take off?

When they emerged into the sun, Eli shielded his eyes. The fresh snow from last night made everything brighter. Next to him was a long train of rockets. Creosote and tar from the tracks filled up his nose. Someone was practicing a trumpet in the SS camp. It was all surprising and surreal.

"Hurry," Möser whistled to the cluster of men he had collected. He tossed the pliers to the ground and pulled out a pistol. A truck with a canvas top idled up ahead. The double-lightning bolts of the SS were on the driver side door and it was spattered with mud. Clumps of slushy snow were caught in the wheel wells.

Möser waved his pistol. "Inside."

There was nothing he could do, so he got in. He wondered once again about the conversation he had overhead in Barrack 118. Were either of those men in the truck with him? Was it too late to organize something? Maybe he had been worrying about his stomach too much and it should have been the rest of his body—and getting the rest of his body free—that he really should have focused on.

When they were crowded in the rear, a gate slammed into place. The canvas top overhead glowed with sunlight and .45 caliber brass shell casings were on the floor. Eli stared down and noticed the other prisoners were doing the same. What was happening? Where were they going?

Someone got in the driver's side—the truck rocked ever so slightly—and the engine was engaged. The bench beneath Eli began to rattle and they lurched forward.

"Where we going?" one of the prisoners asked.

"No idea."

"When Horse Head finds out I'm gone..."

"We'll be fine."

"How do *you* know that?"

"Where are they taking us?"

Eli had heard rumors of prisoners being taken into the woods and shot. Maybe that's what was happening? The Germans had done such things before. When they invaded Poland they forced Jews to dig their own graves—they said they were anti-tank trenches—but when the digging stopped, they shot them all. He studied the faces of the men around him. Did this have something to do with that talk of revolt? Did someone say that he was behind those words? Had a loaf of bread been swapped for his life?

He peeled back a flap of canvas and looked out. They were moving away from the rail yard.

"We're leaving Dora," he half-shouted over the engine. "See?"

They passed the barber-pole barricade at the entrance and bumped down a dirt road. The truck picked up speed. A motorcycle with a sidecar followed them. Its headlamp was on.

"We've left the camp for sure," Eli said, turning to the men who were looking at him.

"But here are we going?"

Eli shrugged. "I don't know."

THEY BOUNCED ALONG FOR HALF-AN-HOUR, and as they rumbled over grooves in the road and went deeper into a forest, Eli decided that he would take off running as soon as he saw a chance. Better to be shot in the back while running away than to be shot in the head while kneeling on the ground. His palms were sweaty and his whole body was a coiled spring. The motorcycle with a sidecar that followed them had a machine gun mounted to it. Eli looked at his feet and prepared for the end. He imagined zigzagging back and forth as he ran through pine trees. Huge chips of bark would explode around him as guns stammered out bullets. On and on he would run, until everything was quiet and calm.

Easy, he told himself. You can do this.

He curled his toes inside his wooden clogs.

The truck downshifted to a stop and the engine was cut. Time seemed to slow down. Two guards opened the back gate.

"Out."

He jumped down to the frozen ground and looked for men with guns. If he had to run, he'd kick off his clogs and worry about frostbite later. Four SS stood in the distance with machine guns, but they seemed totally disinterested in the prisoners. They didn't even look up. Trees towered around him and sunlight filtered down through the branches in thick buttery slants. He couldn't see a freshly dug trench anywhere, nor could he see any shovels so, maybe, perhaps, they weren't going to be shot.

What really commanded his attention was the sight of a V-2. It was in a clearing and it pointed straight up at a cloudless sky. The rocket was on an L-shaped launch pad and it huffed as a truck pumped it full of propellant. It was so strange to see. All the cold steel and electronics that made up the rocket now acted as one and it almost seemed like a living, breathing creature. The fuel was super-cooled liquid oxygen and this made a thin layer of shiny ice appear on the metal skin of the rocket. A team of civilian scientists moved around the base and unhooked hoses. They wore white coats and pointed at a fin.

The smell of bark and old leaves were all around him, as well as something else. He took a deep breath and couldn't place it. And then, it dawned on him that he was smelling a clean world. For almost a year he had been surrounded by thousands of men who hadn't bathed but now, in this clearing, with the wind moving through pine trees, everything was fresh and bright. Pure. He filled up his lungs. It was the first time he had been beyond barbed wire since his family had been arrested in Kraków. There was *so* much space, he thought. Freedom was so close. All he had to do was walk.

As the rocket breathed on its mobile launcher, a group of civilian workers huddled near the engine. They looked at clipboards and pointed at the nosecone.

"Let's go," Möser said, snapping his fingers.

Eli moved toward wooden crates that had PROPERTY OF THE REICH stenciled onto them and he glanced back at the rocket. The civilians didn't seem to notice or care that men in striped uniforms had appeared—slave labor was so deeply embedded in the Nazi economy that the sight of them didn't raise an eyebrow. He was a beast of fieldwork, nothing more. He was just a slave and was looked upon the same way a black man would be in the deep south of the United States. Or maybe not, Eli thought, looking at his uniform. Back then, before the Americans had their bloody civil war, there was at least an economic incentive to keep slaves alive. After all, you could always sell them to the highest bidder when you were finished with them. Some kind of return could be had on your property. Slavery in the Nazi universe, however, was something different. The concentration camps were designed to wring out as much labor as possible from an inmate before they died. They were never sold. The Third Reich took the model of the plantation and brutalized it even further for the modern industrialized twentieth-century. With a constant flow of free labor from the conquered countries of Europe, what did it matter who lived and who died? They were to be used, then burnt.

The men in white coats continued to care for the rocket. All that mattered was this agent of destruction that stood in the middle of the pine trees.

Möser lit a cigarette and spoke to the prisoners without looking at them. "After this thing's shot into the air, I want you to load these boxes on the truck."

One of the civilians shouted at Möser. "Put that damn thing out!"

"Don't talk to me that way. I'm SS."

The civilian raised both arms in disbelief. "Are you kidding me, *Obersturmführer*? Are you trying to get us all killed? This thing's full of liquid oxygen and you're *smoking* like you're in a beer garden? Put that damn thing out!" There was a pause. "And I'll talk to you any way I want. Do you know who I work for?"

Möser's face tightened and he took a step forward. His jaw clenched and unclenched. Slowly, purposefully, he dropped his cigarette into the snow and ground it beneath the tip of his jackboot.

"We're ready," another civilian shouted from what looked like a portable control console. He had a round face and a double-chin. "Clear the area."

A truck honked its horn three times and this made the civilians in white coats move away. Their shoes crunched and squeaked through snow. All was quiet, except for a low hiss from the rocket. Eli wondered if they should be further away. He imagined the fireball that would happen if the V-2 exploded. Surely they were too close. But maybe, if it did explode, maybe he could run into the woods? Disaster could bring opportunity.

The horn sounded again, this time it was a single long note, and then someone shouted out numbers. Eli looked for the voice but couldn't see it. The hiss of the rocket increased.

"Ten…nine…eight…seven…six…"

A low creaking could be heard from the V-2. It sounded like a thunderstorm rumbling on the horizon.

"Five…four… three…"

The man's voice pitched up in excitement and the hiss became a scream. A flash of baby blue appeared in the engine bell.

The final two words of the countdown couldn't be heard because thunder rippled through the air and a spout of flame spilled out in a widening circle. The rocket began to shudder. A crackling vibration hit Eli's chest and the ground beneath his feet shook. His whole body was buffeted by sound and he felt the delicate organs inside his body begin to quiver. The fabric of his uniform flapped and snapped. Heat hit his face. The rocket lifted slowly on a pillar of fire and then it flew up, like it was being sucked into the sky. The flame from the V-2 was now so bright it looked like a band of sunlight. Eli shielded his eyes as the rocket continued to fall up. It became a pinprick and there was the sudden double-crack of the sound barrier being broken. *Ba-boom*! It receded like thunder.

And then?

Silence.

Black smoke rolled through pine trees and the mobile launch pad creaked with heat. The snow around the base had been turned into a circle of burnt soil. Smoke waltzed around it, ghostlike.

"We're not going to lose this war," a guard shouted with joy.

There was a cheer from the civilian workers.

"That's the sound of the future, right there."

Eli thought about guidance controls pulsing out electrical sparks and that, somewhere in the guts of the fuselage, was his circuitry and his welding. He felt both anger and exhilaration as the V-2 climbed higher into the troposphere. To think that Germany, his country, had been the first to build an automobile, the first to discover x-rays, and now it was the first to build—

He looked down at his wooden shoes.

"All right," Möser said, lighting a cigarette. "Work."

THOU SHALT KILL

THE SNOW WAS MELTING FOR good and this meant the roll call square had become a soup of mud. His uniform was stiff—slightly frozen at the cuffs and he found himself looking forward to entering the tunnels. At least it would be dry and arc welding gave off a little heat.

Someone blew into the camp loudspeaker. "Test…testing."

They were ordered once again to snap off their caps in one fluid motion. The movement of thousands of men slapping their caps against the seams of their trousers sounded like a wave crashing against a shore.

"Again," Kempf shouted.

The men put their caps back on.

"Aaaand…*off!*"

The sound of a breaking wave washed over the roll call square again. This wasn't about getting the prisoners ready for work: it was about control, and it went on and on, pointlessly, for thirty minutes. Forty minutes. Fifty minutes. Guards roamed through the ranks as the clouds overhead looked like gunpowder.

Horse Head strolled in front of them. So too did Hans Möser. There was also SS-*Hauptscharführer* Wilhelm Simon, who had the nickname "Simon Legree" after the slave master in *Uncle Tom's Cabin*. He was known for assigning backbreaking work and there was a popular rumor floating around camp that he'd ordered several children beaten to death when they were accidentally sent to Dora instead of the nearby concentration camp of Buchenwald. Legree had a large forehead and a receding hairline. He also had the habit of looking straight through a prisoner. They were like birch trees in a forest to him. He didn't see them until, that is, a prisoner did something wrong. That's when his eyes narrowed. That's when his fury came out.

"At ease," a guard finally bellowed.

Eli could hear the dead being carted away behind him. Six bodies were found in Barrack 118 that morning and they were laid out by the front door.

A team of prisoners was now collecting bodies from all of the barracks. He could hear the rolling wheels of the wagon and, in the distance, he could hear the rumble of the brick crematorium at work. It had been built at the top of a hill so that the black fatty smoke might spill up into the sky. He turned to look at it. Even though it was only six in the morning, a jet of murk poured up from the chimney. It was grainy and as dark as ink.

Eli stared beyond the barbed-wire and chewed on his tongue. The sun was coming up in a brilliant yolk of yellow. A portable gallows had been wheeled before them and Eli wondered if his number would be called. In the last few days it had become popular to call out random numbers and have prisoners step forward. False charges were read out against them and a leather rope was cinched around their neck.

On this particular morning, a prisoner was dragged from a guard tower and forced to kneel in front of everyone. His right eye was swollen and his bottom lip was split. He slumped to the side with his hands tied behind his back.

It was André.

Eli took in a sharp breath and closed his eyes. No, no, no. He hadn't seen André for several days and he assumed that he'd died somewhere in the tunnels. It was clear now that he'd been tortured in the camp prison. He looked wrung out. Spent. He'd been a part of the Resistance so maybe the SS had tried to pry more information out of him? Had he said anything? Had he made false charges against Eli in order to lessen the pain? He couldn't be faulted for that, but—

Möser took out a pistol and aimed it at the back of André's head. The barrel hovered over that spot where the spinal column meets the skull. There was a lingering silence. This was called a *genickschuss*, a bullet to the back of the head.

"This man," he finally said to everyone, "tried to keep secrets from us about a rebellion. There are no secrets here. There will be no rebellion."

Möser stood with his arm ramrod straight and Eli knew that nothing could stop it now. SS-*Obersturmführer* Hans Möser would soon curl his forefinger and this would send lead flying through the air, it would slam into an innocent man's skull and the bullet would keep going until it drilled through a storehouse of memory and burrowed its way through nerve-endings, it would keep on traveling and destroying and shredding until it exited through a bony dam of forehead. Blood would pump out. André would fall. His body would be thrown into a wheelbarrow and a letter would be sent to his family in France. It would say that he had died of heart failure.

There wasn't a sound to be heard from anywhere in the roll call square. There wasn't a cough, or a clearing of a throat, or a sneeze. There was nothing. Nothing at all.

The gun cocked.

When the crack came, it echoed around the square. The prisoner—a former man—fell forward surprisingly slowly. André Laurent had been from Alsace-Lorraine and he'd fought in the Great War of 1914-1918. He'd survived the meat grinder of Verdun only to be captured by the Germans in a new war and then sent away to a secret concentration camp. In spite of the thousands of bullets that had flown around him in the trenches of Verdun and Ypres, he was now dead. It had taken more than two decades, but a German bullet finally found him in the end.

Eli watched all of this without emotion. He was numb. Flat. Ground down. He no longer felt the high and low registers of emotions, there was only this flatness.

Wilhelm Simon strode before the men. "I need two volunteers." He scanned the rows of prisoners carefully. "Who will come with me?"

Eli wondered what Simon wanted. Volunteers for what?

Simon wore his SS cap at an angle and walked down a row of prisoners. "For your efforts, you'll get two fat sausages."

Eli's hand went up as if it belonged to someone else. It was like a doctor had hit his kneecap with a tiny hammer and his auto-reflexive muscles had taken over. It was his stomach that lifted his hand, not his brain.

"You there," Simon pointed. "What's your number?"

"41199."

The man with a swastika armband nodded. "Come along." He turned on his heel and added, almost as an afterthought, "Pick a friend. He will join us."

ALTHOUGH THE SUN HAD ALREADY set, and although the camp searchlights had winked on long ago, he and Moshe were still dragging bodies to the crematorium. Their job was to make sure the number on the uniform matched the number inked onto the forehead of the corpse. Someone in the *Revier* had taken a black marker and written the camp identification number across the brow of the dead and it was Eli's job to make sure the number on the uniform matched the number on the skin. The Nazis were meticulous about records—they wanted to know who was alive and who was dead—and there had been a few cases in Dora where a living man had used a dead man's uniform. This not only made records inaccurate, but it was also hard to tell if an escape had happened. It was therefore decided that numbers would be inked onto foreheads so that uniforms would stay on bodies all the way to the oven.

"If you find a number that doesn't match the rag, put both of them over there," Wilhelm Simon said. He placed a hand on his holster. "And if I find that you've tampered with anything, I'll shove you in the fire myself."

They worked in silence. One of them grabbed the soiled feet, the other, the wrists. In this way they carried a flopping swaying body to the oven. The mouth was often open, as if in surprise, and as they carried each thin hammock of a body, the eyes stared ahead into the abyss. They dumped the corpse onto a pile and went back for more. What horrified Eli, at least at first, was the texture of the dead. Their skin was as cold as rubber and he could feel tendons and bones as he grabbed wrists. The head lolled as they lifted the body. The lungs were empty of air. The brain had gone black.

Eli looked at his hands and wanted to scrub them clean. Once, a few hours ago, his eye itched but he didn't want to touch himself with the same hands that had touched so many of the dead. He wanted to douse himself with disinfectant, he wanted to bathe in oil that would wash his memory clean, and he wanted to walk down the hill and leave the last fourteen hours far behind.

But instead, he went back for another body.

He called out the number on the forehead as Moshe studied what was printed on the uniform.

"41180."

"A match."

The body was stripped. The body was moved.

The crematorium had a large room for storing bodies. A smaller room to the side had a stone table for pathology research, and in the center of the building were two coal-fired muffle ovens that had been built by the Kori Company of Berlin. They rumbled with flame and heat. It was like standing in a desert. Above the entrance of the building was a small cross that had been set into the brickwork. At first Eli couldn't figure out what it was doing there, but as he went in and out of the building, he slowly realized it was a vent. It obviously drew cool air in and helped with air circulation, but someone had decided to make the vent into the shape of a cross instead of, say, just an open square window. Eli looked at the yellow star on his uniform and couldn't help but wonder if the vent was designed to look like a crucifix out of spite.

The bodies came from all over Europe. A Jew from Hungary. A Jew from France. An Italian. A Pole. Another Frenchman. Another Jew. A Russian. He carried twelve women to the furnace and was surprised to see their naked bodies. Women, he thought. Women in Dora. There was the corpse of a little girl as well. He tossed it over his shoulder like a sack of salt and felt nothing, just the flatness.

They stopped every once awhile to stretch their backs. They spit into their hands to wash them.

"Think of the sausage," Moshe encouraged.

Eli nodded as they undressed yet another corpse. A hawk circled around the warmth of the chimney and hogs could be heard squealing for slop in a nearby pen. The SS feed them daily and butchered them for special occasions. They'd put a hog on a spit and then, over loud music, the SS would tap kegs of beer and pick the bones clean.

A truck approached.

It climbed the steep dirt hill, downshifting. Headlights felt their way through tall jack pines and the engine revved high. It came to a sharp stop when it hit level ground. A fan belt rattled, someone got out of the driver's side, and boots could be heard hitting the sandy ground. The headlights were still on and a figure stepped towards them.

"Unload what's in the back," Simon said. He adjusted his SS belt and looked at his wristwatch. "You've got one hour."

And with that he walked away, leaving the truck running. Eli and Moshe didn't know if they should turn it off or let it keep running. Was this some kind of test? They looked at each other and whispered about what to do. In the end, Moshe climbed into the cab and turned off the clattering engine.

"It'll save gas," he reasoned, and that alone might be enough to keep them from being beaten. Just as likely though, Horse Head, Brinkmann, Möser or

Simon could return in an hour—swimming in vodka—and they might decide to hit them for daring to make a decision on their own.

Exhaust hung in the air as they moved for the back of the truck. Eli untied a canvas flap and saw a mound of naked bodies. Arms. Legs. Feet. Skulls. An arm sprouted up like a weed. A body was slumped to the side and it almost seemed to blink. Maybe it *had* blinked?

"Did you see that?" Eli asked.

"See what?"

"Is someone alive in there?"

Moshe climbed in and went over. He lifted an arm and watched it flop back into place.

"No," Moshe said. "They're all gone."

"You sure?"

"Eli, it's the living we have to worry about. The living will be back here in an hour."

They pulled at a pair of hairy legs, which drew out several bodies. One body slipped off the truck and landed with a thud on the ground.

"Let's get this one," Moshe said, reaching for the wrists. "Ready and...*lift*."

As they brought the flopping corpse into the crematorium, it wasn't until they were under a light that Eli noticed something odd. There was a tattoo on the left forearm of the body. As soon as they dropped the naked man onto the pile, Eli pulled the cold skin taunt. Yes, a tattoo, and it was like the one that had been stitched into his arm at Auschwitz.

"See this?" Eli said, rolling up his sleeve.

Moshe turned for the door.

"Look. See? I think they're from Auschwitz." He tapped the inky blue number that had been sown into his flesh. 142757. The moment he arrived into Dora he had stopped being that number and he became something else. 41199.

Moshe, however, had already moved back into the night.

Eli hurried to catch up. He passed his friend and climbed into the truck where he immediately began looking at other forearms. Yes, they were all from Auschwitz. He recognized the placement of the ink. They had all been tattooed.

He stood up, confused. "Why are they here? Why not burn them in Poland?"

Moshe reached for a foot. "If we don't move faster, we'll be joining them. Hurry up."

"It makes no *sense* though. What are they doing here?"

"I don't care. Shut up and grab that foot."

"We don't tattoo in Dora, though. How come they're being sent here?"

"Listen to me, Eli. Look at me. Are you listening? I...don't...care. Now grab that damn foot and help me."

They ferried another body to the stock room and, beneath the humming ceiling light, Eli looked at the man's tattoo. It was blue. 142606. Even though he knew it was crazy, he rushed out and climbed back into the truck. Maybe his father or mother were in there?

He sifted through a tangle of arms and legs and hips. He searched sunken cheeks and cloudy eyes. And while he looked at the dead, a little voice said that he'd never find what he was looking for. Not here. Not ever. Still, he studied vacant face after vacant face. Once or twice he thought he saw his mother's nose, her cheeks, but it turned out to be the face of a stranger. Tears streamed down his nose as he hopped from body to body. His clogs banged against the metal flooring of the truck.

"Stop it. You're going to get us killed."

He didn't listen. He kept on looking.

Finally, two hands pulled him back. "Enough!" Moshe yelled, inches from his face. "They're dead, Eli! Every single one of them. They're gone." There was a pause as he looked around. "Now grab the wrists of that woman. That's it, you've got it. Good...good. Pull. That's right...pull."

He wept as he moved the thin body into the building. Moshe let go of the legs and dropped her onto the pile, but Eli held onto the wrists a little longer until, at last, he let her go gently, slowly, carefully. Eli wiped his nose with the back of his hand. His family wasn't here. He knew this. He accepted this. They'd been burned a long time ago. They were lost somewhere in the ash fields of Auschwitz.

He took a deep breath and felt the heat of the air in his throat. Moshe slapped him on the shoulder in a gesture of friendship.

"Almost done."

Eli walked out and watched his shadow twitch and flicker on the ground. Fiery sparks shot up from the chimney. The smell of burning flesh was overpowering and a greasy black plume lifted into the sky. When the wind picked up, the roar of the furnaces seemed to go up, and bits of grainy ash began to swirl around him.

He went back to the truck.

"I don't understand why they weren't burnt at Auschwitz," he finally said. "It's strange."

As Moshe stared at him, shadows danced on his face. He shook his head and finally said, "No, Eli…nothing is strange. Not anymore."

THEY WORKED IN SILENCE. Sometimes they heard a whistle flare to life in the railyard as engines loaded down with rockets huffed away from the camp, but other than that it was quiet. The bleachy moon swam behind clouds.

The two eventually came to the last body. They kicked it off the truck and heard the thud of its bones on the sandy soil. When they got it to the crematorium they tossed it onto the pile and leaned against a wall to catch their breath. Eli studied his reflection in a window. Ghostly and double-imaged, he saw a stranger. Pale. Empty. Drained. His eyes refocused and he looked out at the woods beyond. Trees flickered in hellish orange shadows. They burned in ghostly fire.

Two other prisoners at the other end of the crematorium continued to stuff bodies into the ovens. There was a rhythm to their work and he watched them without emotion.

"Good evening," came a voice. It was SS-*Hauptscharführer* Simon. He blew into his hands and held them against one of the ovens. He rubbed his palms together and spoke to Eli and Moshe without looking at them. "I have *one* tiny last job for you, and then you can have your precious sausage. Come with me."

They followed him to the back of the crematorium and exited through a wooden door. There was a ravine, and next to it lay a wheelbarrow. Simon clicked on a flashlight.

"Do you see that?" He used the beam as a pointer. It slithered down a hill of grey snow. "There is some waste next to the ovens, dump it here. I'll be back in…let's say, twenty minutes."

When he was gone, Eli and Moshe didn't know exactly what he meant or what they were supposed to do, but when they stepped inside, they saw a pile of ash in a huge metal box. Chips of burnt bone were on the surface. There were two shovels.

They looked at each other and knew what they had to do.

The ash was still warm to the touch, and when their shovels slid into it, it was like scooping up grey cinnamon. The dust of lives got into their nose, their lungs, it coated their tongues and eyelashes, but they shoveled the remains into a wheelbarrow and moved outside where they tipped it down the hill. It floated and drifted like a tripping cloud. When they went back into the crematorium and dug deeper into the huge metal box, they discovered scorched ribs and femurs. There were bits of skull and the wings of hipbones.

It took half an hour, and when they finally finished, Moshe sat against the brick wall. He looked at his fingers.

Eli stood at the edge of the slope and tried to understand what he was looking at. Strangely, he thought of Moses standing on Mount Sinai. Yes, he nodded. A new set of commandments had been forged for the world. New laws and new ways of doing things had been hammered onto stone. The burning bush. The voice of God. *Thou shalt steal. Thou shalt bear false witness. Thou shalt covet. Thou shalt kill.*

Snow fluttered down. It was beautiful and tranquil while, behind them, the chimney continued to roar. Hellish flames spilled up into the night and he couldn't help but think how much the chimney looked like an inverted rocket—a V-2 turned upside down. It rumbled with the never-ending fuel of flesh and bone.

SS-*Hauptscharführer* Simon came around the corner with a half-empty bottle of vodka. He walked over to Eli and took a drag on his cigarette. He swayed on his feet and flicked the butt down the hill of ash before pulling out a package of brown wax paper from his leather coat. He handed it to Eli. "Your reward," he said.

And with that, he walked away, humming. His boots clicked off the concrete path until he rounded the corner.

They looked at each other before unwrapping their meal. They ate the sausages slowly—the meat was warm and greasy—and when they finished, they stared into the darkness. Snow continued to fall through the pine trees.

"It's good to be warm," Moshe finally said.

"Yes, I suppose it is."

Behind them, the chimney continued to rumble.

FUEL

By EARLY 1945, EVERYONE KNEW that Germany was going to lose the war. The British and the Americans were advancing from the west, and the Soviet Union was driving in from the east. As the Third Reich collapsed into itself, the concentration camps in occupied Poland, Hungary, and Ukraine began to send their prisoners deep into the heart of Germany. This mass evacuation meant that an unprecedented number of skeletal humans were shipped to Dora. Trains arrived daily and there was no place to put them. Many were shoved into barracks at the far end of camp where they stayed until they died.

And die they did. In their thousands.

Because this secret concentration camp was in the middle of Germany, it was an ideal place to send prisoners from Auschwitz. It wasn't something the rocket experts particularly wanted nor was it something they thought was a good idea. It was, however, necessary when the Red Army rolled over the frozen wheat fields of Poland in late January 1945. The Soviets soon discovered the most notorious site of mass annihilation in all of human history, but before the USSR entered the gates of Auschwitz, the Nazis dynamited the gas chambers in an effort to hide their crimes. Huge blasts could be heard from nearby villages as brick and iron were sent flying into the air. Paperwork was set ablaze. Stacks of money, diamonds, rubies and gold were taken from strongboxes. An uneasy quiet settled over Auschwitz after 60,000 prisoners were sent on a death march out of camp. Burning rubble crackled and spat near the barracks. Bits of paper skittered across the snow.

The starving prisoners were marched to a small town fifty kilometers away. Many of them were shot in the head if they couldn't keep up. Those strong enough to survive the blowing snow and subzero temperatures were put on freight trains and sent to Bergen-Belsen, Sachsenhausen, and Buchenwald. Others were sent to Dora. A little known curiosity about this secret underground camp is that most of the SS officers stationed at

Auschwitz were reassigned to Dora-Mittelbau by February 1945. In fact, SS-*Sturmbannführer* Richard Baer, the last commandant of Auschwitz, found himself looking at rockets and wondering if they might save the Third Reich. He cupped his hands behind his back and strolled through bright tunnels that were now under his control. Many of the prisoners were already familiar with him. They feared him. They knew what he was capable of doing. And thus, although it is rarely acknowledged, part of Auschwitz was allowed to continue on—at Dora.

The train ride across Germany that winter was a death sentence. Piles of corpses rolled into camp every day, and for those who managed to survive the trip, their fingers were blackened with frostbite. They were ordered to walk past rail cars loaded down with V-2s and they shuffled through a gate that announced they were in a place called KZ DORA-MITTELBAU. They were then pushed into barracks where they were told to lay down until they were strong enough to work. Many of them never stood up again.

The crematorium couldn't keep up. Bodies were stacked around it like cordwood and, at night, the sky overhead was stained an ugly dark orange. The chimney was a stony nozzle with an everburning fiery exhaust rumbling up to the stars.

Still the trains kept on coming, and coming.

Dora had never been so full of fuel.

HE WORKED ON PROPELLANT TANKS NOW. It was his job to crawl inside the large burnished metal containers and make sure the pumps were hooked up properly. This meant he had to shimmy into spaces that would one day be filled with explosive liquids. It was tiring and exhausting work to twist copper strands into place and make sure the ignition systems would pulse to life at just the right time. There were two different tanks: one was for ethanol and water; the other was for liquid oxygen. They were stacked on top of each other and a tangled nest of wires ran between them. Each tank was big enough to hold a Volkswagen. The rockets rested on their sides, and once Eli finished his work, the V-2s would be hoisted upright. They moved down the line where the tanks would be flushed clean, sealed shut, and a final inspection with civilian workers would be done.

As he climbed barefoot inside one tank, he thumped the sides and thought about how strange it was that air could be turned into a liquid. He maneuvered with a flashlight and took out a pair of needle-nose pliers. He had spun so much copper wire in the last few days that his fingertips were raw and painful.

At least the war was coming to an end, he thought. Now it was just a matter of who would arrive first—the Americans or the Soviets? He had recently allowed himself to imagine sitting in a rocking chair with a child in his lap, a granddaughter perhaps. There he was, alive and healthy at some point deep in the future and she would be asleep. They would both have full bellies and maybe a fire glowed inside a potbelly stove while a radio mumbled out something soft and gentle. As she grew into adulthood, she would have questions about her murdered family, and he would talk about Berlin, how his mother lit up an entire room with her smile, how his father taught him mathematics while smoking a pipe, and how his brother had wanted to be a zeppelin pilot. Yes, Eli nodded. He would make them come alive through memory. He would survive Dora so that words might lift them out of the past and carry them into a peaceful future. This could happen. But if he were to die now—?

The thought of survival fired his muscles. He moved quickly because he never knew if a kapo or an SS officer was waiting outside the tank for him to emerge. Sometimes they used a stopwatch. Wasn't it only yesterday that a Russian was shot for taking too long on a gyroscope? The man was pushed against a wall and shot in the face.

"Work," Eli whispered to himself. Work was life.

Inside the dark stomach of the V-2, he dreamed of bread. He allowed himself to imagine a loaf of pumpernickel, fresh from the oven. He'd cut off a slice, spread creamy butter onto it, and it would melt into the grainy texture. Steam would rise up. And then he'd take a long, deliberate bite.

As he shimmied out of the V-2, he found himself looking at the rocky floor for ants and spiders. With so many prisoners being crammed into Dora, Eli now experienced a hunger unlike anything he'd known before. There wasn't enough beet soup to go around and the prisoners were getting desperate. Yesterday he saw one man pick seeds out of diarrhea to eat.

Moshe was working at the back of the tunnel and he had no idea what had happened to Zev. He hadn't seen him for two weeks and this probably meant he was either in the *Revier* or that he'd been taken up the hill. As for the others who were slaving away around him, he had no idea who they were. It hardly mattered, though. Everyone looked the same. They were skeletons in uniforms, they shuffled wordlessly through the tunnels, and they worked as fast as their muscles would allow.

Kempf whistled in the corner. His mouth formed a perfect O as he brought each note to life. He used a knife to clean his fingernails and, as the notes fluttered up from his pursed lips, he sometimes splayed out his hand to judge his work. His uniform was ironed and the white stripes were spotless. Sparks fountained from a nearby arc welder, rivets were pounded into place, and winches groaned as they shunted rockets down the line.

"You there," Kempf said, tapping the air with his knife.

"Yes, sir," Eli said, stiffening his spine.

Kempf stood up and kicked out his clean boots in an exaggerated walk. He moved closer and twirled his knife back and forth in front of Eli's face. Eli saw his reflection in the blade. He was upside down.

"You won't leave this place," Kempf said. "They'll dynamite us in and bring the whole damn tunnel down on top of us. Me too." He looked around and lowered his voice. "Tell me something…I've always been good to you, haven't I?"

"Sir?"

Kempf lowered the knife. "For the sake of argument, if we *do* manage to survive, I've always been good to you, right? I never hurt you. Understand?"

Eli stood there, uncertain what to do. The knife was near his bellybutton. "Yes, sir. You were always nice to me."

"*Nice* to you. That's the perfect word for it. Yes, I was *nice* to you. Remember that if we manage to survive and the Americans start to—I don't know—ask questions. I was nice to you. I was nice to everyone."

"Yes, sir."

With that, Kempf strolled away and began talking to prisoners at another station. Eli let out a long breath and realized his hands were shaking. A line of V-2s marched off into the lighted distance of the tunnel. What was that all about, he thought. Dynamite? Americans? How close was the enemy? No, not *enemy*. Liberators. How close were the liberators?

A group of prisoners lumbered past with a section of rocket shell. It was huge. It was made out of sheet duralumin and weighed over 300 pounds. It was the kind of tank that Eli would later climb into and, now, six men were carrying it up the assembly line. Three prisoners were on one side—three prisoners were on the other. They linked hands and let the giant weight rest on their arms. They grunted as they passed. Sweat misted their faces. Their cheeks were pressed against the cold metal and they huffed hard. One of them, a homosexual from Poland, closed his eyes and gritted his teeth.

Eli looked around and decided to get back to work. One never knew when the SS were watching. He lifted himself into an open rocket and wormed into the belly of a tank with a flashlight. Shadows leaked down the metal wall as he crawled forward, barefoot. The pliers were in his mouth. A moment later he heard a thunderous boom.

The fuel tank must have crashed onto the floor—he could hear it rolling quickly. When it hit the wall it made a *bwaaang* that echoed up and down the tunnel. Eli poked his head out of the rocket and saw the eyes of the prisoners widened in fear.

"Your hand slipped," one of them hissed.

"*Your* hand is sweaty."

"Quick, pick it up."

As they gathered around the burnished metal tank, their reflections moved and twisted on its skin like a fun house mirror.

"Lift on three. Ready? 1…2…3!"

The shiny tank wobbled up to their shoulders, but the front end fell to the floor, bwanging out a loud low note once again. A compressor coupling at the top was bent.

"Shit, shit, shit."

"*Merde!*"

"Again. Ready? 1…2…lift!"

A boy trumpeted out a familiar phrase from one of the sub-tunnels. "Horse Head is coming. Horse Head is coming."

Eli climbed back into the V-2 and turned off his flashlight. He sat in the dark and closed his eyes.

Jackboots slapped closer. The sound grew louder and louder until it stopped. Nothing was said for a long moment. The footsteps did a slow circular orbit.

"What's this?" Horse Head asked.

"Sir," one of the prisoners said. He had a strong French accent. "The tank, he slip on us."

"You've dropped valuable property."

"I regret to agree."

"It's dented."

"The rocket…he slip from our hands, *Hauptscharführer*."

"Do you think you're worth more than this fuel tank?"

There was a pause, and in that tiny fractured opening so many bad things could happen. Eli put his ear against the metal sheeting. His face was so close to the metal skin of the tank that he could feel his breath.

"Well?" Horse Head asked. "I'm waiting for an answer."

"Begging pardon, Herr *Hauptscharführer*, I am not understanding the question. My German, he is poor."

"It's a simple question. Are you worth more than this dented tank? Yes or no?"

There was the sound of a gun being cocked.

A second later there was a sharp ear-splitting crack. The fuel tank thrummed with reverberations and Eli touched the metal with his fingertips to silence the noise.

"Pick up that rag," Horse Head said without anger. "The rest of you, come with me."

Eli sat inside his dark cavity of safety and listened to wooden clogs clatter against the stone floor. The men marched in unison and sounded like a receding train. When it was safe to come out, he shimmied from the rocket and stood in the tunnel.

A puddle of blood was on the floor. It was the size of a manhole cover and it reflected the bright track lighting above. There was no body.

Eli wanted to feel some kind of emotion, he wanted to feel some kind of empathy and compassion and pity, but there was nothing. Just the flatness. He didn't even shrug a shoulder. He just climbed back into the fuel tank and reached for the pliers.

"All is well," he told himself inside the darkness. "All is well."

In the milky dusk of evening he stood once again for roll call with thousands of other men. The great dome of the world hung above him. The wind rolled down through the pine trees and he could feel his heart, his living heart, rock inside his chest. He couldn't feel his toes. He waited for his number to be called, and when it came he raised a dirty hand.

"*Jawohl!*"

More than anything, he wanted to blow heat into his hands but he had to stand with his fingertips pressed against the seams of his trousers. The numbers were called out, one after the other, as the sun melted into the trees.

Beyond the main gate was the SS camp. One of the guards watered hydrangeas while another sat in a deck chair, smoking a pipe. They drank vodka from silver flasks.

When roll call was finally ended, the sky was salted with stars. The crematorium was hard at work as the camp loudspeaker ordered the prisoners back to their barracks. And then? Music fluttered out. It was Mozart's "Serenade for Winds". As warm ash was dumped into the ravine, oboes and clarinets waltzed through camp. And when the prisoners were at last asleep, the northern lights came out. They danced and swirled in greeny-blue and salmon pink. It was beautiful. Mesmerizing. The SS watched it silently while they smoked cigars and drank brandy.

Far in the distance, somewhere on the border of Germany, a foreign army was stacking up artillery shells and pouring gasoline into tanks. The war would soon be over.

The great dance with death was finally coming to an end.

WALKING THE AIR

WORK HAD COME TO A stop and everyone had to stand in rows of five. The dead dangled from cables. Eli refused to look at them. Instead, he stared at the back of the head of the man in front of him. His cap was at an angle and the neck muscles that attached his skull to his shoulders bulged like two ropes.

"Next," someone shouted up ahead. It was Horse Head.

The days lengthened, and Eli had heard the guards talking about how April was just around the corner. Time, though, meant nothing to him. Not at Dora. He was told when to get up, when to eat, how long to work, and when to go to bed. Only the guards and the civilian workers in white coats were allowed to have wristwatches. If a prisoner was found with a watch, he was thrashed with a stick. Just a few days ago, he had seen one man get beaten so hard that his skull cracked open—and this had happened simply because he wanted to know the time. It was such a normal question. So mundane. So natural. What time is it?

Aside from a change in season, other things were happening at Dora too.

The SS had competitions to see which prisoners would survive and which would not. There was a curving dirt road up to the crematorium and the weakest prisoners were now forced to have races to the top. Stragglers who crossed the finish line last were beaten. Some were shot. These sprints to the top—where death waited beside a glowing furnace—were done over and over again. Some prisoners spent a whole morning huffing up and down the dirt road. They had swollen knees, twig legs, and yet they were forced to run in clumsy wooden clogs. The mud sucked at their feet and this made the lumbering all the more terrible. The SS stood on the sidelines and cheered. They made bets. They called out the numbers of prisoners as if they were horses at a race, and when that race ended, they were forced to run again.

"Next group of five."

Eli stepped forward and scratched his left armpit. He licked his dry lips and smelled the mog of body odor that lifted up from the men around him.

Eli's body had become so thin that his chest was nothing more than a webbing of ribs and his hip bones stuck out like wings. Lice had returned to his skin. They feasted. They grew fat.

"Next."

If he was being honest about the situation, he was happy for the break. It was nothing to look upon the dead now, especially if it meant an hour away from his work station. Seeing another body was like seeing a leaf on the ground.

They were Russian. He could see the R on their uniforms and, like everyone else that was advancing towards the husk of their bodies, he knew why they were dangling. They had destroyed a winch near the entrance by soldering the gears of the motor. When the SS found out about this, they marched them over to a different winch—one that worked. It could hold tons of weight and, now, there were twelve steel cables hanging from a horizontal bar. At the end of each looped cable was a man. They had been lined up and lifted by the neck.

Eli imagined the winch humming as it raised them from the earth. These men dangled from where a rocket should be, and for those standing beneath them, it would be like resting at the bottom of a lake and looking up at swimmers treading water high above. These men scissor-kicked and jerked as they went about the business of dying. They walked the air.

Even from a distance, Eli could see their hands tied behind their backs. A dowel of rough wood had been shoved into their mouths to keep them from saying anything rebellious before they were lifted. This wooden gag was kept in place by copper wire—it had been twisted around the back of their skulls like a horse's bit.

"Next."

His row took a step closer.

It was quiet in Tunnel A and Eli couldn't remember the last time he had experienced so much silence in the underground factory. There were no acetylene torches blowing, no hammers striking, no rivets, no shouting. There was just the humming of the fluorescent lights above.

Arthur Rudolph stood against the wall. Straight-backed and serious, his brow was furrowed and he paid no attention to the men suspended from the crane. Instead, he looked at a blueprint. He held it like a newspaper. Rudolph was in charge of production of the V-2s and this meant he was in charge of slave labor. It was Rudolph who recommended that slave labor could be used in the first V-2 factory at Peenemünde—this policy was later adopted for Dora-Mittelbau. He made decisions about how many men were needed for propellant tanks, turbine pumps, combustion chambers, external control vanes, stabilizer fins, azimuth gyroscopes, and the production of warheads in general. He marched through the subterranean factory every day to solve tricky engineering problems. He had a shock of hair and a confident gait. Rudolph joined the Nazi party in 1931 and he was known to walk through the streets of Berlin with a swastika on his arm. Like so many others who buttoned up the brown shirt and sang the party anthem, he had no problem using "subhuman races" to advance the might of the Reich. Not only was he good friends with Wernher von Braun, but he later become indispensable to America's space program. By the late 1960s he was known as "Mr. Saturn." He made sure rockets to the moon rolled towards the launch pad at a steady, reliable, clip.

Rudolph puffed on a cigarette and didn't look at the rows of prisoners around him. A river of white and blue stripped caps lined the tunnel. He blew smoke from his nose and studied the blueprint. He shook his head and grimaced. Someone walked up to him—it was SS-*Sturmbannführer* Richard Baer, the last commandant of Auschwitz. The two men pointed at the top of the blueprint and then looked at the entrance of the tunnel. Baer tweaked the sides of his nose and said something. Rudolph shook his head. The two men smoked causally before they dropped their cigarettes onto the stone floor and walked into subtunnel 40. They stood next to Rudolph's desk and consulted a chart. They looked worried.

"Next."

Eli's stomach was on fire. He was so hungry it felt like thistles were growing inside his guts. He imagined sausages, fruit salad, walnuts, oranges, salmon, and a pitcher of water. He saw slices of lemon floating in ice cubes. Carefully, gently, he reached into the pitcher and lifted out a lemon.

When he opened his eyes, he realized he was sucking his tongue.

Commandant Baer had taken off his peaked SS cap and leaned against Rudolph's desk with his long legs crossed at the ankles. He had his hands in his pockets and he stared at the floor. A case of unopened seltzer water was next to him.

"Next."

Horse Head stood with a wooden club over his shoulders—his arms were draped over the ends as if it were a yoke. Hans Möser was next to him and he used his pistol as a pointer.

"See what happens if you mess with our rockets? You walk the air."

Next to the motor that drove the crane was a plywood sign. A message had been written onto it in sloppy white paint. *Für Hochverräterische Sabotage.* For Traitorous Sabotage. A skull and crossbones was painted beneath it.

"Next," Horse Head yawned. He turned to Möser and added, "What's for dinner? I'm starving."

Möser shrugged. "Duck. I think."

Horse Head lowered the wooden club and adjusted his jodhpurs. "I like duck. Reminds me of home. Maybe we'll have carrots? They were swimming in butter sauce last time, remember?"

The world blurred into double-vision as Eli refused to look at the dead. They were just shapes—sacks really, nothing more—and he decided that when it was his turn he wouldn't look them in the eye. It would be his own small act of mutiny.

"Next."

The man in front of Eli took off his striped cap in order to pay his respects to the dead.

"What's this all about?" Horse Head bristled. He stepped over to the prisoner and asked, "What're you doing? Did we ask you to remove your cap?"

The prisoner said something in Russian and this sent Horse Head into a rage. He kicked and punched and hit. Möser, meanwhile, calmly pulled out a cigarette, tapped it against the side of the winch, and lit a match. Wings of smoke glided around him. He puffed a few times before he put a hand on Horse Head's shoulder.

"Erwin," he said, gently.

The prisoner was nearly unconscious as kicks continued to land on his stomach.

"Erwin," Möser said again.

Horse Head paused. He bent over, gasping for breath and cupping his kneecaps. He spit on the floor, winded.

SS-*Obersturmführer* Hans Möser looked at his wristwatch. "Okay...next row."

It was Eli's turn. He took a step forward and stared up at an invisible spot on a dangling man's forehead. There was a scar. He wondered how the Russian had gotten it. Maybe it had happened when he was a child? Eli kept staring at the scar and imagined the dead man as a little boy—he saw him alive instead of dead. Once, long ago, this man played on a farm. Maybe he tripped against a brick wall and, as blood came pouring out, maybe this man's father bent low with a plaid handkerchief and wiped it away. Maybe he patted his son's shoulder. "You'll be fine," he might have whispered. "I'm here. Papa's always here."

Eli allowed himself to become lost in this woodland of thought. He saw fathers coming to take down the bodies of their sons. They uncinched the metal cables and dusted off the soiled uniforms of their boys. They whispered their names, and when this happened, the freshly dead opened their eyes. They were told that their pain was finally over and they were offered cups of water. The fathers of these men pointed down the tunnel and smiled. They put arms around their sons and said, *Come. Let us leave this place.*

"Next."

Eli walked beneath the bodies and heard Horse Head say, "Don't even *think* about sabotage."

But of course, Eli already was.

A FEW HOURS LATER THE hiss of acetylene torches could be heard, along with hammers coming down onto sheets of duralumin. Eli climbed back into the guts of a rocket and went back to work. So much time had passed that it seemed impossible that the hangings had taken place in the morning. Maybe it had happened yesterday? Or the day before?

From inside his fuel tank he heard Kempf whistling the "1812 Overture". There was a tapping on the side of the rocket.

"Hello, my friend. You're not sleeping in there, are you?"

Eli slithered out and brought himself to attention. "No, sir."

The beefy man in a clean uniform studied him. "How do I know your wiring is up to code?"

"I wouldn't do a poor job, sir."

The word *KAPO* was printed on Kempf's sleeve, and his blue eyes narrowed to slits. How strange, Eli thought. If this well-fed German had only obeyed the law, he might have been allowed to wear the black uniform of the SS. But here he was in a concentration camp, wearing the green triangle of a criminal.

Kempf looked into the tank. "Remember, I've always been nice to you."

"Yes, sir."

"Keep up the good work."

"Yes, sir."

Kempf ran a finger along the metal skin of the rocket and strolled away—dragging his fingertip as he walked—and he whistled loudly to announce his arrival into a subtunnel. He twirled his stick and disappeared from view.

Eli looked at the floor and blinked a few times. It was a strange song to whistle, he decided. Didn't Kempf realize that it was written to commemorate Russia's victory over Napoleon? For a German to whistle that song was very odd, especially since the Soviet Union had recently pushed back waves of German tanks. Just as Napoleon had crashed against the shores of Moscow, the same thing had happened to Hitler. Didn't Kempf realize what that song by Tchaikovsky meant? It meant Russia defeating a mighty enemy.

He stared down the tunnel towards the entrance. There was a small root of sunlight. The lights began to flicker and the electricity in the whole factory seemed to stutter. Eli looked at one of the sodium lights overhead. Yes, it was definitely flickering. It surged bright and then the glowing bulb dissolved into darkness. The whole factory was swallowed by black. When this happened, Eli put a hand in front of his face. He couldn't see a thing. There was shouting and someone up ahead clicked on the spark of an acetylene torch. It flared like an underwater lamp.

Behind him, the bodies of the men continued to walk the air.

Without thinking about it, Eli moved his fingers up the rocket until he found a bolt. It twisted loose easily. He opened a panel, grabbed a tuft of wiring, and pulled.

NORDHAUSEN

As the end approached, supplies became more scarce.

Construction of the V-2s stopped completely when electrical components that were made in Hamburg and Leipzig no longer arrived into camp. The same was true of servo motors, rivets, and sheet metal. There was, however, no shortage of human cargo. That never slowed down. Trainload after trainload of prisoners arrived into Dora and, as a consequence, Eli found himself almost free of work by early April 1945.

As they stood for hours in the *Appleplatz*, he had plenty of time to think about survival. The war was coming to an end so, maybe, perhaps, there was an infinitesimal chance that he might actually walk out of the camp. But even as this happy thought fireworked in his head, he also imagined the SS herding them into Tunnel A and dynamiting the entrance shut. It would be easy to do. All they needed was a truckload of TNT and, for all he knew, the explosives were already in the rail yards waiting for use.

Without the need for slave labor, the SS weren't entirely sure what to do with the prisoners, so they lined them up for roll call. Under a leaden sky, mindless acts of labor and punishment occurred. Sometimes they had to dig huge holes only to fill them back up again. Other times they had to run around camp. The gruel of rutabaga soup stopped flowing, and men turned to eating tufts of grass or crickets they found around their barracks. The SS sat in their villas and clinked shots of vodka together. They listened to music and talked about the good old days when the world trembled at the sound of their goosestepping.

One evening, when peachy blue dusk was pulled across the sky, Eli stood on wobbling legs and tried to focus. A swastika fluttered on a pole and he could tell the guards were already drunk. They wobbled too. Folk music bled from the camp loudspeaker and the rail yards were silent. The only sound was the crackling of two huge bonfires of the dead. The crematorium could no longer keep up, so massive pyres were set ablaze and bodies were tossed onto it. Black smoke rolled overhead, twirling and twisting.

It was all so strange for Eli because it seemed to be happening to someone else. It was like an out of body experience for him. The world was foggy and dim. And yet at any moment Simon, Möser or Horse Head could level their gun at his forehead and click open the doorway to another world. As he stood on woozy knees, it felt like he had shed his skin. It was like the best parts of him had already strolled out of camp and moved beyond the cool woods to someplace far beyond.

As SS-*Hauptscharführer* Wilhelm Simon paced before them, he boiled with drunken anger. A flock of geese honked overhead and they flapped in a lazy broken V. He raised his pistol and began firing wildly into the sky, but he was so plastered he didn't hit a thing. The pop of small arms fire filled the air. It sounded like applause.

After the geese moved away, no one moved. The ompa-ompa of a tuba pumped out from the camp loudspeaker.

"Where was I?" Simon roared.

Möser answered. "The Bolsheviks and the Jews."

"Ah yes…" he said, taking in a deep breath to resume his lecture.

But in that moment of heavy calm, air raid sirens began to whir in the valley below. They started as groans but turned into high pitched yowls. The SS looked at each other with wide eyes, and then they started swearing. A low grumble could be heard on the horizon and when Eli looked up he saw vapor trails etching themselves into the darkening sky. Enemy bombers. They cut the air in a V formation.

Eli couldn't tell if he was imagining this or if it was really happening. Were the bombers coming for the camp? Had they figured out where the V-2s were built? Maybe they were going to hit the rail yard?

Down in the valley, the lights of Nordhausen snapped off, street by street. The city rolled a thick blanket of darkness over itself. Steeples pricked the air, and if Eli squinted he could just make out the brick rooftops. Searchlights flicked on and shafts of milky white began to stroke the sky. The grumbling got louder as the bombers approached. The air raid sirens continued to whir.

The city of Nordhausen was a thousand years old and it was graced with fine medieval architecture. Tourists came from all over to snap photos and admire hanging baskets of marigolds and daisies. There were rumors that Jews once lived in Nordhausen but, like everywhere else in the Third Reich, they had been driven out. The synagogues in town had been razed and the cemetery was currently being used as a garbage dump. Triumphant Nazi parades twisted through streets by day, and beneath the gas lamps of night, restaurants were full of noise. *"Prost!"* someone would shout, and glasses of rye whiskey were raised. Their children, their lucky children, were going to inherit a glorious future—a future run by National Socialism.

That, however, was five years ago, and now a terrible vengeance was about to be poured down onto Nordhausen. Death was flying towards them, and soon it would tumble from the sky.

When the first bombs hit, geysers of silent fire shot up. Eli heard nothing at first because he was so far away, but the sound of damp thuds eventually came to his ear. Blossoms of fire opened up over the city and, if he closed his eyes, it sounded like a clattering typewriter. As he stood at attention, everything seemed to unravel. It was so surreal, so impossible. Was Germany *really* being bombed? It was like watching a color movie. Everything was so grand and furious it was like something Hollywood might make. Fountains of yellow-orange erupted into the sky and a growing hurricane of flame began to spin above the city. A steeple sank sideways into the ground.

The earth beneath Eli's clogs began to rumble and he pressed his toes against the inside of his wooden clogs to feel the quivering. Yes, he thought. This *was* real.

The lights of Dora were still on, and the guards shouted for them to be turned off.

"Blackout!"

"Turn off the lights!"

"Darkness! Darkness!"

The floodlights in the roll call square were doused but those in the rail yard continued to glare, and this sent the SS into a panic. They ran down the concrete road while, up ahead, two bright beams spilled out from the entrances of Tunnel A and Tunnel B. They were rivers of light. They were twin beacons that all but welcomed bombardment. Folk music still danced from the camp loudspeaker and a tuba was hard at work. Someone began singing about a white stag in the Black Forest and this was quickly interrupted by a frantic voice.

"All lights off! Repeat ALL LIGHTS OFF!"

The singing returned. So did the tuba.

Some of the bombers caught in the searchlights banked for the camp. A needling sickness scratched at the back of Eli's throat and he looked at the wooden guard towers. Did they still have machine guns trained on them? Should he run? Should he stay? Mud sucked at his clogs as the bombers got closer and closer. The tunnels up ahead looked like glowing portals to the underworld and it filled Eli with a surprising calm. If he met his end this way, with the destruction of the camp, at least his death would have meaning.

The silhouettes of the bombers grew larger against the orange night. They dropped lower and leveled off. The rail yards of Mittelbau must be in their bombsites. He was sure of this.

Thousands of prisoners began to shove and push against each other. A shot was fired from the main gate and this made everyone flinch. The whole horizon was erupting with blasts and everything was colored blood red and jagged yellow. There were more gunshots from the main gate.

The camp loudspeaker crackled again. "All prisoners to the tunnels, repeat, all prisoners to the tunnels."

The folk music returned. The tuba gave way to a woman's voice about missing home.

The men in blue and white stripped uniforms ran, their ordered rows in the *Appleplatz* dissolved, and Eli was carried forward on a wave of flesh. He was funneled through the main gate—shadows flashed and danced around him—and he started to run down the concrete road. His clogs were loose on his feet and there were so many men running that it sounded like a mighty river hitting a stretch of rapids. He was carried along like a twig. There was screaming. Yelling. Prayers to God. He worried about tripping because if he fell now he'd be crushed. The SS ran too. They held their pistols and sprinted hard. Trucks whined into higher gears and made their way into the forest. One of the SS guards was half in his uniform and half in his flannel pajama bottoms.

"All prisoners to the tunnels!" the loudspeaker said again.

Eli's knees were weak, it was like running on stilts, and he worried about breaking a bone, but still he pushed on. Huffing, puffing. Others were doing the same. The concrete road was littered with wooden clogs—many prisoners had decided to kick them off—and the sound of a raging river that was heard a few seconds ago was replaced by the soft patter of feet.

The bombers were close. He knew this. He could hear their engines.

A whistling came through the sky.

When the first explosion hit the rail yard it shattered the air with light and sound. A cattle car was sent flying into the air as if it were a toy and the force of the blast sent several V-2s clanging and rolling to the ground. One of them crushed a Mercedes.

Eli kept on running. The road was cold against his feet and he stepped on something warm and wet. He was close to Tunnel A and saw that prisoners were already funneling into the safety of its mouth. An SS guard stood on top of a truck and fired a machine gun at the approaching bombers. Huge orange asterisks erupted from the end of his weapon. He screamed, open mouthed. He cursed.

A moment later, something hit Eli across the chest and threw him to the ground. He gulped for air but nothing entered his lungs. He choked and slapped the concrete for help. Wooden clogs and prisoners ran around him, naked feet scurried past his face, he could see ankles, shins, legs, he gasped and felt his throat open wide for air, his tongue curled back but he couldn't scream, he couldn't breathe, he couldn't understand what was happening. And just as he was thinking that he might die, delicious air filled up the bellows of his chest. It was like breaking the surface of a dark rolling sea. He took in another lungful. And another. He checked his body for blood and holes, he looked for gashes and wounds, yet there was nothing. He ripped open his uniform and searched his stomach and chest. Also nothing. He was unhurt. The wind had simply been knocked out of him—nothing more. He found himself laughing as bombs continued to whistle down. Smoke drifted across the rail yard like an army of ghosts. Another cattle car flipped into the air before it came crashing down near a water tower.

He made himself small and watched one prisoner run past him engulfed in flames. His arms wheeled the air as he screeched in animal horror. His pants burned and his arms were wings of fire. A sudden blast sent this man flying across the road and an enormous shower of dirt came pelting down.

When Eli opened his eyes, he saw that the prisoner was no longer on fire. The huge spray of dirt had buried him and spared him. Instead of fire, smoke now lifted from his arms.

A leg was in the distance. An arm too. One prisoner walked around in a daze and picked up wooden clogs.

"All prisoners to the tunnels...all prisoners to the tunnels."

There was a rumbling blast to his right and he stood up to run. He was close now, only one hundred yards away, and he sprinted through smoke. He was surprised by his own speed and when he entered the safety of Tunnel A he kept on running until he found a sub tunnel at the very back. He knocked over a file cabinet and looked around. He hid beneath a desk where he hugged his shins. Puffs of dust sifted down from the ceiling. Just as he realized that he'd lost his cap—Horse Head would thrash him for sure if he found out—the lights snapped off.

The darkness was total.

Eli breathed and heard dull explosions from the entrance. Dust was on his tongue and he worried about the tunnel cracking open and crushing him. He bowed his head and began to think of home. There he was, doing calculus at his parents table. And as he focused on limits, and harmonic series, and prime numbers, his arms relaxed. He thought about Ohm's law and resistance. He thought about taking a nub of chalk and writing on the darkness of a blackboard. He thought about his hand unspooling an equation of stars. Yes. His little life did have meaning.

His breathing slowed.

His head drooped.

And then, exhausted, he fell asleep.

THE RAID ON NORDHAUSEN LASTED twelve hours. The bombers came in waves throughout the night and, for those who survived, it seemed as if the enemy was trying to wipe Nordhausen off the face of the earth. Historians would later say that an unbelievable amount of tonnage fell from the sky on April 3-4, 1945. The firestorm was so great that it blinded the dawn. No one saw the sun come up. The whoosh of fiery tornados could be heard many kilometers away and smoke rolled across the valley. The ancient medieval buildings that had stood for centuries could be heard groaning and collapsing into themselves. As for the guards at Dora-Mittelbau, the unnatural light was so bright they could see their shadows on the ground at three in the morning. They smoked cigarettes and watched the city burn.

When it was all over, when the fires finally turned into piles of smoldering rubble, the prisoners of Dora were lined up and marched down the hill. Eli shuffled in mismatched clogs. A blister was already forming on his right toe, but he tried not to think about it. The smell of scorched wood, tar, and rotten eggs was everywhere.

As they marched next to a burbling creek, the cool waters called out to him. The current was clean and fast, it was fresh snowmelt from the Kohnstein, and he wanted to jump in, he wanted to drink his fill and lower his head to let the grease dissolve away from his skin, but he knew that if he jumped out of line he would be shot. It was as simple as that. There would be no discussion. There would only be a bullet.

He looked around for Moshe. The last time he saw him was in the roll call square before the bombing. Was he dead? Did he make it to the tunnels in time? As for Eli, he had fallen asleep under Arthur Rudolph's desk without realizing it. He woke up when he heard jackboots stomping towards him and he snapped to instant attention. He had been so close to an unopened crate of seltzer water that all he needed to do was reach out and open a bottle. He noticed this only when the boots stomped toward him. Now, the creek was equally close. And equally far away.

"Keep moving," one of the guards yelled. It was Simon. He had a deep raspy voice, like sandpaper.

As they approached Nordhausen, the trees became more splintered and charred. The cobblestone road was punched with craters and many of the homes were scorched—their rafters were exposed like burnt ribs.

Eli had never seen such devastation, such ruin.

A small fire still fumed inside a church. The steeple lay on the ground like a broken ice cream cone. A huge bell—flattened and hissing with heat—lay next to it. Colorful pools of molten stained glass were beneath empty window frames. A little girl stood on the steps in a perfectly white dress and held out her arms. She wept and howled in grief as the wind played with her hair. A body lay next to her. It was a woman's body. The face was smashed in and dried blood was on the woman's chest.

As they walked past her without stopping, Eli looked at the lampposts. Everything else had been turned into waste but, amazingly, the lampposts were still standing. How strange, he thought. A framed poster of Hitler was bolted outside the entrance of a beer garden and it, too, was unburned. Someone had punched the face, and cracks radiated out from it like a spider's web. The Führer glared out as if from inside a kaleidoscope.

As the prisoners walked past what used to be a large train station—collapsed bricks, glass, the cactus needles of iron girders—a group of boys began throwing stones. A prisoner next to Eli was hit in the jaw. Another was hit in the forehead. The SS did nothing to stop this. Instead, they encouraged the boys to use bricks. Möser cheered them on.

"That's a big one there," he pointed. "Use that."

"Aim higher."

"Good shot!"

As they marched around bomb craters and continued up the torn street, the boys lost interest. They chased a black cat around a corner and soon hoots of delight could be heard. A pained hissing shriek followed.

Eli looked around. Most of the building were either scorched or smashed. All of the windows were blasted in and, as they walked, they kicked chunks of plaster and wiring. A man in pajamas watched them trudge past. His face was covered in soot and he began to scream.

"You Jews! You brought this evil upon us!" He sank to his knees and sobbed in wailing huffs. He turned to a ruined house behind him and yelled out names. "Sieglinde, Monika, Maria! Maria...my little Maria."

Eli wondered if he could escape. Maybe it could be done when the guards were distracted? Yes, if he slipped away, maybe he could find some civilian clothes? He just needed a corpse and then it would be a matter of pulling off the trousers, the shoes, and sliding his arms into a jacket. He squinted at the thought. Yes, he nodded. He'd need a hat to hide his shaved head. And thank goodness he spoke German. It was his mother tongue after all. Yes. He could get by. Yes. He could escape. The sun was a murky coin in the sky and he had—what?—six hours before nightfall? After he shed his uniform, he could walk through the night and find a pantry full of bread and pickles and salami. He licked his lips at the idea. All *could* be well if only he was given a chance.

But the charcoal gray uniforms of the SS were everywhere. It seemed like every single guard at Dora-Mittelbau had been sent down to escort them. There were at least fifty of them and they all had machine guns. They held them lazily at their sides, like baguettes.

"Halt!" came the order to stop. "Stand at attention, rags."

Shovels scrapped against rubble. Glass sparkled on the street. Grit and dust floated in the air. He could taste ruin on his tongue.

A family across the street was going in and out of a smashed house gathering up whatever they could salvage. Pots and pans. Clothes. A photo album. A fat woman in a lemon dress waddled out with china plates and put them noisily on a kitchen table. Behind her, the entire front of her house was gone. The bedroom and living room were open to the air, and a toilet was on display next to a smashed sink. Oil paintings were on the wall as if nothing had happened. Eli almost felt guilty about seeing into the private lives of this family, but that feeling didn't last very long.

A body dangled from one of the green lampposts. It was obviously a quick execution without trial. The dead man's face was grey and his neck was at an unnatural angle. A sign had been tied to his right foot that said, *This is what happens to TRAITORS*.

"Why did we stop? What do they want from us?" a prisoner whispered.

"No idea."

"What's happening?"

Eli craned his neck. The guards were talking about something and one of them, Simon Legree, pointed around a corner with the snout of his machine gun. Möser nodded.

"They're not going to shoot us, are they?"

Eli shook his head. "I don't think so. I mean, why bring us down here for that?" And yet, even as he said this, a bolt of ice rode up his spine.

"We're here…f-f-for *some* reason," another prisoner said with a stutter.

Eli looked at him. He was Austrian and wore the black triangle of an asocial. Maybe he used to be homeless and was listed by the Nazis as "work shy".

Another prisoner added, "All of you. Shut up." A gash was over his eyebrow and he was trying to staunch trickling blood with his sleeve. He must have been hit by one of the bricks, Eli thought.

He looked around and sized up his chances. Surely he wasn't the only prisoner thinking about escape? Off in the distance he could see the Kohnstein. A thread of black twisted up into the sky. *There is only one way out of this camp*, Horse Head had said. And yet here he was, outside the camp.

His muscles ached for him to do something. Run, an inner voice said. Do something.

SS-*Hauptscharführer* Otto Brinkmann, that same man who smelled of bourbon, stood next to him with a machine gun. He chambered a bullet.

Hope leaked out of Eli when he saw this. What now? Should he run? Shouldn't he?

A voice came from up ahead. It was a man that Eli didn't recognize. Smoke obscured him at first but, as it passed, Eli could see that the man had a great walrus moustache.

"Grab a sheet, each of you."

No one moved so the voice shouted again.

"Are you fucking deaf? I *said*...grab a sheet!"

As they shuffled forward in their ragged uniforms, Eli's head swiveled back and forth. What if he ran now? The smell of burning wood surrounded him and there was something else—an earthiness. He stepped through puddles that were rainbowed with oil. His ankles got wet and he felt water on his toes.

"Keep moving," the man barked.

As Eli got closer, he could see that this man was a civilian in a brown suit. He wore a hat with a feather sticking out of the back and he had heavy jowls. He also wore a circular Nazi pin on his collar.

"Keep moving. Grab a sheet. Keep moving."

An elaborately carved antique desk had been hauled out from somewhere and stacks of linen sheets were on it. Eli reached for one and worried about getting it dirty. Why had he been handed something so nicely laundered and ironed? As he followed the other prisoners around a corner, he looked at the square of white and marveled at how spotless it was, how clean, how it smelled so beautifully of lavender. Black letters were stitched into one of the corners. HOTEL NORDHAUSEN. The H and the N were looped in calligraphy. He couldn't remember the last time he held something so nice. It was like holding an artefact from another time.

"Over there. Move it, move it!"

They were near a park where most of the trees had been blasted into stumps. Eli glanced over his shoulder and took a step away from the other prisoners. There was a house with a missing front door. It would be easy to dart inside.

Horse Head kicked him in the ass, which sent him stumbling to the ground. Eli stood upright and came to attention. He offered a smart salute.

"What the hell are you doing?"

"Nothing, sir."

"Where's your cap?"

"Lost in the raid, sir."

The man with red hair and a long face leaned in. His breath was hot against Eli's cheek. "Did you know there's a sub camp near this place that makes Dora look like a holiday resort? It's called Boelcke Kaserne. Maybe you'd like to see it, 41199?"

"No, *Hauptscharführer*."

"I can arrange it."

"Maybe tomorrow, sir." A pause and then, "Thank you."

Without warning, the giant made a beefy fist and punched Eli in the stomach. The flashing force knocked him to the ground, and although the pain was terrible, his first thought was of the bedsheet. It was so clean, he couldn't let it fall to the ground. Surely he'd get beaten harder if that happened. He fell in such a way that it allowed the linen to remain pristine and untouched. His eyes watered from the tremendous blow to his bellybutton and he gasped for air. It felt like crabs were opening and closing their pinchers inside his intestines.

"Now fuck off," Horse Head nodded with his chin. "Follow the others."

Eli stumbled up, fingering the linen as he hurried away in a running crouch. He passed open doors and heaps of smoking brick. Maybe he could find another place to slip away?

The guards, however, were evenly spaced. They smoked cigarettes and chuckled with good humor. A few of them sat in plush chairs that had been brought outside and they leaned back with their guns in their laps. Möser and Simon unbuttoned their uniforms and stretched out their legs. A young woman with copper hair brought out bottles of wine from the broken guts of the restaurant and a record player started up. It was forbidden American music—Glenn Miller's "In the Mood"—but in the wasteland of Nordhausen, with the SS tapping their feet, no one cared. They held bottles of red wine as if they were sodas. Occasionally, one of guards would take aim at a prisoner and pretend to shoot. This sent the others into peals of laughter. Another guard raised his gun and yelled out, "I'm going to shoot some Indians. I'm in the wild west!" He moved with cowboy swagger and tipped his SS cap back with a flicked finger. "I'm Jesse James."

"I'm Wild Bill Hicock."

"Kill the Indians. Clear the land!"

"Living space for everyone."

Eli stumbled over fist-sized chunks of brick and he saw gobs of molten glass stuck to the street. Who was still in Dora? All of the guards seemed to be here, so maybe they were all going to this other camp? This placed called Boelcke Kaserne?

As this thought flared like phosphorus in his mind, he also realized the SS were clearly getting drunk and had no plans of moving anytime soon. They were at ease. They were relaxing. Puffs of soot rolled overhead and the sound of brick walls tumbling to the ground could be heard in the distance.

He walked over to the edge of a long trench and stood beside it with the other prisoners. It was huge, and there were bodies in it. *German* bodies.

He paused.

A numbness filled up his veins as he looked at twisted limbs and open-mouthed faces. The earth was damp and smelled of wormy rot. Some of the corpses were completely cooked—not a patch of skin had been spared from the firestorm—and the familiar grapefruit smell of charred skin hung in the air. He covered his mouth and noticed that other prisoners were using the bed linen as a mask. He worried they might be pushed in and shot, but when he looked at the SS they seemed too distracted. More wine had been brought out. One of them put on a lady's hat and strutted around with his hands on his hips. He blew kisses. "In the Mood" still jumped out from the record player. It was all drums and trumpets. American swing.

"Over here," someone yelled.

Eli turned and saw six trucks. Their rear gates were down and piles of corpses were inside each one. Some of the prisoners closer to the grey vehicles were already dragging bodies to the trench. They used their bedsheets as a type of sled. Bodies were pulled over rubble and then, once at the edge of the mass grave, they were tipped in. Each one fell like a rag doll.

As he walked over, he felt nothing. The Germans were reaping what they had sown. He yanked on an arm and watched a woman tumble onto his white sheet. He grabbed two fistfuls of fabric and pulled against the weight. She was surprisingly heavy. A gutted warehouse crackled with fire on his right and dark smoke floated overhead. The SS continued to drain bottles of wine and slap each other on the back. On the Kohnstein, the crematorium was hard at work. He could see a ribbon of black.

Eli pulled the woman's body toward the grave and got ready to roll her in. She had a spray of freckles on her cheeks, her eyes were closed, and her hair was curly. There wasn't a mark on her and it almost seemed like she was sleeping. It occurred to him that she was the first healthy woman he'd seen in over a year, and it had to be said that she was beautiful, mesmerizingly beautiful. He took her right hand and tugged her to the edge. Her fingernails were manicured.

Did she raise this hand to salute Hitler? he wondered. Did she bray for the blood of nations? Did she smile when her Jewish neighbors disappeared into the fog of night?

He shrugged, dropped her hand, and kicked her in. She slid down the side and rolled to a flopping stop. Her curly hair lay across her face.

Eli threw the soiled bedsheet over his shoulder.

He went back for more.

LEAVING THE TUNNEL

AFTER THEY FINISHED LAYERING THE bodies, and after they patted the last shovelfuls of dirt into place, the prisoners stretched their backs and held onto their sides. They breathed heavily. They licked their lips. Some of them looked around for water while others sat down and simply stared at their hands.

It had taken over an hour to fit the dead into the earth—they packed them in like sardines—and then quicklime was spread over their bodies. What a waste, Eli thought. All of those useful shoes. All of those trousers. All of those hats and belts and socks and shirts. What good were they in the ground? A priest pounded a wooden crucifix next to the mass grave and began to murmur prayers. Eli watched him sprinkle a vial of water and make some kind of holy gesture with his hands. So, he thought, Germans aren't invincible after all. They too can become the children of death. How strange.

When an SS officer blew a whistle, the prisoners looked up. It was late in the afternoon and cows could be heard lowing in the distance. Eli couldn't help but wonder how they were still alive. All of these people were dead, but the cows…?

"Get in," SS-*Hauptscharführer* Arthur Andrä said, jerking his thumb to the trucks.

They schlepped and dragged themselves to the vehicles. They didn't feel human anymore. They were bone and sinew, joints and stomachs, they were dried flesh that swung their massive skulls on spindly necks. As Eli watched the others, he considered his own body. His hands were nothing more than knuckles and tendons. If he looked at his kneecaps, he could almost see the bones moving beneath his grey-pink skin.

He was helped into one of the trucks by a prisoner who was already inside, and when he found his footing he held out his hand to aid the next prisoner. They entered the truck, body after body, until the cramped space that once held the dead now held the living.

Horse Head slammed the metal gate shut and the engine started. The fan belt clattered and a plume of dark smoke flushed out from the exhaust pipe. Eli watched it disappear in a wisp of wind.

As they lurched into first gear, the prisoners had to steady themselves. They twisted through streets and bounced over bricks. No one made eye contact. He looked at his clogs and thought about what had been piled in the truck just an hour earlier. As he studied the dirt that was crusted onto his trousers, he noticed a pearl button on the floor. It looked like the moon and it skittered back and forth as they swerved around bomb craters.

Everyone knew they were going back to the Kohnstein. It was obvious because they were heading north, out of the smoking ruins of Nordhausen. The truck shifted into a higher gear and rumbled down a dirt road. They passed the creek once again—glorious, flowing, wet—and Eli thought about jumping out. Sunlight greased the water. As he gauged the distance from the truck to the edge of the speeding ditch, he wasn't sure he'd survive the fall. He squinted in thought. Maybe it could be done. The weeds might be tasty.

A burst of gunfire came from the truck behind them. The stammering of bullets sounded like a hammer pounding against a metal door. It happened again—a longer burst this time—and that's when he saw three prisoners staggering towards the creek. One tripped and fell. Another made it to the other side but as he began to scramble up the grassy bank, his head bloomed open and he crumpled.

The trucks didn't stop. The guns, however, kept sweeping the grass like a scythe for good measure.

It was surprising how quickly everything had happened. One minute Eli was watching a button roll around on the floor, and then there was a hail of bullets. Trees continued to flash beside them. The sun stumbled through branches.

His truck downshifted around a corner and a few miles passed in silence before a gun at the back of the convoy began to tat out a few more rounds. Eli couldn't see any prisoners running away. There was a cow though, a brown and white one, and its tail flicked lazily as it munched tufts of grass. A riddling of red dots appeared on its flank and when it tried to run, it fell.

They climbed a hill and the truck in front of them blasted its horn three times. Moments later they roared through the gate of Dora-Mittelbau and found themselves behind a world of barbed wire once again. The trucks slowed and squealed to a jolting stop. The smell of burning flesh clawed at his nose and he could see SS guards lined up.

"Welcome home," someone yelled.

It was Horse Head. And he was smiling.

IN THE FINAL DAYS of the war, the most secretive and technologically advanced concentration camp in the Nazi Empire was no longer a place of slave labor. The prisoners of Dora had to stand for hours during roll call and then they were allowed to sit down and watch the clouds fluff overhead. If the wind was right, Eli could hear the distant thud of artillery on the horizon. His eyes fluttered to the tree line and he imagined tanks appearing. Occasionally, fighter planes roared and looped overhead.

The SS gathered up blueprints and records, which were then tossed onto enormous bonfires. The flames licked high into the air and paper curled into blackened ash. They dumped petroleum onto the blaze and kept feeding manila folders and ledgers into it. They carried bottles of vodka in one hand and pistols in the other. Some of the SS ripped patches off their uniforms. These too were burnt. The rail yard was silent and rain pattered on nozzles, fins, and propellant tanks. The prisoners bent down to drink streams of rainwater. They searched the camp for weeds, pinecones, and earthworms. Still the rain came. It dribbled at first. It showered down in sheets. It dropped in fat splatting beads. Some of the guards even started to be nice. They offered cigarettes and bits of chocolate.

"When this is over," they said, "remember that I was good to you."

"Here. Take some bread."

"How about a candy mint?"

Other guards become more vicious. Horse Head prowled the camp with his stick. A wild-eyed fury filled him up and it seemed as if he had decided to take as many victims with him as he spiraled down into destruction.

And then one morning, everything changed. It happened when Eli was moving around camp looking for food. He hoped to find a snail on the clapboard of a barrack or perhaps a few ants that no one else had noticed. The sky was green and boiling in the distance. A thunderstorm was on the way and lightning was shocking the horizon. The camp loudspeaker crackled to life as someone blew into the microphone.

"Attention. Attention."

There was a long pause. It was so long that everyone went back to what they were doing.

"Attention. All prisoners report to the *Appellplatz* with a blanket. Repeat, all prisoners to the *Appellplatz* with a blanket."

He looked up. A blanket? Who on earth has a blanket?

A spark of worry filled his throat as he walked down a muddy lane and passed barrack after barrack. Thousands of men began to make their way to the roll call square.

"What's going on?"

"Why do we need a blanket?"

"I've never *seen* a blanket in Dora."

"Let's fall in and see what happens."

"Maybe they have blankets for us?"

Eli let them pass. He slowed down and ducked behind Barrack 92. Prisoners rivered past him and he told himself to stop and think. Something didn't feel right. Be calm. Think. They had all been working on a secret weapon at a secret camp so surely it would be easier to eliminate them instead of letting them live. Secrets can be silenced. Dead prisoners tell no tales. And hadn't Horse Head said, "If things go bad for us, things will go bad for you"?

In a moment of dazzling clarity, Eli saw exactly what the guards might do next. It would be easy to get rid of them, he thought, especially when they were lined up in the *Appellplatz*. He looked at the sticky ground. The SS would only need a few mounted machine guns and they could sweep fire back and forth. Bodies would fall, row after row. Only a few prisoners would need to be saved to help with the clean up afterwards.

He chewed on his lower lip and wondered what to do.

Years later, when Eli was asked about this moment, he would say he didn't have a plan. His feet just started moving. He made a point to walk with a limp and he started to scratch his skin in an exaggerated way. He dug his fingernails into his head, his armpits, and he picked at the seams of his uniform.

The loudspeaker rustled to life again. "Attention…everyone to the *Appellplatz*."

The yard filled up with prisoners and many of them actually held brown blankets. Where had they come from, Eli wondered.

"Everyone to the *Appellplatz*."

He moved around the edge of the roll call square and kept scratching. The gate to the concentration camp was open and he approached it with purpose. Machine guns in the guard towers followed him. He saw their metal snouts sticking out and he imagined, briefly, what it might be like to be shot. The shock would be incredible, so incredible that it might dull the searing pain. Of course, if he were struck in the head there would be no pain at all. It would be an easy death. Fast too. Would he even know that he had died?

He walked up to SS-*Hauptscharführer* Wilhelm Simon and came to attention. He snapped off his cap and tried to click his muddy clogs together. The man in a black uniform put a hand on his holster.

"What?"

Eli gave a Hitler salute and looked at a point over Simon's shoulder. The words came to him as if they weren't his own. "Sir. I've been ordered to get a satchel from sub tunnel 40."

Simon squinted in doubt. "Who ordered you to do this?"

"Horse Head, sir."

SS-*Hauptscharführer* Simon rubbed his thumb against his chin and made a face. He pulled out his pistol and said, "Don't move." There was a long moment before he shouted over to the next guard. "Have you seen Horse Head?"

"He's at the back of camp. Rounding up stragglers, I think."

Simon grunted and returned his gaze to Eli. "What's *in* the satchel?"

"I don't know, sir. I was just ordered to get it."

Simon pushed his tongue against the inside of his cheek and grunted again. "Hans," he yelled to the next guard. "You know anything about this?"

"Nope."

"You think it's the whiskey Horse Head was taking about?"

"Maybe."

Simon studied the Star of David stitched over Eli's breast pocket. "Okay, 41199. You can get the satchel from sub tunnel 40, but make it quick. Bring it directly to me. Understand? I've got my eye on you."

"Yes, sir." Eli nodded and immediately started to walk to the barbed wire fence. He heard the hum of electricity. Thunder roiled in the distance and lightning spread its fingers across the sky.

He hurried past the SS villa and kept his gaze straight ahead. Some of the Nazis were loading suitcases into trucks that waited near a grove of weeping willows. Eli wanted to run but he knew it would draw too much attention. There was another crack of thunder and this made a few of the guards look at the horizon with worry. The clouds were green and angry. Rain was beginning to fall.

The rail yard was full of rockets and cattle cars. A steam engine sat quietly next to a glistening pile of coal and there didn't seem to be anyone in the industrial area of camp. Up ahead, at the very end of the concrete road, he could see the main gate. He counted ten guards, and they all had their weapons drawn.

Eli turned left and followed the rail track to Tunnel A. Blasted bits of white gypsum were on either side and a cool breeze made the pine trees on the slope sway back and forth. The temperature was dropping. Rain fell more quickly. Up ahead, the lights of the tunnel were still on.

"Attention…everyone to the *Appellplatz.*"

Eli looked over his shoulder and broke into a jog. The mouth of the tunnel was so close. Two enormous iron gates were wide open and camouflage netting was still strung above the entrance like an awning. When he stepped inside, a coolness wrapped around him and he wasted no time moving down into the assembly line. V-2s were suspended from cranes and he took off his wooden clogs—he kicked them behind a generator—so that he could move quickly, quietly, tiptoeing at a run. The lights were on at the front of the tunnel and he moved to the growing shadows at the back. He looked for the orange glow of someone smoking a cigarette and every few seconds he stopped to listen for footfalls. There were voices up ahead but he couldn't tell where they were coming from.

He hid behind a work bench and closed his eyes. The voices were German, he decided. One of them had a Bavarian accent.

"Come out and show yourself," came the voice.

Eli opened his eyes and looked at a V-2 laying in front of him. It was a long torpedo and he could see the metallic guts behind the open service panel. He took a step towards it and listened hard. The voices were coming closer. He worried about accidentally kicking a tool on the floor and told himself to slow down. His hands felt the cold metal of the rocket. The rivets beaded up beneath his fingertips. When he found the access panel, he opened it with care. He put one foot inside the V-2 and wormed into the fuel tank. He used a pipe that ran through the middle of it to shimmy himself further into the heart of the rocket. He curled into a ball and waited.

The voices grew louder. Jackboots scuffed against the stone floor. Eli didn't move. He held his breath and pinched his eyes shut. He told himself everything would be fine. Just breathe, he thought. Breathe quietly. All is well. All is well.

In that moment he got to thinking that if someone were watching him in a film they'd think it was a great adventure. Was God watching him go through this terrifying moment? Was he observing this? And if so, why didn't he stop it? His life was at stake and every cell in his body quaked with panic. This wasn't an adventure. It wasn't some kind of grand journey. No. It was a moment that thousands of souls had experienced at Dora-Mittelbau. Life or death? Here or hereafter? The coming seconds would give him either the future or nothing.

In that chamber where liquid oxygen was supposed to go, Eli let the rocket surround him and contain him. He was deep in its belly and he found himself asking God to shield him. The tunnel had tried to kill him many times before but now, perhaps, it would save him. Even as these thoughts flashed through his mind he remembered what happened to Delacroix when he was found inside that wardrobe.

A pale light began to swell and he cursed himself for not closing the access panel. The guards were obviously walking the tunnel with a flashlight. It would be so easy for them to look into the rocket and find him.

One of the voices yelled out, "The camp is being evacuated. If anyone's hiding here, show yourself. We're going to dynamite the tunnel." There was a deliberate pause. "If you wish to live, show yourself. We're sealing the tunnel."

Eli blinked. What should he do?

"We're going to blow up the entrance. Come now...show yourself."

The voices were right next to the rocket and the beam of light was just outside the access panel. The two men stopped.

"Is anyone here?"

Cigarette smoke wafted into the propellant tank. Eli saw ghostly fingers reach towards him. The men shuffled their boots.

"Look at the time," one of them said.

"Already? We'd better hurry."

They walked away, dragging the light with them, and they shouted out that the entrance was about to dynamited. Their voices receded, like they were falling away. A heavy quiet surrounded Eli and it was now so dark that he couldn't see a thing. Would they really blow up the entrance? Would he be sealed inside? He didn't move because he wondered if other guards were waiting to catch hiding prisoners.

Part of him wanted to jump out of the tank and run towards the outside world, but the other part said that it was better to hide. Yes, he counseled himself. Be patient. Maybe there isn't any dynamite and it's all a big lie.

He couldn't see his hand in front of his face and, as he hunched into a motionless ball, he heard the soft feet of mice. Or maybe it was muffled gunshots. It was hard to tell.

HE SLEPT INSIDE THE TANK and had no idea how much time had passed. It was like being buried alive and whenever he thought about leaving the safety of the rocket he shook his head. Who knew what was happening outside of the entrance. It was better to stay put. One thing was certain: Eli couldn't remember the last time he had dozed off and didn't need to worry about who might wake him up. In the overpowering darkness, his body slipped into the warm waters of nothingness. His limbs twitched as he fell asleep. He did not dream. He simply sank away.

When he woke up, it was with a start. The black was so pure, so total, that he began to lose all sense of his own body. He floated out of his skin and lived entirely in the mind, and because he couldn't see himself, he wondered if he had ceased to exist. Perhaps he was dead?

In this new bodyless world, he allowed himself to think of the past—his childhood in Berlin and growing up in Kraków. He thought of Germany before the National Socialists began marching through the streets with their brown shirts and brass knuckles. Since he was hiding in a rocket, maybe that's why he kept thinking about a movie he saw as a child. It was Fritz Lang's *The Woman in the Moon*. In a darkened theatre on Friedrichstrasse, he watched this silent film splash out a giant window of light against a screen. A piano played in the corner as he sat in unblinking fascination. A rocket lifted up through the atmosphere and headed out into the black where it carried a crew to the dark side of the moon. They found gold and breathable air. It was an undiscovered world of mystery and beauty. He imagined riding to the moon and leaving Dora far behind. Up he lifted in his V-2 and he was suddenly transported somewhere else, someplace safe. He saw himself orbiting the ashy greyness of a pocked new world. Hanging in the black void of space was the blue and white Earth. It was the same color as his prison uniform and now he was speeding away from all the pain that his home world had caused. The moon was untouched by human hands and he dreamed of landing on its surface where he would walk among strange trees and dip his face into cool waters. Food was everywhere and no one was forced to work. He could do as he pleased. He was a moon king.

When he jerked awake, he sat up. Or at least he thought he sat up. Without seeing his body, it was hard to match the reality in his head against the reality of the world around him. His stomach popped and clacked for bread. Not a crumb was inside him and he was beginning to feel lightheaded. If he didn't eat something soon, the rocket would become his tomb.

He scooched forward and let his legs hang out of the access panel. The ragged ends of his trousers were stiff with dried mud. He listened but couldn't hear a thing. Even the mice were quiet.

Slowly, as if he were stepping onto the surface of a new world, he dropped to the stone floor. It was cold against his bare feet. He touched the casing of the rocket and steadied himself. Strange yellow and purple blobs floated before him as his mind tried to make sense of the inky blindness. He saw no light and wondered if the Nazis had kept their promise to blow up the entrance. They were good at keeping promises, after all. Hadn't they sworn to destroy the Jews of Europe?

He searched for the nosecone of the V-2 because he knew it was pointing towards the exit. When he found it, he touched his way down the wall and moved back towards the world. His fingers read the bumpy chiseled surface of the tunnel. Thousands of workers had chipped away at the rock and thousands more had built futuristic weapons under the mountain. And now, as far as he could tell, he was the only soul in this secret underground factory. He had the whole wicked place to himself.

He moved around generators, cranes, and work tables. He stubbed his toe on wrenches and hammers. A rivet got stuck to the fleshy sole of his foot as he continued to read the wall and move forward. A few minutes later he tripped face first into a cold pile of bodies. His hand went into someone's open dry mouth—he could feel teeth. He got up and kept moving.

When he saw it, he thought his eyes were playing another trick on him. He had gotten so used to seeing floating blobs of color that it seemed like the yellow dot hanging before him was a figment of his imagination. And yet, as he took a few more steps, the light got brighter and he knew it was the entrance. He stopped to listen for boots, or the clearing of a throat, or a shout for him to put his goddamn hands up. He approached the future gently, and walked as if he were on a high wire.

When he emerged into the bright blinding sunlight, he squinted and looked at the ground. Dried clog marks were everywhere. He followed the rail tracks and enjoyed the sun's warmth on his skin.

It was quiet. Noticeably quiet.

He shielded his eyes and blinked. Bodies were everywhere but he couldn't see any SS officers. The whole world was still and hushed. Dora sounded different and he couldn't figure out why this was. He nodded in understanding when he knew what was missing. The constant low rumble of the crematorium couldn't be heard. He looked at the wooded hill and saw no thread of smoke. Wind rustled the pine trees and a robin called from somewhere in the distance. There was also a new sound he couldn't quite place—a low zuzzing of flies. They shook like dots over the dead.

He stood with his arms at his sides and felt nothing. It was like his brain had turned off. He was numb. Emotionless. Beyond caring. The barber pole barricade of the main gate was raised, which meant that he could leave if he wanted to, but he just stood there, staring. He couldn't understand what he was looking at. An open gate?

From somewhere beyond the borderlands of the camp, he heard an engine. It didn't sound like a truck—it was too high pitched—and it was approaching fast. He looked around for a place to hide but the tunnel was too far away. The engine came closer and closer. A vehicle unlike anything he'd ever seen suddenly appeared at the gate and roared into the camp. Two soldiers were in it and they were dressed in olive drab. One of them pointed at Eli and they drove over in a cloud of noise. They parked but didn't turn off the engine.

Eli stood at attention because he wasn't sure what else to do. He wavered on his feet. One of the men got out with a rifle and looked around in horror. He stared at a body on the ground for a long lingering moment.

Eli tried to concentrate. They were Americans. They had arrived in a jeep—a big white star was on the hood and the front grill was spattered with mud. Tufts of brown weeds were caught in the fender and the windshield had a bullet hole in it. The solider who stared at the corpse was well fed and he had stubble on his face. He turned to Eli and when he spoke it was in flawless German. "What is this place?"

Eli's tongue didn't move. He was afraid that if he spoke or looked away from the Americans this new reality might flutter away. He worried that it was a hallucination.

"Do you speak German? What is this place?"

Much later, in the years to come, Eli learned that Dora-Mittelbau was liberated on April 11, 1945, and that these two men were from the 104th Infantry Division. At that particular moment though, he could do nothing more than stare at the name stitched onto the man's uniform. VOGEL. It was written in the same spot where 41199 had been printed on Eli's uniform.

"My God," the soldier said. "Is this another camp?"

Eli dropped to his knees. A sharp pebble was beneath his kneecap but he didn't care. He slumped sideways. The soldier, Vogel, came over and lifted Eli. He propped him against his leg and fumbled for something in a knapsack. A dented silver canteen. It was caked with dried mud. He unscrewed the top with his thumb and gave it to Eli. The water was warm and metallic—he drank it all in.

The man dug around in a side pocket and pulled out a bit of wax paper. He handed over a bit of warm salami. As Eli began to chew, the man said something in English that he couldn't understand but he knew that the words were full of kindness and compassion. He could see it in the man's hazel eyes. It had been a long time since someone had looked upon him in such a way, and it made Eli feel so very strange. He tried to sit up, but broke down in tears.

He was free.

PART II

"I believe that this nation should commit itself
to achieving the goal, before this decade is out,
of landing a man on the moon and returning him safely
to the Earth."

—President John F. Kennedy

SON OF APOLLO

IT TOOK A YEAR BEFORE Eli allowed himself to believe that he was still among the living.

His hair came back in tufting patches, the weeping sores on his legs began to scab over, and when he was given an old suit—one that was mercifully free of lice—he felt himself walk a little taller. Even though it was strange not having the scythe of death hanging over his head all the time, he still found himself looking over his shoulder for Horse Head. The Americans built a plywood cafeteria and he ate with his back against the wall. His eyes darted to the left and right. He covered his food bowl with one hand and ate quickly with the other. After a month, he was taken to a Displaced Persons camp in Nuremberg where he scanned the barracks and worried that guards might rise out of the ground to place a pistol against his forehead. As for the American soldiers, he found it difficult to believe that men in uniform could actually be kind.

After a few months of freedom, a voice began to echo in the dark tunnels of his memory. It was something his mother often said: *We are who we love.* Now that his entire family tree had been reduced to ash, he had no one. He was without love and he wanted to start over someplace new, someplace safe. When he asked to emigrate to America, a lieutenant with a clipboard wanted to know his reason for leaving Germany. Eli's answer was simple and full of raw truth: "I'm the last of my name."

"There must be someone. An aunt or an uncle, maybe?"

"There is no one."

The young man with red hair considered this for a moment. "Where do you want to live?"

"New York. I want to live in New York City."

Years later, long after he sailed past the Statue of Liberty and stepped into a new life, he still couldn't relax in his own home unless the front door was double-bolted and chained. He stored dried lentils in the cupboard and stacked cans of tomatoes, sweetcorn, and asparagus tips in the garage. He walked around with sweets in his front pocket. Whenever he fell asleep at night, he was grateful for a full stomach and, always, he kept an apple next to his bed in case he woke up in the middle of the night. He drifted into the foggy land of sleep with an air conditioner brumbling in the window. Such simple pleasures were a wonder. They were beyond belief. His nightmares, however, were vivid and crisp. He often woke up panting and had to remind himself that he was safe, that he had outlived Auschwitz, Dora-Mittelbau, and the Third Reich. His pajamas were made of silk and they looked nothing like the uniform he was forced to wear.

"All is well," he told himself, examining the alarm clock. "All is well."

It was the summer of 1969 and the "big one" was scheduled to liftoff in three days. His nightmares about Dora had mysteriously increased over the past few months and the same dream kept stealing back into his mind. There he was, in a striped uniform, and the SS slowly paced the tunnel—their boots clicked against the stone floor like a metronome. In the dream, he's hit in the face with a truncheon and, as blood pours over his lips and down his chin, he watches his wife and daughter get dragged away. Horse Head pulls them by the hair and—no matter how hard Eli tries to catch up, no matter how hard he tries to run after them, no matter how hard he wills himself forward—he just isn't fast enough. His feet are caught in quicksand and his legs won't move. When he finally struggles free and reaches the tunnel, his wife and daughter are already in a wheelbarrow, dead. They gaze up at him, naked, opened-mouthed, their hair shaved off. A hooded figure reaches for the wheelbarrow and yells out that he's going to win the chariot race. Eli watches his new family roll towards a glowing furnace where their essence curls away from a brick chimney. As he stands there, Horse Head hooks a long arm around his shoulder and gently escorts him back to the tunnel. "This way," he says. "Come back to the underworld. You shouldn't have survived in the first place."

Slowly, deliberately, Eli reached for the alarm clock and pushed the nightmare aside. He got out of bed and could hear water splashing against a plastic curtain in the bathroom. His wife was alive and in the shower.

"You are in Florida," he told himself. "*All* is well."

A mountain of data waited at work and, as he thought about blueprints and propellant and the vectors of heavenly thrust, he dressed. He reached for his plastic NASA badge and pinned it to his shirt. He put on a suitcoat and snapped wrinkles from the front. He leaned into the bedroom mirror and smoothed a hand over his jaw. Should he shave? The press were crawling all over the Cape and who knew when the *New York Times* or *The Washington Post* might step into his office.

He moved down the hallway and walked through a warm bank of steam—she was singing in the shower—and when he reached the living room he noticed that the TV was on. Her bathrobe was tossed onto the avocado colored sofa and he imagined her walking naked down the hallway. She did this kind of thing when they were alone. A morning show was on and an attractive blonde with poofy hair was talking about a new movie while the man next to her held a cigarette. He blew smoke sideways out of his mouth and shuffled paper.

America was such a dazzlingly strange and wonderful place, he thought. It was full of speed and commerce and wide avenues and baseball and cars and an absolute faith in the future. He remembered the first time he walked down Broadway. There were so many neon lights competing for his attention it made him dizzy.

MAKE CAMPBELL'S SOUP

Betz's Better Beds
from Ah-ha! to Zzzz

Hersey's Chocolate

ALMA BAKERIES

Boraxo Hand Soap

CHESTERFIELD TOBACCO
For that smoooth taste

Television, he thought while staring at the morning show, was the bonfire around which America gathered and the shows he saw were so very odd. *Gilligan's Island, Bewitched, The Munsters, I Dream of Jeannie.* They had absolutely nothing to do with reality. These shows, if you could call them that, were designed for people to detach and disconnect. It was cheerful propaganda, a way to let forgetfulness fill up living rooms and numb the realities that were happening beyond the manicured lawns. Who remembered Auschwitz now?

The show that stunned him the most was *Hogan's Heroes*. In this, the Nazis were portrayed as harmless buffoons, and when he saw it for the first time he could not believe a laugh track was running while men in swastikas barked out orders that no one obeyed? Orders that no one obeyed? He couldn't imagine such a thing. It was simply beyond belief. And when he saw this show leaking into his own home, his finger jabbed the OFF button and he stared at the black mirror of the television.

Imagine. A comedy. About Nazis.

When the attractive blonde finished speaking, his eyes refocused on the television.

"Everyone's talking about Apollo 11. At this very moment, the rocket that will carry Neil Armstrong, Buzz Aldrin, and Michael Collins to the moon is being moved to launch pad 39-A. We have some live coverage of this, don't we? Do we have that?" There was a pause as the man looked down at his desk. "I'm afraid we don't have that for you but history *will* be made this coming Wednesday, July 16, when Apollo 11 blasts off shortly after one o'clock eastern standard time. If all goes according to plan, Neil Armstrong will become the first human being to set foot on an alien world."

Eli glanced at the plastic NASA badge on his shirt. Seeing it made him smile. An advertisement for frozen TV dinners came on and it showed a happy man peeling aluminum foil away from a tray—steam puffed up from sliced pork, mashed potatoes, a nest of peas, and something called applesauce cake.

He weighed 93 pounds when the Americans found him. A medic with a red cross on his helmet took Eli aside and said, in broken German, "You must the weight more have. Feed on eggs." Over the coming months he was given eggs by the dozen. They were scrambled and fried and boiled and poached. He ate them in sandwiches. And as he waited for his immigration paperwork to clear, he opened tins of chipped beef and drank pear juice. He was given corned beef, bowls of potato salad, and real coffee. His stomach went to work on this necessary fuel and his body slowly grew stronger. One day, not long after he stepped away from Dora, he found himself before a full-length mirror. He hardly recognized the grotesquely malnourished person he had become. His reflection was nothing more than a skeleton in a suit. It made him reach for more eggs, more bread, more chipped beef. To eat was to live.

History would say he had been liberated but, for Eli, this wasn't technically true since the SS had fled Dora-Mittelbau and taken most of the inmates with them on a death march, hundreds murdered along the way. What really haunted Eli, though, was what happened at a tiny village called Gardelegen. It was here that over one thousand prisoners—men Eli had known and stood in roll call with—were all stuffed in a barn and burned alive. Padlocks were put on the doors, straw bales were lined against the outside walls, and gasoline was splashed out. The guards stood back and shot anyone who tried to burrow their way out. They smoked cigarettes as flames lifted into the blue, blue sky. As screams filled up the air, the SS talked about what they'd do after the war. The air grew hazy with heat. The killers stayed until the only sound was that of crackling fire. They made sure the prisoners were dead before they took off their uniforms and stepped into new lives as electricians, bankers, and plumbers.

No, he thought, the only thing he'd been liberated from was hunger, brutal work, and the fear of being beaten to death. When the Americans rolled into Dora-Mittelbau, there was no one for him to be liberated *from*. All of his tormentors had all fled.

Wind tickled a curtain near the kitchen sink and this made him scowl. Had she left the window open again last night? He went into the kitchen and latched it shut. He glanced at the front door and wondered if she had forgotten that too. He walked with purpose, his shoes clacking against the linoleum, and he checked the locks. Good, he nodded. Everything was buttoned up.

He paused to look at the framed jigsaw puzzles lining the hallway. There was one of Big Ben. Another of Paris at night. One of Brandenburg Gate and another of Mount Rushmore. From a distance they appeared like oil paintings but up close they were fractured pieces that had been painstakingly fitted back together again.

An advertisement for Folger's coffee blared from the television.

"Henry?" a woman asked. "Do you want anything special for your birthday?"

"A decent cup of coffee would be nice. Your coffee is undrinkable, dear."

"That's pretty harsh."

"Well…so is your coffee."

Another voice, overly friendly and confident, chimed in about the wonders of freeze-dried instant grounds. It made Eli look at his wristwatch and go back into the kitchen. He reached for a red metal can and peeled off the plastic cover. The incense of morning lifted around him, and he bent low to smell. He dug for the metal scoop inside the can and enjoyed the raspy scrunch it made moving through freeze dried coffee.

She was taking a longer shower than usual and singing something by Billy Holiday. Eli imagined his wife standing before him, naked. She dropped her pink negligee and cupped her breasts. There was a scar over her belly where their daughter had been plucked out.

"Lover maaan. I'd give my sooooul just to call you my oooown."

Other visions of naked bodies flashed before him, and he reached for a packet of cigarettes. Pall Mall. He lit one and considered the glowing fire at his fingertips. Fire. Flame. Furnace.

"Lover maaaan…where can you be?"

He told her nothing about Dora. He kept the poison of that place stored deep inside his tissue—it was locked in the very molecules of his being. Oh yes, he nodded, he had scars. You couldn't see them, but he had scars in his brain.

The shower thwanked off and the curtain was slapped aside. "My lover maaaan…oh, where can you be?"

Her name was Paulina. Lina for short. They met in New York after he enrolled at Columbia University to study astrophysics and rocketry. He chose those fields not only because of what he had seen at Dora, but also because it calmed him to see that the world was governed by fixed forces. She worked in the library and smiled at him as she walked by with a cart full of returned books. They got to talking and went out for coffee, which turned into dinner, which turned into a walk around Central Park. Although she couldn't understand the mathematical hieroglyphics of his textbooks, she asked about them anyway. She was curious, bright, and her smile filled Eli up with July sunshine.

As he got to know her, he learned that the war had marked her too: her fiancé had died when his parachute failed to open on D-Day and her brother was killed at Anzio. Like so many Jews in New York, she lost distant family members in the camps. Sometimes Lina was quiet and broken, and other times she would grab Eli's wrist and drag him into the bright lights of Time Square. "Isn't it beautiful?" she would say, spinning around. "Isn't it beautiful in spite of it all?" As she turned in a slow circle, Eli watched her and felt something like joy fizz in his chest.

They were married six months later. It was a small celebration because he had no relatives, and after he stomped on a wine glass wrapped in a linen napkin, everyone patted his back. "Welcome," they said. "Welcome to the family."

That night, when they stripped off their clothes and finally saw each other's naked bodies, she stroked the messy blue tattoo that had been stitched into his forearm. She traced the numbers with her finger.

"Auschwitz?"

"Yes."

She cupped his face and looked deep into his eyes. "You are an amazing, talented, good, and kind man, Eli Hessel. Do you hear me? You're amazing."

The coffee commercial on television turned into a local ad for a car dealer, and this brought him back to the present. He picked up the coffee pot and moved to the sink. A rope of water splashed out of the faucet and he placed the metal pot beneath it—the tone inside went from deep and tinkling to high and burbling as it filled. A baby carrot was in the sink and he cleaned it off. He placed it in the fridge next to a browning apple and a half-eaten stalk of celery. When he plugged in the coffee maker, he found himself staring at the socket.

Back in the 1950s, he was given shock therapy. It was his doctor's idea, something about knocking his memories loose and cleaning out the conduits of his brain with electricity. Men in white coats attached wires to his forehead, they placed a brown rubber bit into his mouth, and then they filled him up with sparks. A lightning storm detonated inside his skull and when he came to, when it was finally over, a single thought butterflied around the grassy meadow of his mind. He was back in Neue Synagogue on Oranienburger Strasse and he could hear the cantor. He could hear the cantor so clearly. His father was next to him, deep in prayer. As the doctors unhooked the wires and helped Eli sit up, he thought about how his family had been turned into ash. He didn't even know where they had been scattered.

"All better?" the doctor in a white smock asked cheerfully.

Eli shrugged and allowed himself to be lowered into a wheelchair. When Lina drove him home, he placed his head against the rumbling window and closed his eyes. Spark. Fire. Ash. These words orbited around his skull. Spark. Fire. Ash. He thought about the acetylene torch he used at Dora and he thought about the welder's mask he wore to protect his eyes from what was before him. Spark. Fire. Ash. He had three more sessions of high voltage but the cloak of depression just wouldn't lift. That's when Lina bought him a jigsaw puzzle. She cleared the dining room table and dumped out the broken pieces. They scattered like rubble from a bomb blast.

"Here," she said, pointing at the mess. "Make it whole again."

"I really don't think—"

She held up a hand. "Just do it."

That night he sat down with a large whiskey and began to move fragmented parts around the table. Pieces clicked into place, a picture slowly emerged, and when he was finished—after he slotted the last piece home—he coated the back with glue. Now it was a single piece of cardboard and it was no longer something that had been broken. He slid it into a frame and hung it in the hallway by the front door. Finished jigsaw puzzles were soon everywhere. They were in the bedroom, the living room, the kitchen, the den, even the garage. He liked doing portraits of famous people and he often held up pieces of jaw or slivers of eyebrows to figure out where they might go. He tapped these pieces into place with a single finger. It was about control. He knew this. He accepted this. He didn't question it.

"There'll be no more electroconvulsive therapy for you," Lina said, shaking her head one night. "You need to build things, Eli. That's what'll help…it's not a cure, but it will help focus your mind."

He was soon publishing academic articles and attending conferences and he became an adjunct professor at Columbia. And then one day, he got a call from NASA. They wanted to know if he was interested in the manned space program. It was new territory and new problems to solve, so after talking about it one evening over a fancy dinner with Lina, they packed everything into a small truck and left New York. The jigsaw puzzles were thrown away because Eli was determined to leave the past behind. The Russians had just launched a man into space—a cosmonaut, they called him—and America needed to catch up. Only the future mattered now. Yes, he told himself as he drove south on

Interstate 95. He would live in the future. Florida. A fresh start.

They bought a house near the ocean, and at first he worried that his new colleagues might ask him unwanted questions about what he did during the war. Hardly anyone asked though. He was just another immigrant, he was just another displaced person who had made America their home. If they *did* ask about his past, he told them he was in a concentration camp.

"Where? Dachau?"

"No."

"Buchenwald?"

"No."

"That other place. Bergen-something-or-other."

He shook his head.

"Where then?"

"Dora-Mittelbau."

They scrunched up their mouths and shook their heads slowly. "Naw. Never heard of that one." They might shrug and offer him an *hors d'oeuvre.* "Did you catch the game last night?"

Whenever this happened, Eli told himself the past was no longer important and he couldn't let it rule him forever, especially now that everyone at NASA was gazing at the moon. He needed to bury everything that had happened in the tunnels. He needed to spark the dynamite of forgetfulness and walk away.

"It's Hannah's birthday next week," Lina called from the bathroom. "We need to get a card."

"Mmm-hm," he half-shouted.

The coffee maker bubbled and rumbled. Steam lifted from the spout.

"I'll pick one up at Crawford's," she said.

"Pick what up?"

"A card." There was a pause and then, "Are you listening to me?"

Their daughter was pulled into the world on July 24, 1949. She didn't scream, and Eli took this as a sign that her life might be easy. "We are who we love," he whispered into her newborn ear. "Can you hear me, little one? We are who we love." In what seemed like the blink of an eye, she grew into a woman. He saw how men leered at her when she walked across the street but he didn't know what to do about this. Should he say something? Should he tell these men they ought to be ashamed of themselves? She had tight curls and a mist of freckles across the bridge of her nose. Her smile—it still made him buoyant.

Now that she was a sophomore at Berkeley, the house felt quiet and sleepy. He'd gotten used to her friends coming over, their heated talk of politics, their homework sessions, and their loud music. She wore low cut dresses and enjoyed wearing pink tinted sunglasses. Her room still had posters of The Beatles on the walls, and her bed still had stuffed animals lined up on the pillow. How odd, Eli thought for the millionth time, she was both a girl and a woman whenever he thought about her. The younger her and the adult her were braided together. He hoped she might come home for the summer but that boyfriend—an activist against Vietnam—had convinced her to stay in California. He was majoring in political science. "Poly-sci," he called it. (Whatever *that* was.) He had muttonchops, wild hair, and trousers that had swirls of green and yellow on them. He wore necklaces and bracelets, which Eli found very weird. They were probably—he took a deep breath at this disturbing thought—they were probably sleeping together.

He reached for a mug and poured steaming coffee into it. He dropped in a cube of brown sugar and then tapped in a single drop of vanilla extract. The spoon clinked off the sides as he stirred and stirred. The tan liquid spun like a galaxy.

Hannah wasn't interested in being a Jew. Oh sure, he nodded, she knew about Passover, Rosh Hashanah, Yom Kippur, and Hanukkah, and she had her bat mitzvah like any other girl, but she took no interest in her roots. In fact, a few months ago, she declared that she was a "cultural Jew" (whatever *that* was) and on the very few occasions that she did ask about Dora, he held up a hand and simply shook his head. "I do not want it in your eyes." More than anything, he wished that his mother could have met Hannah. She would have wrapped her granddaughter in love, she would have poured her whole being into making her happy. Did Hannah ever wonder about her murdered relatives? Did she ever wonder about the ghosts that came before her? Maybe she was asking about the camps because—

"Eli…? Are you listening to me?"

He turned and shouted up the hallway. "Yes, of course." His voice was loud, perhaps too loud.

"Then tell me what I just said."

"Something about Crawford's."

"Right…and?"

"I will sign the card tonight."

The closet in their bedroom clattered open and he could hear something being tossed onto the bed. Another something was tossed.

He went into the living room and stood before the shimmering television. The camera framed a handsome newscaster and, beside him, was a plastic model of a Saturn V. The man with perfectly cut hair held a cigarette and smiled.

"In the next few days Apollo 11 will lift into the history books, and sitting with me is a man who is making this impossible dream, possible. Professor Wernher von Braun, welcome to the show."

The camera panned to the left and, sitting in a dark blue suit with his fingers laced together, was the same man Eli once saw examining V-2s in the railyard of Dora. His hair was smoothed back, streaked grey, and he had a winning smile.

"Professor von Braun...the Saturn V is the highest of high technology and your rocket has already carried several of our boys into lunar orbit. Tell me, what got you interested in space?"

Eli flicked off the television and watched the picture shrink into blackness. A pinprick of light glowed in the center before it too winked out like a dying star. The TV clicked and ticked as it cooled. He stared at where von Braun's face used to be and saw his own reflection.

"I made coffee for you," he said, picking up a leather satchel and moving for the door. "It's in the kitchen, just the way you like it. Don't wait up for me. We have lots to do before launch."

Ever since President Kennedy challenged the nation to land a man on the moon and return him safely to Earth, they had been working relentlessly towards this moment. NASA had taken baby steps with the Mercury program, much had been learned about living and working in space thanks to the Gemini program, and now? Now they were about to land on the moon. They were carrying the fire of knowledge and he liked that NASA used mythology to name its programs.

It made him think of Orpheus and Eurydice. He related to this ancient tale of the underworld all too well. It started when Orpheus was playing his lyre and his wife, enraptured by the beautiful notes, stumbled into a nest of vipers. She was bitten and dragged down to Hades. Heartbroken, Orpheus journeyed down to find her. He climbed down through rocks and entered a world of cool darkness and pale souls. When he found Persephone, the queen of Hades, he charmed her with his music and she made him an offer. "You may bring your wife Eurydice up to the land of the living on one condition: you must walk ahead of her and if you look back for any reason your wife will remain dead." Orpheus agreed and began to walk. He sensed his wife pacing behind him and he kept on moving. He scrambled up the rising path and imagined the delicious warmth of sunlight splashing onto their faces. He wanted to glance back and see how she was doing—was she okay?—but he did not do this. Instead, he kept moving forward, upward, forward, and when he finally climbed out of the cave and returned to the land of the living, Orpheus turned back and yelled, in great excitement, "You're almost there, my love. Only a few more steps now!" But Eurydice was still in the cave when he did this and she was not yet in the sunlight, so in one terrible moment she was pulled back into the gloom. She was lost forever. Orpheus, Eli knew, was the son of Apollo. He understood tunnels. He understood darkness. And he especially understood the world of the dead.

He gripped his satchel and moved for the front door. Yes, in order to save his loved ones, he couldn't look back. He had to keep moving forward and focus on the future.

Lina came padding down the hallway, but he didn't look over his shoulder at her.

"We still need to chat about the whiskey," she said. "Don't think I've forgotten about that."

He opened the door, and stepped into the world of the living.

MOON FEVER

As HE DROVE ACROSS a one lane bridge, the sun was on oily streak on the Banana River. His tires thrummed on the metal grating. He pressed down on the accelerator and thrilled at the sudden burst of speed, the open road, the raw power of his American built engine. Palm trees tufted up on either side as he blurred past bait shops, bars, and whitewashed churches. JESUS IS LORD! REPENT YE SINNERS! He ignored this and stared instead at the looming hulk of the Vehicle Assembly Building on the horizon. The VAB was the largest structure on earth. It could swallow the Pentagon, it could absorb the bulkiest pyramid on the Giza plateau, and it could comfortably hold three Empire State Buildings. It was so immense, so echoing, so colossal, that it created its own weather system. Huge openings had to be drilled into the ceiling to churn up the air. It was, Eli thought, a palace of technology. It was where the rockets were built.

A wide-winged anhinga lifted up from a gully and he watched it sail over his car. The wildlife around the Kennedy Space Center still amazed him. He knew that hidden beneath palm trees were pelicans, armadillos, bobcats, loggerhead turtles, deer, and thousands upon thousands of alligators—they floated just beneath the surface, their primordial eyes narrowing at the human activity which disturbed their land.

He was startled when a white jet appeared on his right. Its landing gear was down and it bobbled lower for the runway. Its shadow flashed over the car and he leaned forward to get a better view. A blue NASA symbol was on the tailfin and the engine shrieked as it disappeared behind a clutch of palm trees. There was a roar of airbrakes. Probably one of the astronauts flying in from Houston, he thought. That's where they all lived and trained. They often commuted to Florida in these stubby-winged jets whenever they were needed or whenever they were about to strap themselves into a rocket. Maybe that was Neil Armstrong who had just flashed overhead? It was possible, Eli thought, looking at his watch. After all, they were going to the moon in a few days so why wouldn't the crew of Apollo 11 already be here? How strange, he thought, gripping the steering wheel. The Wright Brothers made the first flight in 1903 and now, a mere sixty-six summers later, humanity was about to fly to the moon.

"*Wunderbar*," he whistled.

Another jet with stubby wings appeared and it, too, bobbled in for a landing. Sunlight flashed off the canopy and he stared at the cockpit. Was that Buzz Aldrin? Michael Collins?

When it was out of sight, he sat back and realized that he'd slowed down to 40 miles per hour, so he pressed down on the accelerator. He floored it and imagined himself lifting into space.

"Star sailor," he half-shouted. Astronaut. He looked up at an ocean of sky and nodded at the word. Yes, astronaut was so much better than that other word, Cosmonaut.

A silver Corvette shot past him as if he were standing still and the sudden movement—not to mention, noise—brought him back to the road. He wiggled his fingers on the steering wheel and checked his speed. He was going seventy and that Corvette must be clocking at least one hundred. Maybe one ten.

He watched the Corvette shoot up the road and his eyes fell on an approaching green sign.

KENNEDY SPACE CENTER, 1 MILE
CLEARANCE NEEDED

When President Kennedy said, "We choose to go to the moon in this decade and do the other things, not because they are easy, but because they are hard," he almost certainly had no idea what he was asking of the country. When he uttered those words, much of the technology and materials needed for a moonshot hadn't even been invented yet. No one had the slightest idea how to rendezvous in space or how a person could survive in the unforgiving black void for more than a day. It wasn't even known if the dusty surface of the moon wouldn't just swallow up a landing craft whole. What if it sank? No, Eli thought, when Kennedy spoke those words, the United States had only sent up one astronaut—a single man—and that flight lasted just fifteen minutes. Back in 1961, Alan Shepard was fired straight up, he arced over the Kármán Line, and he came roaring straight back down before he splashed into the warm waters of the Bahamas. He hadn't even orbited the earth, and yet Kennedy announced that America would go to the moon. It was crazy. It was insane. You want us to go *where?* Eli remembering thinking at the time. We've only managed to send an astronaut to the Bahamas, and now you want us to go to the moon?

As he pulled up to the barricade, a guard came out of a concrete hut with a clipboard. He wore sunglasses and had a sidearm. His cowboy boots were made of ostrich leg leather. They were buffed to a high shine.

"Number?"

Eli wanted to say that he was a man, not a number, but he wasn't in the mood for a debate, so he simply pointed to the badge on his dress shirt. The guard clicked open a pen and continued staring at his clipboard. He hadn't noticed that Eli had pointed to his shirt.

"Number?" the guard asked again.

"VAB ML 119."

The man scribbled on the clipboard and nodded at an unseen colleague in the booth. "Go ahead."

The pole was raised and Eli drove through, slowly. A squashed pelican was in the middle of the road and he swerved as he gathered speed.

To rest of the world, the sprawling complex around him was called the Kennedy Space Center but for those who worked inside its buildings and on its launch pads it was affectionately known as "The Rocket Ranch." White cars with government plates zipped around, trucks hauled massive parts from one building to another, and everyone worked towards a single unchanging goal: getting a man on the moon. Although it didn't look like it, he was at the front line of the Cold War. This was where American scientists were determined to beat Soviet scientists. There was constant worry about spies infiltrating the ranks and, over lunch, there were rumors of sabotage. It wouldn't take much, people said. If the right agent was in the right place at the right time, all they needed to do was pull a tuft of electrical wiring.

As he pulled into the VAB parking lot, he glanced at the American flag painted onto its side. The morning sun made him squint. The flag was bigger than a football field and each star was the size of his Buick.

He pulled in and turned off the engine. It promised to be a hot day, so he rolled down the window a few inches, grabbed his satchel, and hurried for the office. Buzzards rode the air currents that lifted up from the side of the VAB. There were at least twenty of them rising, diving, falling, rising again. Like the alligators in the swamp, they had ruled this land long before NASA tried to tame it. Just beyond the parking lot was a wild world of mouths and teeth. Eat or be eaten.

Eli opened a glass door and stepped into air conditioning. It felt good—not just the coolness on his skin but the idea of being part of something bigger than himself. A tide of energy pulled him forward when he heard typewriters clacking and pinging. Photos of astronauts lined the walls and a laugh came from behind a closed door. When he passed a restroom he heard a toilet flush. He enjoyed the quick movement of his legs over the checkered floor and he noticed secretaries making mimeographs. They wore flowery dresses, they had horn-rimmed glasses and, every now and then, they reached for a cigarette. Around them were cabinet-sized computers with spools of whurring magnetic tape. A soft hum was in the building. It was like being inside a beehive.

His secretary, Jessica, looked up from her electric typewriter as he approached. She had copper blonde hair and wore a peace symbol around her neck. A framed photo of a soldier was on her desk.

"Good morning, Mr. Hessel."

"Any messages?"

"Just this," she handed him a piece of folded yellow paper. "PRT wants to know if you're doing a secondary final on the F-1s before the LUT moves."

He looked at the note and handed it back. "Thank you," he said, already stepping away. "If anyone asks for me, tell them I'm doing another final on the F-1s. We want to give our star sailors on 11 a smooth ride."

He worked in a world of mystifying acronyms and abbreviations. He knew this and enjoyed it. What did LUT, CSM, LEM, SA-506, LOX, and MSOB mean to an outsider? Even the name of the place had been compressed down to three simple letters: KSC. This wasn't done for secrecy, it was done for accuracy. With over two million moving parts on Apollo, coded language was the only way to keep everything straight and checked. Even the bolts were numbered. How else would you know which one to tighten? To work here, he thought gliding over the floor, one has to earn the password of language.

He stopped at a table of doughnuts. The best ones had already been picked over so he reached for two that didn't have sugar. He wrapped them in a napkin and read the headline on a badly folded copy of the *Orlando Sentinel*. 23 DEAD IN VIETNAM. There was an inky picture of a soldier firing a machine gun into a jungle. Only twenty-three, he thought. Not even half a cattle car and yet it's front page news.

The fear of unwanted memories made him walk quickly past an empty hat stand and step into a cramped room full of desks and cabinets. Three-ring binders were everywhere. An ashtray overflowed with butts, a radio was on a shelf mumbling out a weather report, and pinned to the far wall was an enormous map of the moon. Even from this distance he could see the red pin that someone had put into *Mare Tranquillitatis*. That's where Apollo 11 was going to land. *Mare Tranquillitatis*. The Sea of Tranquility. His colleagues were busy with slide rulers and charts and blueprints. Cigarette smoke hung near the stucco ceiling and someone—probably Gordo Woods—was crashed out on a sofa. His shoes were off and a copy of yesterday's newspaper was tented over his face.

When he moved for his desk, his colleagues didn't look up or say hello. Charlie Greenfield, the youngest, was from the cattle belt of Texas and he bent low over a chart. Gene Presnell hadn't touched the cigarette in his ashtray for so long that two inches of powdery ash were suspended from the end—he glowered at a print out. Skip Rezner wore sunglasses and was busy crossing out numbers on a yellow pad. As for their boss, Gordo Woods, he snored softly and rhythmically on the sofa. It made the newspaper flutter.

Eli put the doughnuts in the bottom drawer of his desk. There were three apples in there, along with a banana and a fistful of caramels. There was also a half empty bottle of vodka under a manila folder. He slid the drawer shut and locked it. He remembered something his father had once said, "Eating always satisfies your hunger, but drinking never satisfies your thirst. Beware the bottle."

Eli pushed this unwanted thought aside, grabbed a clipboard, and moved for the door. When he spoke, it was in something like a strangled whisper so as not to make too much noise. "I am doing another final on the F-1s. Did he go home last night?"

Charlie shook his head. "Naw. He's been working on those nozzle fixes for 12."

Skip Rezner glanced up from a pad of paper. His voice was also low.

"Didn't you inspect the F-1s last night?"

"Yes," Eli nodded, running a hand through his buzzcut hair. "But I want to check again. If the boss asks," he nodded to the sofa, "tell him where I am, yes?"

"You Germans. Always the perfectionists."

Gene puffed himself up and spoke in a fake accent. "Ve haf vays of doing the rockets."

"*Ja, ja*," Skip added.

"Und after dee rocket go zooming up, ve haf the bratwurst and sauerkraut."

"Und beer."

"*Ja, ja*, und plenty of beer."

Eli tried to smile but it was yet another reminder that he wasn't one of them, nor would he ever be. They came from the fields of America and, because of this natural fact, they moved around the office with an easy swagger. They used baseball phrases that felt foreign and strange on his tongue. They said things like *touch base*, *home run*, and *struck out*. They spoke about *swinging for the fences* and *touching 'em all*. He knew what these phrases meant, but if he said them in his thick German accent it was something to be mocked, something to be ridiculed, and if complained about being teased they would say he was too sensitive. Lighten up, they'd say. We're joking, they'd say. In America, people didn't listen to what you said—they listened to how you said it.

As Eli walked back into the secretarial area he muttered, "Ve haf vays of doing the rockets" and tried to sound more American. "We havah waaays of doing the rock-its."

Typewriters clacked around him and a flight of soft music came from a desk radio. It was a popular song. By the Beatles? Or was it the Monkees? He couldn't tell them apart but his daughter would surely know. Something about getting back and belonging.

He hurried down an overly bright stairwell where, after opening a stiff door, he stepped back into the sun. Muggy heat rolled over him and he heard frogs singing from a nearby swamp. Cracks in the sidewalk floated beneath his shoes as he thought about fuel pumps, compressor valves, and liquid oxygen. He walked over a strip of grass and kicked at fuzzy dandelion heads. When he passed into the mighty shadow of the VAB, the air around him became cooler. The buzzards were still riding the air but he ignored their rising and falling—he hurried for a door and stepped into the VAB. Even though he had been inside hundreds of times, it still thrilled him to enter the cavernous echoing space. It was like being swallowed.

A lattice of girders and beams lifted up from the concrete floor and, high above him, tiny fans stirred the air. To ride one of the many industrial elevators to the top meant that your ears popped, and even the most hardened engineers got a little woozy with vertigo. His eyes, though, weren't drawn to the ceiling. Instead, he focused on what stood before him. It was a hulking grey crawler that loomed up several stories—it weighed millions of pounds— and stacked on top of this mighty crawler was a Saturn V rocket. Before him was what the entire world was talking about: Apollo 11. It was the size of a skyscraper and the words UNITED STATES were painted down its side. In the next two hours, the tank treads on this powerful crawler would inch forward and deliver the rocket to launch pad 39A. There, gantry arms would lock into place and the crawler itself would become part of the launch system. It was the base from where Apollo 11 would rise. The crawler and the Saturn V were so colossal that Eli had to tilt his head back until the base of his skull touched the vertebrae of his neck. It was immense. It was awe-inspiring. It was—there was no other word for it—a wonder. Around him he could hear the low rumble of moving cranes and he saw men in white suits moving around the gantries like ants. A door closed somewhere on the right—the sound boomed off the high walls and echoed into silence. Even though the rocket wasn't yet filled with fuel, it felt like it could thunder to life at any moment. Already, it was straining for ignition.

Eli allowed himself to feel a moment of pride that he was here, that he was playing a small part in such a grand adventure, and then he walked into a nearby room to put on a white coat. He fitted a surgical mask over his face and snapped on a pair of rubber gloves. A coffee pot gurgled in the corner, and along one of the walls was a huge bank of blue metal cabinets—each one of them housed a hive of circuitry and transistors. Lights winked on and off. These were some of the most powerful computers the world had ever seen and the room was warm from all the vacuum tubes. Eli adjusted his mask and glanced at the sign over the door.

SAFETY & SECURITY
IS EVERYONE'S BUSINESS

Squaring his shoulders, he walked back onto the floor and made his way to the most talked about object in the world. A shaft of sunlight filtered down from the ceiling and, for a moment, he wished that he had thought to bring his camera. Taking a photo was of course forbidden but, in the decades to come, when America had colonies on the moon, history might appreciate some secret photos of the beginning.

Entering the crawler was like entering a submarine. Everything was painted warship grey and gauges seemed to be everywhere. He liked hearing the clang of his shoes on the steel staircase as he climbed up. The smell of cold metal and oil surrounded him. He moved for the huge F-1 engines on the Saturn V and stood there with a clipboard. They hung before him like bells in a cathedral. In front of him was a massive square hole in the crawler. In a few days, a waterfall of flame would pour down through it but, now, in this particular splinter of time, he strained to get a good look at the valves and pipes that would carry liquid oxygen and kerosene. When these two super-cooled gases were mixed together in a thrust chamber, a hypergolic explosion flashed into an inferno. These gases ignited on contact and the five engines suspended before him would nozzle out an eruption of fire. They would create 7.5 million pounds of thrust, and in less than three minutes—less time than it takes to make a slice of toast—the rocket would be in space. Each engine was a masterwork of design, and he paused to admire what he was looking at. Thanks to an elaborate twisting and coiling of metal, liquid oxygen cooled the engine bells and kept them from melting; it acted like icy fingers moments before being funneled into the path of kerosene, also known as RP-1. Thus, the fuel itself was used to cool the engine bells hundredths of seconds before it became flame. It was ice then fire, coolant then propellant, it was a dance of chemicals.

He unclicked a pen and looked for fractures, missing bolts, and poor welding. He ticked off boxes. And while his hand placed initials here and there, he saw floaters cross his field of vision. Black dots swam before him and, whenever he tried to focus on one, it scurried away. When he looked at an intake port on an engine bell, a floater skittered away. It made him think of a tooth skittering away from a prisoner's mouth. It had happened when Horse Head kicked a man in the face.

Eli closed his eyes at the memory.

He listened to the bellows of his lungs and felt the great anvil of his heart.

The past is over, he told himself. He worked for NASA now and he was doing something good. He took another deep breath and went back to work. The checklist needed to be done right because he would almost certainly be the last person to stand this close to the F-1 engines ever again.

He stared at the clipboard and thought about the future.

IT TOOK FORTY MINUTES OF focused work but he was finally able to tap the clipboard against the seam of his trousers.

"Well done," he told himself. Once Apollo 11 rolled away into the sunlight, he could turn his attention to Apollos 12 and 13. If Armstrong failed to land, they still had two moonshots lined up before the calendar ticked over to 1970. Maybe President Kennedy's goal would be met after all? A sudden twinge of pain came from his lower back, and he massaged his lower vertebrae. This sometimes happened if he stood for too long and, during a physical a few years ago with his doctor, it was discovered that his L4 had been badly cracked at one point in time. "It must have been one heck of a blow," his doctor said. "You should have been in a back brace. You can see in this x-ray that it didn't fuse properly. What happened?" His doctor looked at him for an explanation but Eli just stared at him blankly. He didn't want to mention Auschwitz, or the waiting train, or the kick from a hobnail boot. When the door of the cattle car rolled shut, he knew something was broken— but what could he do?

As he rubbed and massaged his lower spine, he saw a group of suits moving across the concrete floor down below. Were they reporters? Politicians? He paused and heard them speaking…German. Yes, it was definitely German. They spoke loudly and with easy confidence. Eli stepped closer to the grey railing and stared down. There were five of them and they huddled around a single man. When Eli realized it was Wernher von Braun he stumbled backwards and felt something curdle in his chest. His heart began to beat faster and he could feel his palms getting wet. He'd seen von Braun a few times at the Kennedy Space Center but the sight of him—here—now—on the verge of his greatest triumph—filled Eli's chest with spiders. He felt dizzy and gripped the railing. Were the floaters increasing? Was he beginning to black out? He took several forced breathes and counted to ten. His back sizzled with pain.

"One...two...three," he counted.

When he felt in control of his body once again, he noticed that Arthur Rudolph was standing next to von Braun. He was the project director of the Saturn V program and he made sure his workers met deadlines. Shortly after the first Saturn V lifted flawlessly away from a launch pad, he transferred to the Marshall Space Flight Center in Alabama where he worked shoulder to shoulder with von Braun. It was strange seeing them both here, both smiling. There is Arthur Rudolph, Eli thought, squinting with hate. This was the same man who made sure there were plenty of prisoners to build the V-2s. He strolled past stacked bodies and snapped his fingers for the rockets to roll out faster, faster. Eli knew that pinched face well. He'd seen Rudolph in subtunnel 40 many times.

Kurt Debus was also down there. He was the first director of the Kennedy Space Center, and the fact that he once wore a Nazi uniform had been totally forgotten about. Although Eli had no memory of seeing Debus, maybe he had walked through the tunnels? Hitler had personally appointed Debus to the V-2 program so it was hard to believe that he never saw Dora. Eli squinted harder. No, it's *impossible* to believe he was never there.

As the men looked up at the engines of the Saturn V, Eli shrank into the shadows. The iron wall was cool against his back. He felt like a gargoyle looking down on them and he wondered if anyone cared about what these men had done during the war. Did it matter? Did the history behind the Saturn V matter on the eve of such national hope? What did the dark truth about Dora mean to the world now?

In a rush of movement—he didn't know what he was doing—he watched his polished brown shoes clang down the metal staircase. He adjusted the mask on his face and made his way to the men that hadn't been put on trial for what they had done at Dora. When he reached the bottom of the crawler he walked faster, faster. Hard words formed on his lips and his sweaty fists tightened. He marched beneath the engine bells that would soon spew out unstoppable fire. As he got closer to the creators of Dora, the words he wanted to say got gummed up in his head and he saw two security guards take an interest in him, but this didn't slow his pace. His mouth twisted wormlike beneath the surgical mask, and as he approached Arthur Rudolph he bumped into him, hard. He almost knocked him over. He thought about wheeling on von Braun and using his clipboard as a weapon but, instead, he focused on the massive grey treads of the crawler and marched on. Behind him, he could hear the Nazi scientists speaking in German. Their voices were bright and full of something like amusement.

"You see, gentlemen," von Braun laughed heartily. "Everyone is so focused they do not apologize for being rude."

There was chuckling at this.

Someone added, "Focus is good."

Eli circled around the crawler and boiled with anger. He considered turning around even as one of the security guards gave him a frosty stare. The guard with copper colored hair adjusted his belt and put his hands on his hips. The other guard crossed his arms. They both stared at Eli, daring him to do anything other than walk away.

He hurried for the exit and stripped off his rubber gloves—they came loose like pulled taffy—and he felt talcum powder on his fingertips. He took off his mask and tossed it in an aluminum garbage can. Apollo is bigger than you, he told himself. Take it easy. Calm down. Getting that machine into the heavens is all that matters now. Be Calm. All is well. He looked at the clipboard and considered that he just needed to pass it over to Gordo, who in turn would send it up the bureaucratic food chain. A series of signatures would then send the crawler out into the sun and into the pages of history.

He pushed against a door and left the VAB. The late morning sun warmed his skin and it felt good to be outside. Looking at the sun made him sneeze— once—twice—three times—and he wondered why this sometimes happened. Did everyone sneeze when they looked at the sun? In Dora, he often sneezed when he came out of the tunnels.

He walked across dry grass and watched jewels of light flicker in the faraway trees. He felt hot and wanted to roll up his sleeves but this would mean having to explain the number tattooed onto his left forearm. He frowned at this. No, he thought, it was better to be hot than to deal with questions. He couldn't remember the last time he had been outside in short sleeves.

An elderly black man was trying to drag a garbage can out of the building. Eli rushed over to hold the glass door for him.

"Thank you," the man nodded. He wiped sweat from his forehead and let out a long whistle. "It's a furnace today."

Eli smiled and continued to hold the door. It made him feel good to help this man. And when the garbage can was wrestled away, Eli stepped inside and walked past a blue NASA flag. The soft rumble of air conditioning came from ceiling vents. The smell of hamburgers was in the air. Eli sniffed. Was it lunchtime already?

He moved past framed photos of Mercury rockets lifting off and went into a break room. A fat man he'd never seen before shoved Chinese food into his mouth from a white box. The smell of chicken and noodles was strong. Charlie Greenfield and Skip Rezner sat around a table and talked about an engineering problem. They spoke in the language of mathematics and didn't look up. A loaf of pumpernickel was on a cutting board along with a plate of salami. Coffee simmered in a pot. Someone had stacked styrofoam cups into what looked like a rocket and they had drawn a window at the top—a stick figure looked out. The worried man with exclamation points for hair had a thought bubble coming out of his head. "No comrade, Russian rockets no good!"

The television was on but no one paid any attention to the movie. Eli watched for a few minutes and saw that it was *The Great Escape*. Steve McQueen threw a baseball inside a prison cell while a Nazi watched him at the door.

Eli went over to the cutting board and tore off a chunk of fresh dark bread. He chewed and swallowed. He ripped off another wedge.

"Ah for Pete's sake," Skip said, making a face. "There's a *knife* right there, Eli. Use it, man. Come on."

"An old habit. Sorry."

Skip shook his head and studied the television for a long moment. American and British prisoners of war lined up for roll call while a Nazi ordered them to come to attention. A swastika flapped in the background.

Skip pointed a finger at Eli. "Say...weren't you in a camp?"

Eli swallowed the last of the bread. "Yes."

"Which one?"

"Auschwitz," he said in a small voice. "And then someplace else."

"Where someplace else?"

"You wouldn't know about it."

"Try me," Skip said, removing his glasses and polishing them with a napkin. The florescent lights overhead reflected off the lenses.

"Dora-Mittelbau."

Skip stopped rubbing and put his glasses back on. "Nuh-uh. Haven't heard of that one."

Charlie Greenfield jumped into the conversation. "Here's what I think.

If'n you Jews had guns, I reckon things would've gone different. Know what I'm saying?"

"Guns?" Eli asked.

"Yeah, guns! If y'all had guns, you could've fought back."

Eli looked at his colleagues and had no idea what to say. He blinked. He opened his mouth to say something, anything, but no words came out. Charlie was young and hadn't been drafted for Vietnam because he was considered an essential service to the United States government. NASA was quite literally saving his life. He was—what?—twenty-two?—twenty-three years old? He'd never been tested and he didn't know the first thing about the ways of the world. He was a child pretending to be an adult.

Look, Eli wanted to say, all of the guns in France didn't stop the Nazis. And what about the Soviet Union? They had plenty of guns and they *barely* stopped the advance on Stalingrad. They lost millions and millions of men, and they were heavily armed. Guns? Are you kidding me? All the guns in Europe were needed to stop the Nazis.

"Yeah," Skip nodded in agreement. "Guns would've stopped Hitler before he became too powerful. Whole different ballgame then."

Such a simple and stupid thing to say, Eli thought. Hitler came to power in 1933 but it wasn't until five years later that the *Waffengesetz*, the Weapon's Law, came into effect. If taking guns away was what allowed the Nazis to come to power, why did they wait so long to put such laws into effect? Five years. They waited five years! Hitler's rise to power had very little to do with who had access to guns. It was about fear and hate.

Charlie reached for a slice of salami. He folded it into his mouth and added, while chewing, "If'n you Jews had guns, you could've fought back."

Eli thought about the Warsaw Ghetto Uprising and wanted to mention that even when Jews did manage to buy guns on the black market, even then, when they rose up and attacked the criminals who had stolen their lives, even then they were outnumbered. Flamethrowers were brought in. Buildings were turned into rubble. Survivors were lined up and shot. Nothing was left and every living soul was murdered. Every. Last. One. The ghetto was erased from the map.

"Whole different outcome," Charlie repeated.

A depth charge went off inside Eli and this time, when he spoke, his voice wasn't small. He shook with anger. "Little man, you know *nothing* of war and pain. France had guns. Poland had guns. Denmark had guns. None of them could stop Hitler. Do you think a few of us with pistols could stop him?"

Charlie bobbed his head back and forth in thought. "Not sure. But I suppose Hitler got what was coming to him in the end. That's the main thing, right? Good riddance, I say."

The room was silent except for Steve McQueen's baseball hitting the side of a prison wall.

Eli continued, "You know nothing. How can you work here and know nothing of Dora? Did you know that—"

But Eli cut himself off. He didn't want the past leaking out of him again and he was worried that if he started talking about what he had seen in the tunnels he might not be able to stop. He was already shaking. He gritted his teeth, grunted in frustration, and opened the door. He tied all of his memories of Dora to an anchor and tossed it down, deep inside himself.

He walked down the hallway and heard nervous laughter behind him. Charlie and Skip were no doubt making fun of him. They were probably using a German accent. Ve haf vays of shooting the guns.

As he moved through a maze of desks, witty comebacks floated into his mind and he wondered why they came to him now, when it was too late. When he reached his office, he saw a stack of fresh paperwork on his desk. All he wanted to do was go home, open a bottle of whiskey, and listen to the ocean lap against the shore but, instead, he dropped into his swivel chair and stared at the clock. Gordo Woods, his boss, had taped a sheet of paper beneath it as a not-so-subtle reminder they only had until the end of the decade to get a man on the moon. Written in immaculate handwriting, it simply said, *Waste anything but time!*

No one was a clock-puncher at NASA, he had to agree with that. You stayed at your desk until the job was done and if that meant working twenty-four hour days, so be it. They were in the trenches of high technology and they were creating the future of space flight. This intense focus was called "Moon Fever" and it made everything else fall away.

"A wonderful sickness," Gordo once said. "But be warned…Moon Fever can only be cured by one thing: success."

Eli dragged both hands down his face and turned his attention to the new folder on his desk. APOLLO 12: F-1 DIAGNOSTICS. The gears for the next mission were already being oiled.

Oiled, he thought. His eyes slithered to the lower drawer and he considered the bottle of vodka hidden beneath a manila folder. A little drink might help his back, he thought. It might loosen his muscles.

Charlie Greenfield appeared in the doorframe, which made Eli jump.

"Didn't mean to startle you, man. I just…I just wanted to say…well, back there. I didn't mean to be a jerk." He held up his hands in contrition. "We good?"

Eli chewed the inside of his cheek, and though he didn't feel like forgiving, he thought about how they needed to work together. Now wasn't the time to let squabbling get in the way of getting things done. "Yes. We are good."

Charlie smiled and jerked his thumb towards the exit, "Good because ACE says we're getting some weird data off S2-10. We should look at it."

Eli stood up, tucked a pencil behind his ear. "Let's go. Let's get it right."

On his way out, he grabbed a tube of blueprints and patted his colleague on the shoulder. He didn't want to touch him or offer comfort, but it seemed like the mature thing to do. As they moved for the EXIT sign—talking about aperture openings and rates of flow—they walked past a framed photo of Apollo 10 taking off. Another photo was next to it and it showed a more primitive rocket blasting away from the Florida coastline. It had men in the foreground with movie cameras. A brass sign was beneath this framed photo. In bold lettering it said:

FIRST ROCKET LAUNCH FROM CAPE CANAVERAL
July 1950

It was a V-2.

THE COLUMBUS
OF SPACE

HE PULLED INTO THE cul-de-sac and parked on his brick driveway. He got out, slammed the door with a satisfying thump, and stood there with a sense of pride. He had laid every single brick. All 547 of them. It had taken longer than Lina expected—over three weeks—because he stopped often for raspberry ice tea and sandwiches that were thick with pastrami. After Dora, he made a promise to himself that he would only do manual labor when he felt like it, and even then he would take plenty of breaks in the shade. No one was going to make him do backbreaking physical work ever again. Not even himself.

He looked up. The night was warm and clear. As wind flowed through the palm trees in his front yard it made a rustling scratching sound, like falling waves. A lime green dune buggy with a surfboard attached to the roll bar was parked in the neighbor's driveway. Their son had just returned from Vietnam a month ago and he was always at the beach. As far as Eli could tell, the young man didn't have a job and he had a habit of smoking pot. Eli could smell it wafting through his open windows.

He walked over the bricks to a stone mailbox and opened it—empty. Not even junk mail. Wind chimes tinkled from a neighbor's front door and he glanced over his shoulder to make sure no one was behind him. The street was quiet, at peace, and there were the soft steady waves of the ocean coming from his backyard. Streetlamps cast skirts of yellow light and, when he looked higher, he saw the pale coin of the moon. He thought about the star sailors who readied themselves to climb into a capsule and take aim at it. He looked at the Sea of Tranquility. It didn't seem so far away lately. Just three short days of travel. Funny, he thought, it would take much longer to sail from New York to London.

He crossed the yard, opened the door with a shove of his hip, and nodded

160

happily that the lights were on. Lina knew he didn't like to come home to a dark house. He dropped his keys in a porcelain dish and went from room to room to make sure the windows were locked. It was past ten o'clock and she was at a bridge tournament with her friends. No doubt cheese fondue bubbled in a pot as they'd talked about their children, their husbands, and other things he wasn't sure he wanted to know.

A birthday card was on the dining room table. Lina's bubbly handwriting was already on the inside, and he reached for a pen. He clicked it open and wrote, perhaps too quickly and perhaps too sloppily, *Love Papi.* He took twenty dollars from of his wallet and slipped it into the card before sealing it shut.

He rounded for the television and saw a note taped to the screen.

Dinner in freezer
♥ L

He was hoping for tuna casserole or maybe a thick slab of meatloaf but, no, it was another TV dinner. What really made him grumble was the mess in the kitchen. Dirt was everywhere. So were green beans and heirloom tomatoes. She had obviously harvested them from the garden and dumped them into the sink to deal with later. A spade crusted with dirt was next to the toaster.

Such were the politics of marriage, he told himself, undoing his tie. Since moving to Florida, she had taken up canning food in Mason jars. He liked how she stocked the garage full of peaches, raspberries, pickles, and asparagus. And when she wasn't doing this, she enjoyed long hikes in the muggy heat. She put on a wide-brimmed hat and marched out into the swamps with binoculars to look at birds. She once said she was earthy and needed to be around nature in order to feel alive. He lived too much in his head, she said. All that science. All those books. She was of the soil and he was of the clouds. "No," Lina corrected herself, "not the clouds. You're way higher than that. Most of the time you're in space." She laughed to hide the stinging criticism.

Opposites attract, Lina often said, and he believed this. He believed that couples fell in love because they saw qualities in each other they knew they would never find in themselves. She was everything he could never be, and he loved her for it. Maybe she felt that way too?

"My better half," he smiled, reaching into the fridge for a beer. He cracked off the pull ring and tossed it into the garbage. Suds foamed up. He drank the entire beer in a series of gulps and reached for another. He turned on the oven to 450° and, as he heard the electric coils clicking, he considered that zinc, tin, and lead would all melt at that temperature. But aluminum? That didn't become runny until 1221°. No wonder TV dinner trays were made of aluminum. He shoved one of the frozen meals into the oven, kicked off his shoes, and walked with sweaty socks into the living room.

He fell into his favorite chair and crossed his legs at the ankles. A yawn took him over as he fumbled for the remote. The damn thing cost a fortune but with a name like "Space Command 600" how could he say no? Plus, it was a *color* television in a fine oak cabinet. Now he could sit back and move through all three channels without getting up.

When the TV crackled to life, he saw an image of Apollo 11 on the screen.

"We bring you special coverage of man's conquest of the moon. Brought to you by Tang. Tang…it's what the astronauts have for breakfast. Natural tasting and high in vitamin C."

Eli studied his socks, and when he looked up, the announcer was holding a photo of the crew.

"Neil Armstrong is the commander of the mission and if ever there was someone who loves flying, it is this man. Armstrong got his pilot's license before he got his driver's license, and he flew 78 combat missions in the Korean War before becoming a test pilot." The man with a clean cut smile put the photo down and turned to another camera. "We have a special guest with us tonight. Dr. Wernher von Braun was at the Kennedy Space Center this morning doing a final inspection of the F-1 engines that will launch America to the moon. Welcome, professor."

Eli couldn't help but snort.

Von Braun had slicked-back peppery grey hair, and when he smiled his whole face lit up. He wore a double-breasted suit and looked at the camera briefly as if to say hello to the audience at home. Eli finished his beer and padded into the kitchen for another. Von Braun's voice followed him to the oven.

"I looked at the rocket personally myself. Everything is progressing very smoothly. The inspection went well."

Eli returned to the living room and dropped back into his chair. Sudsy beer rivered over his tongue.

"They call you the Columbus of Space. Why is that?"

Von Braun opened his arms and offered a wide smile. The charismatic man was then asked about what made him interested in rockets, and although he was clearly reading from a familiar script in his head—one that he had no doubt used many times before for interviews—he made it sound like this was the first time he had been asked such questions.

"Your first success was the V-2, isn't that right?"

A nod and then, "Yes, we learned many things from that rocket. I was strictly on the developmental side of things."

Eli waited to hear more, but the conversation shifted to how von Braun and his fellow scientists surrendered to the Americans because they didn't want their knowledge falling into Soviet hands.

"For the safety of the free world, I decided we *must* give our knowledge to the West. My team and I were eventually brought to Huntsville where we built rockets for the Air Force. After many trials and a few—" he looked at the camera with a knowing grin "—a few explosive errors, we arrive where we are today. The Saturn V is the most powerful rocket ever built."

Eli stared out the window into the black of night. There had been no mention that the V-2 was a weapon that killed thousands, nor was there any mention of the secret underground concentration camp that used slave labor. There was no mention of Dora-Mittelbau at all. Instead, there was only talk of how von Braun had launched America into space. He was a hero. He was someone to be respected and admired. Somehow, magically, von Braun had transformed himself from a weapon maker into a cheerful explorer.

Eli considered Wernher Magnus Maximilian Freiherr von Braun to be nothing more than an opportunist whose career had profited off the murder of thousands. The version of history on television—the one that had been broadcast into millions of homes—was sanitized and von Braun's problematic past with the Third Reich had been bleached clean. The bargain for the United States was simple: ignore von Braun's involvement with Nazism, and in return he would deliver the most advanced rockets the world had ever seen. Heroes, Eli thought while tipping back the rest of his third beer, cannot have a dark past. If the truth is troublesome, the truth needs to be revised.

"No one wants a Red moon," von Braun said seriously on television. "The Soviets have built the Zond 5 which theoretically could put a man on the moon sometime this year."

"But we're going to beat them?"

"We *are* going to beat them." There was a reassuring smile before he added, "If all goes according to plan, we will walk on the moon this Sunday."

The newscaster bowed his head in smiling disbelief. "Amazing. I'll bet you can't wait to see it."

"I have waited my whole life for this," von Braun beamed. "A few more days is no problem."

Eli remembered the first time he saw him on American television. It happened when Walt Disney made a six-part series called *Man in Space*. It aired in 1955, and as Hannah played with her Lincoln Logs, he watched von Braun use models to explain how a space station could be built. Cartoons about zero gravity appeared on the screen. Von Braun had boundless enthusiasm as he held up model rockets and said that it was possible to conquer space. A few years later, he launched America's first satellite into orbit, Explorer 1. He made the cover of *Time* magazine and was hailed as "America's Missileman". At the time, Eli couldn't help but think how much Missileman sounded just like Musselman, a term they used in Dora to describe a prisoner who had given up on life. Missileman. Musselman. The two words echoed off each other. He bought a copy of *Time* and sat in a New York deli where he looked for the word "Dora" and the word "Mittelbau" but he couldn't find them anywhere—it was like the camp never existed. He walked out into the bustling city and moved through gently falling snow. A homeless man warmed himself before a fire in a garbage can. The man stomped his boots and held his hands to the flame. As Eli walked past, he tossed the magazine into the crackling fire and stood there for a moment to watch von Braun's face curl into the blaze. The Missileman smiled back up at him.

The oven clicked, and Eli turned his head to take in the smell of beef.

As he walked into the kitchen, he took off his already loose tie and tossed it on the table. It skittered to a snaky stop. His hand moved to the liquor cabinet and he brought out a bottle of whiskey. He poured a generous measure into a tumbler—at least four fingers worth—and drank it all in one pull. He gave a sour shudder and splashed out more of the amber liquid.

When he opened the oven door, a wave of heat rolled up his chest. He stumbled backwards and knocked a few heirloom tomatoes onto the floor. The dirty spade clattered into the sink and it took him a few angry seconds to find the hot pads—why couldn't Lina put them back where they damn well belonged? When his dinner was out of the oven he peeled back the aluminum foil. Steam rose. Gravy bubbled. He mixed butter into the mashed potatoes and gave the peas a dusting of salt. The peach strudel got some nutmeg.

He returned to the television and enjoyed imagining von Braun's face burning away into heat and flame. The man was so famous, so well known, it's amazing that a former prisoner hadn't already shot him dead.

A courtroom drama was on television and he watched witnesses come to the stand. Hands were raised, the truth was told. The food in his tray was segregated into little compartments and he ate each one in turn. The strudel was saved for last. When he was done, he wiped his mouth with the back of his hand and dropped the empty tray onto the floor. He burped. The room was warm and he realized that Lina wouldn't be too pleased with the state of him. *Are you slurring?* she would ask.

His eyes closed and a dream flickered in the movie house of his mind. He was standing before a large house, the grass was finely cut, and little magnolias waved in clay pots. A crowd appeared around him and they began to shout von Braun's name. The famous man opened the screen door and came out in a suit. Eli found himself being pushed inside the house along with a reporter. She pulled out a steno pad and asked, "Professor von Braun…do you admit that you're a war criminal?"

"No, no, my dear. I'm merely a scientist. I was simply following orders."

A spotlight illuminated von Braun as if he were on stage. He sat on a leather sofa with his wife as more prisoners crowded into the room. A camp loudspeaker crackled to life. "Attention. All prisoners to Tunnel A."

When von Braun's wife heard this, she placed a nervous hand on her husband's arm. "Tell them it's not true, darling. Tell them you had no choice. You're a genius, not a war criminal."

The walls of the house dissolved into blowing ash and the reporter with a steno pad turned to Eli. She asked him what the camp was like, but when he tried to answer, his jaw turned to ash. He lifted an arm and watched himself scatter into the wind. He blew away into nothing.

When he jolted awake, his breathing was hard. Heavy.

The courtroom drama was still on and a lawyer stood before the defendant with an accusing finger. "Why did you shoot the victim?"

The mousy man in a chair looked at his hands. "Because I knew a trial would happen. I shot him so that people would have to listen to me and learn about what he'd *done*."

Eli glanced down the hallway. There was a gun in the closet. Yes, he nodded. The whole world would be watching and it would be easy to do. If von Braun was killed now, wouldn't that mean cameras and reporters?

He let the idea slosh around in his head.

Yes. It would be easy to do.

He got up, went to the bedroom, and reached for the gun on the shelf. A Walther PPK. German made. *Polizei Pistole Kurz*. 7.65mm. It felt good in his hand, like an extension of his fist. He walked back to the kitchen and held it while he poured himself another whiskey. He looked at his satchel.

Yes. It would be easy to do.

"Very easy."

SECRETS

WE'RE SO USED TO SEEING our pale neighbor float across the sky that we can't imagine the heavens without its waxing and waning shape and yet, at one point, we orbited alone. We were moonless. There was no night sun above.

Some five billion years ago, our home was a place of cooling lava, warm rock, and hissing gas. Clouds thickened the sky. And then a stray planetoid the size of Mars smashed into Earth. The impact was apocalyptic and obliterating. A plume of fiery debris spewed out in all directions. The cores of these two planets were wrenched apart and the molten debris twisted around each other, caught in an unbalanced dance of gravity.

Over millions of years, the cooling matter created a larger and a smaller orb. We may not think of the moon as a companion planet, but it is one. It came from us, and we came from it.

Other moons in our solar system are not nearly as large as the planets they orbit. Our own moon is monumental by comparison. It is enormous. And because it is a quarter of our own size, it steadies our orbit and keeps us spinning at just the right speed. The moon offers stability, it pulls on our tides, and it has sheltered us from thousands of cosmic impacts that might otherwise have crippled the development of life. To look at the moon's surface is to realize that it has shielded us and protected us. Together, we pirouette through the dark.

Every culture on Earth has gazed up and wondered what it might be like to walk among its grey dunes. We have lifted our arms, imagining the distance to be just a short hop, a little dream of flight, and yet our nearest neighbor rides beside us at an incredible distance of 240,000 miles. If the Earth were the size of a basketball and the moon was the size of a baseball, they would be 23 feet apart. Getting humans to travel across this mighty void is not only dangerous, it is audacious. It remains the greatest adventure we have yet undertaken as a species.

The moon goes by many names and lives on many tongues. *Luna. Kuu. Mēsic. Mwezi. An Ghealach. Marama. Bulan. Dal. Al-Qamar.* From the first moment that humans looked up at the moon's luminous disc, it has become a furnace for the creation of our monsters and gods. It is a shapeshifter, a form wanderer. It is said to influence rational thought and that is why we talk of "lunacy" and "lunatics." If someone is deeply in love, we say they are "moonstruck." After a wedding, we send the couple on a "honeymoon" where, according to Anglo-Saxon tradition, the newlyweds are to stay in a hut for the cycle of a moon and swig bottles of mead, an alcoholic drink made of honey and wine. Hence, a honeymoon. Of all the things that make us different on earth, the moon is a constant hanging above us all. Gazing at its bruised surface is something we all share, no matter where we stand, no matter what language we speak.

As for Eli, the moon had two different names: *Mond* and *Yareach.* German and Hebrew. As he lifted his gaze at night, he often thought of the old belief that the moon was the final resting place for everything that had been lost on Earth. Up there were missing keys and books, suitcases and watches, teeth and gold. It was a place where the lost could be found. It was a place of grey ash and memory. He often stared up and imagined his family there among all the things that had vanished. *Yareach.*

A world of dust and silence.

The sun wasn't up when he rolled out of bed. There was only the moon.

He held his head in both hands and felt the stab of a headache. His mouth was dry and his tongue was fat, sandpapery. Memories of last night came in flashes. He didn't remember her coming home. But at least she was curled in bed next to him—a good sign—and the duvet was pulled up to her chin. She had forgotten to take off her makeup and the pillow was blotted with mascara.

"Lina?" he whispered. A pause before he tried again, "…Lina?"

He rubbed bits of grainy sleep from his eyes and fell into his morning routine. Aspirin (two). Brush teeth. Shower. Coffee. Toast. Half a grapefruit. He reached for his satchel and tip-toed for the door. Because Lina was still in bed he jotted a note next to a half-finished jigsaw puzzle of Vermeer's "The Milkmaid."

Home late
♥ *E*

A thin band of orange was smeared across the horizon as he climbed into his Buick. Pelicans pulled themselves into the sky—their great wings swooping—and his tires hummed against the highway as he picked up speed. The moon was to his right and he searched for the Sea of Tranquility, the Ocean of Storms, and Fra Mauro. Soon, spidery spacecrafts would touch down in these unknown places and men would emerge in bleached white suits to crawl down a ladder. When their boots touched the undisturbed loam, the dust of the moon would splash away, it would arc up gently and fall sluggishly, as if in slow motion. Gravity was softer on the moon so Armstrong would almost certainly have to hop to get around. What, Eli wondered, would it be like to hold moon dust? Would it be as fine as ground cinnamon?

He imagined standing in a spacesuit and staring back at Earth, the whole planet suspended in the darkness of space, like a little blue marble hanging in the void. To see the blinding sun and look into space, the infinity, surely that has to do something to a man, he thought. The moon was a place of impact sites, ejecta, and dazzling rills. There were craters big enough to swallow football stadiums and there were mountains higher than the Rockies. There were even—he shook his head in wonderment at this—there were even debris slides that would dwarf the highest skyscraper in New York. Great powdery plains of grey stretched all the way to the horizon. The view would be—

"Unbelievable."

He came to the badging station and slowed for the guard. Bugs jittered in his headlights.

"Number?" the guard asked.

"VAB ML 119."

The guard sniffed and nodded at someone in the concrete hut. The barber pole was raised in a squeaking arc and Eli drove through. The squashed pelican from yesterday was still there.

He jutted his elbow out the window and enjoyed the rush of cool rumbling air. The pale blue of morning made the VAB seem even more dark and mysterious. The parking lot was already full. With only one day until launch, everyone was working longer hours. Guilt filled him up for going home and doing something as selfish as drinking.

"Stupid," he said aloud. He admired the cantaloupe sunrise behind a cluster of palm trees and thought, yes, a new start. A new day. He'd dump out the remaining vodka in his desk when he got a private moment.

Two blinking red lights made him come to a stop at a railroad crossing. A bell dinged as he moved the gearshift on the steering column to P. He stared ahead, ignoring the clattering train and how its iron wheels chunk-chunked over sections of track. The cars rolled by, illuminated by the puddles of his headlights. He didn't see faces behind barb-wired. He didn't see hands reaching out into the morning air for water. He didn't hear guard dogs snapping and straining against their leashes. He saw none of this. He only saw silver boxcars and each one of them had a NASA logo on it.

"NASA and Dora," he said, as if testing the words.

They were the great poles of his life. The darkest and the brightest. How strange that an arcing of a rocket linked them together. As the train rumbled away, it dragged images of the Holocaust behind it. A wave of guilt crashed over him when he thought about all of those who didn't leave the camps. Why did he survive? He wasn't any stronger or better or wiser. There was no reason for him to have been saved when millions of others had perished. Why was he allowed to take off his uniform and step beyond the crematorium and barbed wire?

The red lights stopped flashing and he reached for the gearshift. He put it clunkingly into D.

Forward, he thought. It was all he could do.

Apollo 11 was on his right and it was nearly at launch pad 39-A. It weighed millions of pounds and it gingered its way forward on two huge lanes of river rock. That was the only thing that could absorb the vast weight of the crawler—concrete or asphalt would be pulverized, but river rock acted like nature's ball bearings. Eli drove slowly and marveled at the towering white needle atop the crawler. Soon, the rocket would be filled with fuel.

It had been decided to move Apollo at night because it was cooler. All that metal beneath the baking sun would make the job miserable for the crews that had to walk alongside the crawler and make sure everything was rolling along perfectly. They monitored the massive treads as it inched forward. The rocks below cracked like popcorn.

He pulled into the back lot, slung his satchel over his shoulder, and slammed the car door. When he reached the glass door of the annex to the

VAB, he couldn't remember walking from the car. The last minute found him thinking of nozzles and tunnels and treads.

He showed his badge to another guard—an elderly black man with a fuzz of white hair—and he jogged up the stairs two at a time. Before he entered the office, he smoothed his dress shirt and straightened his shoulders. Right, he thought. Let's do what needs to be done. He adjusted his satchel and opened the door.

It was busy, and there was the smell of stale coffee and burnt out vacuum tubes. A young man with blonde hair was fitting a new roll of magnetic tape into one of the wheels of the computer. Many of the secretaries had their hairs in a beehive and there was—he took it in—the smell of hairspray and perfume.

He walked over to Jessica. "Any meetings?" he asked.

"Oh, good morning." She glanced up from her typewriter but didn't stop clacking the keys. She had long painted fingernails and Eli wondered how she typed with them. She sat at an angle so that her legs were crossed at the knee and her long sun-bronzed leg bobbed up and down. A sandal dangled off a big toe. A beautiful girl, he thought. His gaze glided to the framed photo of a solider on her desk. A boyfriend.

"How's he doing over there?"

"Good, I guess…I mean, I don't hear much."

"When's he coming home?"

Her forehead creased. "Fifteen weeks and two days."

"It must be hard for you. No one is talking about Vietnam, especially now that we're going to the moon."

She glanced at her lap for a long moment. "Thanks for asking, Mr. Hessel. I think about him all the time—"

"Of course you do."

"—but my friends only want to hear about what happens here. They never ask about Miguel. It's always the astronauts they want to know about. Have you met Neil Armstrong? What about Buzz Aldrin? Can you get an autograph for me?"

Their eyes focused on each for several seconds and it looked as if she were going to cry. This embarrassed him so he asked, a bit too brightly, "Any messages?" As soon as the words were out of his mouth he felt badly and wanted to try again with more tenderness. But it was too late. The moment had gone. He reached for a stack of manila folders.

"You're with Mr. Woods and the ML close out crew at ten."

She held up a note but Eli wasn't sure how to grab it because his arms were full of folders. He opened his fingers, scissors like, and she slid the note in. He nodded his thanks and backed away. He wanted to say that things would be okay, and that Miguel would come home safe, but he thought it might be too awkward. He hurried along the tiled floor and thought about the close out crew meeting. Would—he squinted at this thought—would von Braun be there?

He passed one of the new secretaries and felt her frosty gaze upon him. She had a large gold cross dangling from her neck and her face puckered as he approached.

"Good morning," he said with a nod.

The woman, Francine, kept on typing. Her fingers danced on a little stage of letters. She was a miserable lemon of a person, almost certainly an anti-Semite the way she always glowered at him, and he stopped walking in order to make her uncomfortable. It gave him pleasure to use friendliness as a weapon.

"Good morning, Francine. How are you?"

"Morning," she offered in a slow monotone. She didn't look up and kept on typing. A pack of Pall Malls was on the desk along with a coffee mug. Lipstick traces were on the rim. She wore a flower patterned dress and sat bolt upright.

"Lovely sunrise, wasn't it?" he added, letting his eyes fall to the gold cross.

"It's Florida. We get 'em all the time," she said flicking the roller of the typewriter, which made it ding. The clacking returned, faster now.

The cross was meant to advertise her faith. It was an announcement of her worldview. Crucifixion, Eli thought. Those in power nailed a Jew to a tree while soldiers stood around, taunting him, watching him die. He was placed underground when it was all over. But who could really believe that tall tale of him coming out of the tunnel, healed and alive? Crucifixion and resurrection? More like cruci*fiction*, he thought with a smile. Surely the man's teachings were more important. Did this woman even see her Jesus as a Jew? What, he wondered, would she be like in Dora? Would she still believe in a loving God?

He hummed loudly at these inner thoughts and this made Francine look up.

"What *is* it, Hessel? Why are you bothering me?"

The manila folders clutched to his chest were beginning to slip so he backed towards his desk, only to realize that he should have corrected her. That's *Mr.* Hessel, and I'll bother you if I want to.

His small shared office with the huge map of the moon was empty. A freshly extinguished cigarette smoldered in a glass tray. Doughnut crumbs were on a napkin. He plopped down into his chair and rolled around to get it in the right spot. He considered the manila folders and didn't feel like getting to work. Coffee maybe? He glanced at the lower drawer and thought about what was hidden there.

A paperclip was next to his slide rule and he picked it up. He considered its bent shape and tapped it against the desktop. Within months of the war ending, a secret program called "Operation Paperclip" brought hundreds of Nazi administrators, chemists, and engineers to the United States. The numbers these men had locked in their heads were keys to new frontiers and new possibilities. And because their knowledge was in danger of falling into Russian hands, a blind eye was cast upon any crimes these gifted men may have committed. As they went about building jets and rockets and high-performance aircraft, any sticky questions were made to disappear. The dead were dead, the Cold War was turning hot, and it was a time for practicalities. For these reasons, Wernher von Braun, Arthur Rudolph, Walter Dornberger, Kurt Debus, Herbertus Strughold and scores of others became citizens. America opened its arms to these men. They enjoyed barbeques and baseball. They tended gardens and raised their children.

Eli stopped tapping the paperclip.

His hand wandered to the lower drawer and he jiggled the half-empty bottle back and forth—legs of clear alcohol run down the sides. A NASA coffee mug was on his desk and he slid it over. He was about to pour some of the burning liquid in when he glanced at the door—he felt eyes on him—and, sure enough, Francine gave him a disapproving stare.

"Can I get something *else* for you, Hessel?" she asked. "Coffee maybe?"

He put the vodka back in the lower drawer. "No," he said. He was about to say something else when a tremendous thud came from the wall that separated the office from the cavernous space of the VAB. There was the shriek of a pneumatic drill. He stared at the wall and imagined what was happening on the other side. The engineers must have started working on Apollo 13 in one of the high bays.

When he turned back to Francine she was still a thunderhead.

There was another thud, this time much louder, and it was followed by an ear-shattering bang. He jumped to his feet and stared at the wall. What was that? An explosion? He half-expected a piece of rocketry to collapse into his office. The secretaries looked in his direction and Jessica held a hand over her chest. Francine leaned forward as if she were thinking about pushing off from her chair and running for the stairs. There was a softer clanging whump—like a garbage truck lowering a bin—and Eli walked out of his office in order to stand in front of the secretary pool. The grey computers hummed and winked.

When the pneumatic drill returned, he knew that everything was fine and he offered a reassuring smile. "One of the crane operators is banging the water tank," he explained. "That would be my guess. Please go back to work. All is well."

Slowly, the typewriters began to clack again. A murmuring of voices lifted and it sounded like birds in an aviary. Snatches of speech came to Eli.

"I thought a bomb went off," one woman laughed, adjusting her necklace.

"Wouldn't the Russians like that?"

"My goodness, that gave me a start."

"Here, have a cigarette, honey."

When Eli turned back to his office he noticed something odd poking out of his leather satchel. He didn't recognize it at first and he stood there for a moment trying to figure out what he was looking at. He must have jostled the desk when he stood up in a rush because most of the manila folders were on the floor and paperclips were scattered everywhere. He stared at his satchel. Why was a lead pipe in there? Had he placed it there last night when he was…?

He reached for the pipe and brought it out.

At that very moment, Gordo, Charlie, Gene, and Skip all appeared at the door. They were talking about the loud bang and offered suggestions on what might have caused it.

"Water tank practice."

"Maybe stage two is being fitted into place?"

"No, no, no, I think it's—" Gordo held up a hand to stop the others from entering the office. "What are you holding? What the hell is that?"

Eli slid the gun back into his satchel. "I forgot it was there."

"You brought a *gun* into the VAB?"

"I'm sorry. It was a mistake."

"You're goddamn right it's a mistake. What're you thinking? We've got heightened security around us and the whole damn world is watching. The last thing we need—the very *last* thing we need—is a security issue. Why did you bring a gun into work?"

"I put it in my satchel last night. I forgot it was there."

Gordo shook his head in disbelief. "Why the hell'd you put a gun in there in the first place?" He paused and pointed an accusing finger. "Are you saying you *meant* to bring that to work?"

Eli shrugged, which he immediately knew was the wrong thing to do.

Gordo dragged a hand down his face. "Sweet Jesus." There was a pause before his eyebrows raised at a new thought. "You weren't going to bring that to our ten o'clock meeting in the blockhouse were you? Tell me you were not thinking about bringing a loaded goddamn gun into a restricted area that close to the launch pad. Tell me I'm wrong, Eli. I mean...Apollo 11 is going to be fueled up soon. What if APIP found about this? Holy Mary, a *gun*? That close to Apollo 11?"

"Like I said, I forgot. I am sorry."

"Sorry don't cut the cheese here. Why'd you bring it in the first place?" Gordo walked over and snapped his fingers. He held out an open palm. "Give it to me. Is it loaded?"

Eli blinked.

"I *said*...is it loaded?"

When Eli shrugged, because he couldn't remember, Gordo pushed him aside and reached into the satchel. He made sure the chamber was clear before he pulled out a clip of bullets.

"Seriously, man. What the fuck are you thinking? The whole world is expecting Neil Armstrong to put his size ten boot on the moon and you're wandering around like a goddamn cowboy. You know the Rocket Ranch doesn't allow firearms. What the hell? We got high explosives all around."

"I am sorry."

Gordo put the clip into his front pocket and slid the gun into the small of his back. He flapped his charcoal grey business suit over his belt and adjusted his tie. "I mean, come on!"

Charlie stepped forward and raised a hand as if he were in class.

"Um…Eli? You're not still sore about what I said yesterday, are you? You didn't bring that in to prove some point about Jews and guns, did you?" His eyes widened. "You weren't planning on…using it…were you?"

Eli remembered standing in his kitchen last night and pretending to shoot von Braun and Arthur Rudolph, but he had no memory of sliding the PPK into his satchel. Maybe he had though? Well, *obviously* he had, he corrected himself, but he didn't mean to bring the pistol with him. He realized everyone was looking at him for an explanation. He cleared his throat and looked around at the desks, the green sofa, and map of the moon.

"It's all very simple. Look, I was cleaning it last night and I, maybe, put it in the satchel by accident."

"Back up a sec," Gordo said, rewinding the air with his finger. "What happened yesterday between you and Charlie? Is this something I need to know about?" Gordo glanced back and forth at the two men. "Why are you sore with each other? Talk to me guys. No…wait. Let me close the door first."

As the glass door shut, Eli looked at the secretaries, all of whom were gaping at him. Francine gave him a dirty look and picked up her phone. She stared at Eli, and began to dial.

WHAT HAPPENED IN
THE VAB

THE SATURN V WAS MONSTROUS. Colossal. It towered up thirty-six stories and when it was filled with super-cooled gas, it creaked and groaned like a living creature. When the engines ignited, Eli always found himself thinking of Carl Orff's *Carmina Burana*. That song captured the power and majesty of the engines in a way that words never could. The cantata started with the low demonic chanting of a choir, then moved into a rising soundscape of cymbals and grumbling drums and then, finally, a flight of trumpets. When it debuted in 1937 it was hugely popular with the Nazi Party. It was often featured on state radio. Back then it meant something dark and terrible but, now, now that he was a citizen of the United States, it meant something else. It was the soundtrack of a Saturn V rising through the atmosphere and thundering into the heavens.

Although he'd seen many rockets take off, Apollo 8 was the one that affected him the most. The three men who climbed into that cramped capsule were absurdly brave because they ventured into unknown territory and they voyaged further from home than any other soul ever had done before. The moon was 240,000 miles away and they traveled fifteen times faster than a bullet. Eli tried to imagine such speed, such swiftness, such velocity. His brain, however, just couldn't process it though. No human had ever moved that fast before.

Three days later, the men of Apollo 8 entered lunar orbit and became the first souls to see the dark side of the moon. They snapped photos of gigantic pock marks and rills that rolled beneath them. Their photos of a tiny Earth suspended in the infinite blackness of space caused a sensation when they returned. It was on the cover of *Life* magazine and Eli kept thinking about how it was such a beautiful planet even though it was home to so much evil. Pride swelled within him as he looked at those photos. He had helped build that Saturn V. He had worked on the engines. His fingerprints had gone into space.

When Apollo 8 took off, he stood in front of the VAB and watched it climb. Later, when Lina asked what it was like to experience the launch, he thought about it for a long time. He looked at the shag carpet and chewed his upper lip.

"Well," he finally said. "There are three parts to it, I think. See it…hear it…feel it."

See it, hear it, feel it. Yes, that was the best way to describe the launch. First there was a silent scorching orange plume from the launch pad, and this was quickly followed by mighty shockwaves that rippled across the swampy water. Crackling thunder filled the air. A moment later, hard reverberations hit his chest. His necktie vibrated. Quarters and dimes jingled in his front pocket. And although people were cheering all around him, he couldn't hear their whoops of joy. As the rocket climbed, it got louder and louder. People had to plug their ears. The Saturn V was unlike anything he'd seen before. It was pure flame, pure heat. Compared to what rose above Florida that day, the V-2 was little more than a bottle rocket.

When the launch was over, and the astronauts were safely on their way to the moon, that's when the parties started. Crawfish and lobster were brought out. Chips and dip. Huge pots of creamed corn and boiled bananas. Beer too, there was plenty of beer. Everyone glanced back at the empty launch pad and smiled at what they had done. People gave each other high fives and hugs. It was one of the best days of Eli's life, and when it was all over, he went home to his wife. The launch was replayed on the news that night but the orange flame wasn't as bright on color television. There were no reverberations and no sense of velocity. He turned to Lina and tried to explain what it was like, but the words stumbled out of his mouth. At last, he gave up and simply said, "You need to see it. I'll try and get you a visitor's pass for the next launch. I want to share it with you."

But there had been no extra visitor's passes for Apollo 9. Or Apollo 10. And visitor's passes for 11? They were impossible to find.

"—ee?"

He looked over at Charlie, who was in a white smock. They were in the VAB and Eli tried to act like his mind hadn't drifted. "What was that? Sorry, I was thinking of something else."

178

Charlie rolled his eyes. "I said, we should look at the LOX intake valve. Do you agree?"

Eli nodded and snapped wrinkles from his white smock. The NASA logo on his breast pocket had a loose thread and he pulled at it. When it came loose he dropped it into a nearby garbage can. As it fell and twisted, he thought of lunar gravity. What would falling look like on the moon?

"I agree," he said, clearing his throat. "That valve was sticky for 11 last month, and we don't want a similar problem for 12."

A high-pitched hum came from overhead and this made Eli glance at the impossibly high ceiling. One of the cranes that was used for stacking the rockets was lowering its cables. There was a massive grey ballast tank filled with water on their right and, as they walked by it, he studied its swollen shape. It was as big as a house and the crane operators often used it as practice. They were so skilled at moving huge bits of rocketry around the VAB that they could lower this ballast tank onto an egg without cracking it. That was the challenge: get the ballast tank as close to the egg without cracking it. It was only a matter of millimeters, and when a crane operator got the tank so close that the egg couldn't be moved—and it wasn't damaged—that was a sign he was ready to stack Apollo into shape. These men had nerves of steel cables. Not everyone could ride the swaying open elevator up to the little birdcage of a control cab at the top of the VAB, and not everyone could perch in that seat and look straight down, forty-two floors. Just the thought of it made Eli sweat.

"Boy howdy, Gordo sure was *miffed* you brought that thing into work," Charlie whistled.

Eli kept on walking and studied his clipboard. The silence between them continued for so long that he thought he should say something. "A simple mistake. I forgot."

"But why bring it in the first place?"

Eli found himself looking at the dots of men moving across the gantry walkways. He always found it difficult to make his feet listen to him when he was that high up. The flooring of the gantry was grated mesh and it felt like you were walking on air. The VAB was no place for someone with vertigo.

"I understand why Gordo wanted to keep everything hush-hush," Charlie said, clicking and unclicking a pen. His voice was nasally and high pitched. "I mean, with security being what it is right now…if he filed a report it would—"

"Can we talk about something else?"

"Well sure. I'm just saying I can understand why Gordo wants to keep this a secret. No need to file a report."

The smell of oil and arc welding was in the air. Their shoes continued to clack off the floor as they moved around the grey ballast tank, which was hovering just inches above the ground. One of the engineers was laying on the concrete and eyeing the space beneath the tank. He pointed a flashlight and swore. "Naw, he cracked it. Get me another egg and tell him to try again."

"Francine sure gave you the stink eye," Charlie said, obviously still thinking about what had happened back in the office.

"I know."

"She doesn't like you."

"I know."

"Why is that?"

As they walked into High Bay 3, the white skyscraper of Apollo 12 stood before them. It was scheduled to launch in November, and now that 11 was out of High Bay 1, work could begin on Apollo 13. The VAB, Eli thought while lowering his clipboard and beginning to walk faster, was a rocket factory much like Mittelbau. Oh sure, it was a larger and slower, but inside this mountain of American steel, winged missiles were built.

"Why is that?" Charlie asked again.

Eli adjusted the cuff of his dress shirt and considered the blue tattoo on his arm. "It is an old hatred," he finally said.

Up ahead, a group of engineers clustered beneath a walkway. They all looked up. Eli wondered what was going on so he, too, stared up. A beautiful blonde in a plaid mini-skirt was standing on the gantry and she wore a wide-brimmed hat. A pink purse was tucked into the crook of her arm and she pointed up at the height of Apollo 12. Two men in suits were standing next to her and they seemed to be answering her questions. The engineers below followed her as she walked across the mesh gantry. Eli looked up at her sun-browned legs and saw underwear.

The men stared up, nudging each other and smiling.

Charlie Greenfield didn't seem interested in this at all, and Eli found himself liking the young Texan a little bit more for it. He glanced at the blonde and wondered if she was famous. A movie star, maybe? With the wide-brimmed hat, it was hard to tell.

A thought came to Eli and he turned suddenly to Charlie. "Do you have a girlfriend?"

The young man who graduated *summa cum laude* from Rice University seemed flustered and even taken aback. He shook his head and adjusted his fashionable glasses. "W-w-why do you ask?"

"Just curious."

"I guess...I guess I haven't found the right gal yet."

As they walked beneath the attractive woman, neither of them leered up. They came to a large computer and began to study green numbers on small screens. Spools of magnetic tape whirred gently back and forth. Eli was about to say more about finding the right woman—that it happens when you least expect it—but Charlie cut him off. It seemed like he wanted to change the subject.

"I had a strange insight last night."

"Oh?" Eli asked.

"Something must be in the water in Ohio."

"Why's that?"

"Well, think about it...the Wright Brothers came from Ohio and they built the first airplane. John Glenn came from Ohio and he was the first American to orbit. And now Neil Armstrong is going to be the first man on the moon." There was a pause before, "I'll give you one guess where he's from."

"Berlin?"

Charlie didn't laugh. "No, silly. Ohio. He's from Ohio." He leaned in as if to tell a secret. "Armstrong must be already here, don't you think?"

Eli tapped a black gauge and wrote down a number on his clipboard. "I saw him arrive the other day."

"Really?"

"I think so." He stepped sideways to look at another gauge, a voltmeter. "We launch in twenty-four hours so he must be here."

"Did you know the Russkies are calling Armstrong the 'Tsar of Apollo'? No matter what you call them, those guys sure are brave. Can you imagine bolting yourself on top of a rocket? Man, that takes courage." There was a short pause as Charlie transcribed data onto his clipboard. "Say, Eli...I've got a question for you."

"Okay."

"How do the astronauts get into their spacesuits?"

"What?"

"Yeah, how do they get into their spacesuits with such gigantic balls."

Charlie barked out a laugh and this made Eli laugh as well. They both snickered, and it felt good to have a light moment in this place of such necessary seriousness.

"Gigantic balls," Charlie said, amused by his own joke.

Eli reached for a three-ring binder and flipped to subsection twenty-three. He used his finger as a pointer to scan down a column of numbers. Well look at that, he thought. That LOX intake valve *hadn't* been examined. Good, he thought. We caught it. He made a note of this and turned to subsection twenty-four. He studied numbers and flow.

A crane moved overhead and the long thread of its chain began to shake. There was a soft rattling. A shower of sparks drifted down the side of Apollo 12. Someone was arc welding a joint into place. There was another spray of falling light and the pretty blonde in a wide-brimmed hat pointed at it. She *did* look familiar, Eli thought, scratching his cheek. Was she in that movie about a train robbery? As she stared up at the rocket with a hand on her hat to keep it in place, Eli considered the men in business suits around her. One of them was Arthur Rudolph. He could see that now, and in a flash of memory he also saw a pile of tangled bodies heaped in sub-tunnel 40. Arthur Rudolph stood over the dead and ordered the mess to be incinerated. He then went back to his desk to fill out paperwork that would bring in more workers, more bodies. Rudolph was an enthusiastic Nazi, a true believer, and as chief of production for the V-2s it was his job to make sure there were enough prisoners to keep everything moving. Due to the rarified knowledge in his head, he was given a clean slate after the war and was asked to build missiles for America. Eli felt woozy from the weight of these ghostly thoughts and steadied himself against a bank of computers.

The blonde laughed and touched Rudolph's arm playfully. He held out a hand as if to say, *the tour continues this way.* Another spray of sparks drifted down. Hot. Angry. Dissolving away.

"Eli? Buddy. You okay, man?"

A hand touched his shoulder.

"You look like you've seen a ghost."

He closed his eyes and took in deep breathes. "Tell me," he finally said. "Do you know that man on the gantry? The one with white hair?"

Charlie took a step forward and squinted. "Ah sure, that's Artie Rudolph." He seemed star struck and added, "Wow! Mr. Saturn, in the flesh. He used to be the director for all the Saturn Vs and he made sure these babies got *built*. From what I hear, he ran a tight ship and had rockets rolling out of here." He grunted at a thought. "I guess he's come out of retirement for the big show tomorrow."

Eli steadied himself and watched Rudolph walk away with the slender woman. No doubt there would be parties for him tonight, and champagne, and toasts.

Charlie snapped his fingers at a thought. "Do you guys know each other? You're both German."

Eli looked at his shoes and imagined his old wooden clogs. He looked at his hands and saw dirty fingernails. He felt lice nibbling in the nest of his armpit. He put down his clipboard and turned to Charlie with the idea of explaining something about the tunnels, but from over Charlie's shoulder he saw two men in dark suits running towards them. They sprinted and seemed worried. Eli looked around and wondered if something was on fire.

"You there," one of them shouted. He had a round face and blue eyes. The other man was tall, black, and lean. They both slowed to a jog.

"Are you Eli Hessel?" the round faced one asked.

"Yes."

They looked at each other and seemed relieved. "Come with us."

"But I have a meeting at ten."

"Not anymore you don't."

They grabbed Eli by both arms and pushed him for the exit.

"What's going on? Is something wrong? Who are you?"

"CIA. Stop wriggling. We have some questions for you."

Eli looked over his shoulder and shouted back at Charlie. "Tell Gordo about this! This is some kind of mistake." He looked at the man with a round face and tried to sound reasonable. "What kind of questions?"

"You already know."

ROOM 2B

HE WAS TAKEN TO A dented red Oldsmobile and thrown into the back. It was hot inside, muggy, and the leather seats were painfully hot. In the distance was Apollo 11, waiting like a needle on the horizon. The two men said nothing as they got in, slammed their doors, and cranked the engine over. He sat in the back, on the passenger's side and tried to decide if he should say something or be quiet. Which was better? One thing was sure: whatever this was about, he just needed to talk calmly and rationally. Yes, he nodded. He looked at his ghostly reflection in the window and saw that his tie was loose. He straightened it, sharply and with dignity.

Palm trees flashed by and an eagle orbited in the cloudless blue. Beyond the marshy slipway of the road he knew there were alligators and wild hogs. Slippery sunlight glittered off water in a ditch. He balled up his hands and thought about what he might say. This must be about the gun. It had to be. All would be well, he told himself. Just tell the truth.

The office block of NASA's Administration Headquarters loomed on the horizon and it seemed like ages until they reached it but, when they did, they pulled up to the front door and stopped. Although he hadn't spent much time in this part of the Rocket Ranch, he knew there were health facilities, a training center for the flight crews, a fire station, and a large building that housed the astronauts in their final days before liftoff. Somewhere inside this building, maybe just beyond the windows, was the crew of Apollo 11. Security would be tight. He was surprised he was here. But maybe that's exactly *why* he was here. Security was tight.

He was told to get out of the car.

"What's this about?"

The men in dark suits said nothing as they grabbed both of his arms and ushered him roughly to a side door. Dead earthworms were crusted on the sidewalk and there was the smell of freshly cut grass. The round faced one tapped numbers into a keypad and a lock clicked open. They pulled him down a tiled corridor and he had trouble keeping up.

"What's going on?" he tried again. "Where are you taking me?"

They came to a black door and told him not to move. Four letters were stenciled in gold. APIP. Beneath it was something else. 2B.

"In," Round Face said with a shove.

He half-expected to find himself in a jail cell, but it was a normal conference room with grey carpet and a wide wooden table. A glass ashtray with several spent matchsticks rested in the middle. Fluorescent lights hummed overhead. There were no windows.

"Sit," Round Face said.

They turned around, closed the door, and left him alone in the room.

Eli didn't sit. Instead, he put his ear to the door and tried to listen to what was being said on the other side. He could hear mumbling but couldn't make out the breakage of exact words. He tried to turn the knob—left, then right—but of course it wouldn't move.

"Locked," he whispered. It was comforting to hear his own voice, even though he could also hear a tone of worry.

He turned around to look at the room. It was a perfect square of painted cinderblocks. There were no pictures. There were no bookshelves. There were, however, three chairs on one side of the table and a single chair on the other. He strolled around, tapping his fingertips on the wooden tabletop, and sat down in the lone chair. This was clearly meant for him. Maybe it was best to cooperate? Show them the smiling face of an innocent man, he told himself. Tell them a mistake has been made. He folded his hands before him and stared at the door. Now what?

The charcoal grey carpet smelled new and he noticed bits of black woven into it. The ceiling tiles suspended overhead reminded him of the surface of the moon. Grey and pocked.

Voices came from the other side of the door. He thought about standing up to greet whoever was about to enter. *Hello, I'm Eli Hessel. How can I help you?* Was that the right approach? he wondered.

He twirled his platinum wedding ring around and around and wondered how Lina would feel if he didn't come home this evening. That's when he remembered the note, the one he'd left next to the jigsaw puzzle of Vermeer's "The Milkmaid". *Home late, love E.* She knew Apollo 11 was taking off tomorrow—he glanced at his watch—so she wouldn't miss him for at least a day. The thought chilled him. It made the room feel small and cell like. They could keep him here for a long time before she would start to ask questions.

When the door finally opened, he stood up and held out a hand. The two men who brought him from the VAB walked in quickly, followed by a third man. This new man was reading a document and he sat down without looking up or acknowledging that Eli's hand was out. The third man was handsome and misted with cologne. None of them smiled.

"Sit," Round Face said.

He did what he was told. The door swung shut and a bolt was driven home. There was the clicking of an external lock.

"Mr. Hessel, my name's Mike...this here's Keith, and the guy down at the end is Johnson. He's with APIP, not the agency."

Eli nodded. The Apollo Personnel Investigation Program. They were the internal service that investigated issues that might endanger the security of Apollo, as well as the Kennedy Space Center. He looked at the two men in dark suits. "The agency?" he asked. "What's that?"

The black man, Keith, put a briefcase on the table and flicked open the brass clasps. "We already told you, Mr. Hessel. We're CIA. The Central Intelligence Agency."

The round-faced man said, "We have a few questions for you."

"I am ready to help," Eli said, lifting his forearms in an act of openness.

The handsome man named Johnson tapped his fingertips together. He had copper colored hair and high cheekbones. His gaze was as sharp as a drill.

"Did you know we found a homosexual last week? Married, two kids. The wife didn't know he visited fairy bars. The week before that, we found a man who owed $75,000 to the mob. Gambling problem."

"I'm afraid I don't understand."

Johnson looked around the room. "Did you know there are more than 20,000 men and women at KSC? That's a whole lot of people that can be bribed, blackmailed, and extorted to sell secrets to the Soviets."

Eli leaned back and crossed a leg over his knee but he felt that it was too informal so he sat up straight. "I – I'm afraid I still don't understand."

Johnson flipped open a file. "Mr. Hessel, a lot of people have been working very hard to get the United States to the moon before the Russians, and we can't have one person foul that up because they have a—" he looked at the ceiling as if searching for the right word—"a *lifestyle* that could be leveraged against them."

Eli blinked a few times. The men across from him wore suits that were freshly ironed and they wore their authority like armor. He glanced down at his wrinkled white smock and touched the badge over his left pocket. VAB ML 119. He held it up.

"Gentlemen…see this? I have been here since 1964. I am a good worker, and I have nothing to hide."

"You hid a gun," Johnson smiled.

The air conditioner rumbled on and a vent above spilled cool air onto the table.

"That?" Eli laughed nervously. "That was a mistake. I had—and I will be honest with you about this—I had too much to drink the other night and—"

Keith held up a hand. "Is drinking a problem for you, Mr. Hessel?"

"No."

The three men stared at him and waited for more.

"It isn't! And please call me Eli."

Keith reached into his open briefcase and pulled out a leather binder. He flipped for a page and tapped a sentence. He spoke without looking up.

"Someone in your office heard you talking badly about Professor von Braun. You said he didn't pay for his so-called 'war crimes' and that maybe he *should* pay a price? Did you say that on July 2nd?"

Johnson jumped in before Eli could respond. "You said the same thing about Arthur Rudolph."

"I may have said these things. America is a free country though, yes?"

"Mr. Hessel…you brought a loaded gun into a restricted area. Why is that?"

The air conditioner continued to rattle and Eli felt sweat form on the back of his neck. In a flashing moment he saw von Braun in his SS uniform and, next to him, was his longtime colleague, Arthur Rudolph, dressed in civilian clothes. They held champagne glasses and walked down a wide tunnel that was illuminated by sodium lights. The two men strolled next to an assembly line of V-2s.

But there were so many others with similar backgrounds, and they had all been given clemency for what they had done to other human beings.

Operation Paperclip brought over Walter Dornberger, Kurt Debus, Konrad Dannenberg, Hermann Kurzweg, and so many others. There was even Dr. Hubertus Strughold. Although he wasn't connected with von Braun or Dora, he was brought to the United States because he knew a great deal about how the human body reacted under extreme conditions. He wore bow-ties, smoked a pipe, and his friends affectionately called him "Struggie". Much of his early understanding of what happened to human tissue in the void of space was learned from human medical experiments that occurred at Dachau. There, men were used as lab rats. The Luftwaffe, the German air force, wanted to know what might happen to pilots at high altitude, so prisoners were chosen at random for lethal tests. They were pushed into a large metal ball called the "Sky Ride Machine" and the oxygen was sucked out. After they died, their bodies were then dissected to see what had happened to their muscles. Medical reports sent back to Berlin referred to these test subjects as "adult pigs". At NASA, Strughold played a significant role in making spacesuits for the Mercury, Gemini, and Apollo programs. In fact, he became known as the "Father of Space Medicine" and what he learned from the "Sky Ride Machine" would keep men alive on the moon. It wasn't that much different than what von Braun had learned about V-2 trajectories, payload capabilities, and how these deadly arts could be transformed into lifting human beings off the planet. There was a secret history to such high technology. A price had been paid.

Eli looked down. His fingers were interlaced into a ball of knuckles. The criminals, he thought, closing his eyes, were alive and well. They lived under their own names, they had fulfilling careers, and they spoiled their grandchildren. For all he knew, Horse Head might be enjoying a stein of beer somewhere in Munich at this very moment. What price had these men paid? Were their souls as cracked and damaged as the survivors? Did the tunnels keep them awake at night?

"Mr. Hessel. Are you listening? You brought a gun into work, and you just admitted von Braun and Rudolph should pay for their so-called war crimes."

Something dark and oily flipped in his stomach and he knew that he had to take this seriously. Eli took a deep breath, looked up, and asked a simple question:

"May I have a cigarette?"

HE STARED INTO HIS SWIRLING coffee. Powdered creamer was dusted on the table and he took a moment to wipe it on the floor with the plow of his hand. A freshly stubbed out cigarette was in the ashtray and he watched the last of its smoke wisp up.

"Mr. Hessel? Please answer the question."

"Why are you asking me such things? I helped launch Apollo 8, 9, and 10."

Johnson offered a wry smile. "Apollo 11 is *landing* on the moon. That's the difference."

The black man, Keith, leaned into his shorter and wider colleague, Mike. They muttered about something until Keith nodded. He took of his glasses and cleaned them with a handkerchief.

"What are your feelings about the United States, Mr. Hessel?"

"My feelings? America saved my life. America freed me from Dora, and gave me a home, and allowed me to start over again." Eli held the coffee mug in both hands. It was warm and comforting. "My wife is American. My daughter is American. This country gave me a second act."

His throat tightened and he was afraid of what might tumble out. The tunnels, the barracks, the crematorium, the chariot races, the rutabaga soup, the lice, the standing for hours in the *Appellplatz*, bodies dropping into snow, the well-fed guard dogs, the wild eyes of the SS, the train whistles, the eating of a sausage near a slope of human ash. He was afraid it all might tumble out. But how could language hold all that he had seen? How could he explain in words the images that swirled in his head? The Holocaust was beyond words. A whole new language needed to be invented to help explain it. Could it even be explained?

"I just want to go home to my wife," he finally said in a half-whisper.

Keith looked at the men on either side of him and shuffled through a mimeograph that had been paperclipped together. The smell of fresh ink floated up. His fingernail tapped at some words, and he slid it over to Johnson.

"Why don't you take this one, Franklin?"

Franklin? Eli wondered. Who's Franklin?

Johnson ran a hand through his copper hair. "Sure," he said, circling a word with a pen before he spoke. "You said you were in a camp called Dora. That's not what our records show."

Eli frowned. "What *do* your records show?"

Johnson glanced down. "That you were in a place called Mittelbau from October '44 to April '45."

The idea that the word "Dora" didn't have the same draining effect on them as it did on him made Eli groan. He had to admit that different words carry different freight for us all. Words are just vessels, they are just railcars into which we place our emotions.

"Mr. Hessel?"

"*Ja.* Yes," he scooted his chair closer. "I was at Dora between October 1944 and April 1945. I was a slave there." His German accent was stronger now, and he wondered why this was.

"Not at Mittelbau?" Keith asked.

"They are the same camp. It was called Dora-Mittelbau, sometimes Mittelbau-Dora. Those of us who were prisoners called it Dora because that was the area of camp where we slept. A few people called it Kohnstein, after the mountain we were forced to work in. The underground network of tunnels...where we built the V-2s...that was called Mittelwerk, but only the Nazis called it that. That was the official name of the factory, you see. Calling it Mittelwerk erases the concentration camp outside the tunnels, *ja*? So to be clear, Dora was where we slept, ate, and stood for roll call. Mittelbau was the factory and the railyards."

"But how—" Johnson began to ask.

Eli talked over him. "After the Americans freed me, I learned the camp was also called Dora-Nordhausen by some of your soldiers. Others called it Nordhausen because it was close to that town." Eli focused on the crushed cigarette butt and let the words flow. "There was a sub-camp near Dora named Boelcke Kaserne and that's where thousands of bodies were found. There were 39 sub-camps around Dora with names like Ellrich, Harzungen, Blankenburg, and Rottleberode. Many people died in these places too." His hands were warm against the coffee and he paused to take a sip. "I use the word Dora, but the camp is bigger than that little word. It is a massive zone of death, *ja*?"

When he put his coffee down, his hands felt empty and naked. Eli cracked his knuckles and wished that a jigsaw puzzle was in front of him. He wanted to slot broken pieces back together again.

When Keith spoke, his voice was a honeyed baritone. "I can see this is hard on you, but how can one camp have so many different names?"

Eli waved an upturned hand at the room. "What is the name of this place?"

Mike and Keith answered at once, but said different things.

"Cape Canaveral."   "Cape Kennedy."

Johnson added, "KSC."

Eli nodded as if to say, *there is your answer.* After a moment he added, "Dora was the future, you must understand this. It wasn't just another concentration camp. If you want to know what Europe would look like under permanent Nazi rule, it would be full of Doras. This camp was something new and terrible. The Nazis, they finally figured out how to extract every ounce of work from a body. Auschwitz? That was nonsensical. Why kill people who can work? Dora fixed that problem. Dora was the future."

He tried to inflate his heart with love for the men sitting across from him, but how could they possibly understand what he had seen? The forces of hatred had not swallowed them whole. He lowered his voice and added, "Do you understand me? They worked us in Mittelbau. They burned us in Dora."

The room was silent.

"Ya-huh," Johnson said. "But Mr. Hessel, none of this explains why you brought a gun into a restricted area."

He wasn't listening to them now. Instead, he was thinking of fire. He saw whitened bone chips glow in an incinerator. Flames twisted around open mouths, limbs cracked like popcorn, and heat broke down vertebrae and muscle. The great storehouse of a person's memory was spun into smoke. Had things gone a little bit differently, that could have been him in an oven.

Several years ago, Eli read an article about how trauma changes the way the brain processes memory. Trauma scrambles the details, confuses the understanding of time, and makes it harder to recall the proper order of things. Had he eaten that sausage before or after the hangings in Tunnel 40? Or the showers—was that before or after Horse Head quizzed him about Ohm's law? Memory wasn't linear. No, it wasn't linear at all. Memory had an undertow all of its own, and it pulled him down, down, down into the darkness.

And yet, he felt responsible to remember it all, everything. The big things stood out easily enough—the hangings, the beating of Delacroix, how he hid in a rocket—but the other things, the normal everyday things, like Horse Head's nicotine stained fingers, all of *that* was becoming opaque and shadowy. At times, it felt like the smaller parts of a darker whole were disappearing on him. If, for the sake of argument, he had been in Dora for just one day, would the overwhelming shock of it be seared more brightly into his memory? But he had been in Dora for seven long months, and over that time he had been made into a different person. It was an erosion of the self, he thought. The Eli of his childhood had been ground down, scoured away. Killed off.

"The Nazis, they took everything from me," he said. "Nothing escaped Dora. Not even God."

They looked at him as if he were a scared little boy. Their eyes told him that, yes, war was terrible, but suck it up. Be a man.

"The gun, Mr. Hessel. Talk."

THEY EVENTUALLY GAVE HIM A small bag of potato chips and a warm Coke. He wasn't hungry or thirsty but he polished everything off because he didn't know when they might feed him again. Grease from the chips dotted the paper plate, and he used the tip of his finger to pick up crunchy crumbs. As he waited for the door to open, he nudged bits of potato out of his molars with his tongue.

When they entered the room again, they didn't speak. They sat in their chairs and opened their folders. His eyes snaked from one man to the next. Johnson was handsome, slender, and had a high forehead. Keith had wide shoulders, glasses, and his hair was clipped short to hide early baldness. Mike was stocky, a barrel of a man.

Keith cleared his throat and this seemed to bring his colleagues to attention. "Mr. Hessel, have you ever thought about sabotage?"

Eli let out a bark of laughter. "What?"

"Sabotage. The willful disruption of a system that is done in order to aid a foreign power."

"I know what the word means, Mr...?" He paused because he realized he didn't know Keith's last name.

"Doyle."

"I know what it means, Mr. Doyle. Apollo is my life's work. Why would I sabotage it?"

Mike pulled out a sheet of paper. His finger moved down the page. Even though Eli knew it was petty on his part, he enjoyed the small moment of power he had in asking for Keith's last name. He looked at Mike. "And what's your last name?"

"Azzara. Mike Azzara. You already know Franklin's last name—Johnson—so let's stop the nicey-nice bullshit and get back to work." He circled something and glanced up. "You worked on V-2s?"

"Yes. In fact, I got into Columbia University because of it."

"You were saved from Auschwitz for this job?"

Eli sat back, surprised. "I wouldn't say I was 'saved', Mr. Azzara. One day I was taken from Auschwitz, loaded onto a train, and sent across Germany."

"To Dora-Mittelbau?"

"Correct."

"You didn't know ahead of time you were going to build V-2s?"

"I'd never seen a rocket before. When I arrived at Dora, I thought they were torpedoes for a submarine."

"You're saying you had no knowledge of the V-2s prior to your arrival?"

"That is correct."

"And yet the Nazis trusted you to build them? Why were you saved when others were not?"

"I wasn't trusted to build them. I was *forced* to build them. If you didn't work quickly enough or well enough you were beaten or hanged or shot. We were slaves, Mr. Azzara." Eli found himself glancing over at Keith Doyle. "If I didn't do what they ordered me to do, I would have been killed."

"And yet in spite of the possibility of death you still committed sabotage?"

"Ye-es," Eli said, stretching out the word. "Dora was a Nazi camp."

"A Nazi camp full of communist prisoners, ye-es?" Mike Azzara said, also stretching out the word, but in a mocking way.

"I'm not sure I understand."

"Simply that you are…" he smiled, "*familiar* with sabotage. You've done it before. Your father was a communist sympathizer, was he not?"

Eli put his hands on the table as if to steady himself. Small bubbles inside the can of Coke could be heard popping.

"My father was no communist. He was a professor. A democrat. He worked with Einstein." A reservoir of unspoken ideas were dammed behind his lips, and he opened his mouth to let everything spill out. "My whole family was murdered at Auschwitz, Mr. Azzara. They were sent to the gas chambers while I, I alone, was saved because I was young and could be used as slave labor. They were murdered in the first hour of our arrival and I never saw them again. I was taken to Buna, the factory of Auschwitz III, where I was forced to make synthetic rubber. This was done against my will. I was then taken to Dora-Mittelbau, also against my will, where I was forced to build rockets. I saw people die in ways that would shock you. I saw hangings. I saw the SS shoot people in the back of the head. I managed to escape death not because I was smarter or better than the others, I only managed to escape death because I had a greater amount of luck. It was luck that saved me, Mr. Azzara. And yes," Eli looked directly into the eyes of his accusers, "I did commit acts of sabotage in Dora. I am proud of this, and I did it because I wanted to fight back. I was a corpse on vacation, Mr. Azzara. You must understand this. I did not expect to see the end of the war, and I thought it was only a matter of time before I was sent up the chimney. The rockets I damaged may have saved lives in London or Brussels or Paris. Whole families might be alive today because of what I did."

Keith Doyle held up a hand. "Take it easy, Mr. Hessel. We're just asking questions here. This isn't a trial."

"It feels like a trial."

Johnson grunted and looked at his watch. "Let's cut the shit here. Hessel? Are you listening to me? It would be a whole lot easier for the Soviet Union to destroy an Apollo rocket than for the USSR to actually *go* to the moon. You'd just need one spy in the right place at the right time. Why spend millions of rubles when you can make sure America fails...right?"

"You are suggesting I'm a spy?"

"You've said things that make me question your loyalty. Plus, there were plenty of communists in that Dora camp. Maybe you stayed in touch with some of your comrades? Maybe they've asked you to do a few things, hmm? Plus there's the gun. What about that gun, Hessel? Tell me about that gun."

Keith Doyle knocked on the table. "Let's dial this down, fellas." He pushed his glasses up on his nose with his finger, and when he spoke, his voice was gentle. "Mr. Hessel, I'm sure you're aware of the radio signal on the range safety code plugs?"

Eli nodded. If the Saturn V went off course for any reason while it climbed through the atmosphere, the crew could jet away on an emergency booster and the remaining rocket below could be blown up. All you needed was the proper radio signal. For obvious reasons, this was highly secret and classified.

"If the Russians got that code…well then…they would only need to send the right radio signal to Apollo 11 and then," he spread his hands wide as if to mimic an explosion. "We'd have a problem, yes?"

Before Eli could answer, Johnson piped in. "Like I said, you're familiar with sabotage."

Mike Azzara rapped the table for attention. "You were the last person to check the F-1 engines. It'd be veeerry easy for you to crimp a line or turn a valve the wrong way."

Eli rubbed his forehead. "Gentlemen, I have no reason to harm Apollo. I've devoted years of my life to landing a man safely on the moon. I want this to happen. I love my country. America gave me life when Hitler gave me nothing but death, death, and more death."

The men stared at him.

"I am no spy," he said, calmly.

"Are you in the Communist Party?" Johnson asked.

"Have you been listening to me?"

"It is a reasonable question, Mr. Hessel. The Kennedy Space Center is the front line of the Cold War."

Eli rubbed the stubble on his chin. "Did you ask von Braun and the other Germans these questions?"

"We're not talking about them. We're talking about you."

He reached for the Coca-Cola. It was warm and syrupy. He finished it in three long gulps and replaced the can, carefully. "Von Braun was a high-ranking officer in the SS. The S…*S*," he said, enunciating the last letter. "They murdered us. I am the victim here, not the threat."

Eli wanted to add that von Braun did many great things for space and that he was undoubtedly gifted, but his background had been edited, cleaned up. The future couldn't be hopeful if the man leading the way had a dark past. Maybe von Braun pointed at the stars because it kept people from looking at the ground, and all that had been scattered on that ground.

"You hate Professor von Braun, don't you, Hessel? Is that why you brought the gun into work? You were going to kill him, weren't you? Answer the question!"

"Hate is a strong word. I know what sorrow hate can bring. Von Braun created rockets that I was *forced* to build, and now he is creating rockets that

I *choose* to build. My feelings about him are complicated. I do not wish to kill anyone. I have seen enough of killing."

"Nevertheless. The gun."

"Like I said, I forgot it was in my satchel. That's the tru—"

Keith interrupted by reading from his notes. "You had electroshock therapy in 1957."

"Yes."

"Would you call yourself balanced, Mr. Hessel? Mentally stable? *Compos mentis?*"

"Given what I saw, yes."

"What does that mean?"

"I'm fine."

"Have you thought about suicide?"

A pause. "I'm fine."

"Can a psychologist confirm this?"

He closed his eyes and began to massage his forehead with both hands. "The real madness happened in Germany." Eli pointed to the badge on his shirt. "Look, I just want to go back to work. Apollo will be the single greatest achievement of the twentieth century and I am proud, very proud, to be a part of it."

Johnson pointed to his APIP badge. "I don't think America will require your services anymore, Hessel. You're finished at Kennedy."

Something inside him cracked when he heard this. It felt like he was being sucked down into a whirlpool. He stood up quickly, involuntarily, and the chair behind him tipped backwards. It thudded against the new carpet.

"I am trying—I am trying very hard—to keep the past from eating me. I'm not a danger to you or anyone else. Please, you must let me work on Apollo 11, 12, 13, 14 and beyond. It helps me. I see rockets differently." He hesitated and added again, "It helps me."

Grief nipped at his throat and he worried that he might break down if he didn't immediately change the subject. He pointed at the empty can of Coke and said, "You have kept me here for many hours. May I use a restroom?"

"Oh, yes," Johnson said with a smirk. "Your drinking problem. We still need to talk about that."

"Please. A restroom."

The men consulted each other without words. Keith finally nodded and stood up. "Follow me."

Eli walked straight-backed and proud to the door. It felt good to leave the room, and even though the air in the hallway was no different than the air in Room 2B, he found himself taking deep breaths as if he had just stepped outside. Keith pointed to the right. They passed a fire alarm and a water fountain. A FALLOUT SHELTER sign was bolted to one of the walls and, when they passed a clock, Eli stared at it, surprised at how late it was. Ten o'clock already? What was Lina doing? Was she worried? Probably not, he had to conclude with a frown. She knew it would be a late night for him and she probably didn't expect him to come home at all.

"O-kay," Keith said, opening the restroom door with a single arm. "Do your business."

"What's going to happen to me? Afterwards, I mean."

Keith shrugged. "The range safety code plugs have been changed, just so you know."

"You really don't trust me, do you?"

"You got five minutes."

When the door closed, he went to the sink and splashed water on his face. His eyes were bloodshot and he looked, my God he thought, shaking his head, he looked unnaturally old. He had hollow eyes, deep wrinkles, and a wattle of skin sagged turkey-like from his neck. Thanks to Dora, he sometimes felt like he had lived a century. After all, there wasn't anyone who knew what he had experienced. This must be how old people felt, he concluded, chewing on his lower lip. With family and friends dead, no one knew how things used to be. They were marooned in time.

He pulled a brown paper towel from the dispenser and held it to his face. He thought he was going to cry, but seeing himself in the mirror gave him an unexpected bolt of strength.

"You didn't survive by being weak," his reflection scolded him. "You're stronger than anyone else here. You lived through Dora."

He considered the men interviewing him—no, *interrogating* him—and he thought about their uniforms. In America, business suits were a type of uniform; they were the trappings of power. He looked at his white smock and the little numbered badge. The man in the mirror narrowed his eyes.

Keith knocked on the door. "Hurry it up."

His heart felt like a hand grenade and his palms prickled with sweat. It had been a long time since he'd had a panic attack but he knew the signs. He wanted to run and keep on running. He needed movement. He needed motion. Standing in the restroom felt like he'd been tossed into jail, and the idea of going back into that stuffy room for more talk? No, he'd had enough. He needed to leave, to escape. But how?

There weren't any windows. Just the door. He looked at the false ceiling and then at the grey toilet stalls. His body moved, and it almost felt like someone else was telling his muscles what to do. He swung the metal door of the toilet stall open, quietly, and stood on the seat. The silver pipe that led into the wall was thick, and he tested his weight on it. He hoisted himself up onto the wooden wall that divided one toilet from the other—he pulled himself up as if he were getting out of a swimming pool. Balancing, he straddled the wooden divider and silently removed a ceiling tile. The wooden wall beneath him wobbled as he slid the tile to one side. It was dark up there and, as he stood up gently, like a tight-rope walker, he felt like he was climbing into the belly of a V-2. A large pipe was overhead and he put his hands around it. As he lifted himself up into the darkness, there was the smell of dust. It was easy to pull up his legs and hang like a monkey from the thick pipe. It was also easy to slide the fiberglass ceiling tile back into place. The pipe was warm and he wrapped both arms and both legs more tightly around it.

Keith's voice was muffled. "Hurry up, Hessel. You got one minute."

They'd check the rooms on either side—they weren't stupid—and if he shimmied forward that would put him directly above where Keith was standing. But what if he followed the pipe away from the bathroom?

Cobwebs brushed his face as he moved like an inchworm in the cramped space. The pipe came to a joint—he bumped his head against it—and with a free hand he groped in the humid dark to get an idea of what was around him. The false ceiling of the bathroom was no longer beneath him and he worried that he was above some kind of deep shaft. Impossible, he thought. They were on the first floor of the administration building and basements didn't exist at KSC. It had been built on a swamp and the water table was high. No, he reasoned, wherever the shaft went, it couldn't be a far drop. Could it?

Keith's voice was far away and muffled. He said, "Let's go…did you hear me, Mr. Hessel?"

Toilet doors slammed open one after the other. The noise got louder and louder. There was a pause before Keith shouted a single word. "Shit!"

Footsteps raced away as Keith roared for Azzara and Johnson.

Eli lowered his feet and hung from the pipe, wondering what to do next. Going home and pretending everything was fine couldn't happen, especially now that he was being investigated by APIP. Everything was over. It was only a matter of time before they asked him to clear out his desk and turn in his badge. This little stunt? This running away? It only made the end arrive more quickly. As he dangled from the pipe he almost smiled at how ridiculous he must look. His hands were sweaty and he was beginning to slip. Time to let go, he thought.

And so, he did.

The fall must have been ten feet and when he hit the ground, he crumpled. A sharp pain hit his lower back and he let out a cry. His lower vertebra. The hobnail boot from so many years ago. He stood up and held out his hands, fumbling for a light switch or a door knob. The walls were cool and he felt dirt on his fingertips. He sniffed. There was the smell of disinfectant and pine trees. His foot kicked a metal bucket and a pole clattered to the floor. His hands patted the cold cement walls until, at last, he found a small plastic box. A light switch.

When he flicked it on, a light bulb sizzled awake. It swayed on a single black cord and created odd moving shadows against the walls. He was in a janitor's closet. There were shelves of bottles and rags and squeegees, there was a mop, a bucket, and a steel garbage can with wheels on it. Hanging on a peg was a blue smock. A Yankees baseball hat was on another peg.

His white NASA smock was veiled in cobwebs and he slapped it clean. When it seemed presentable, he folded it neatly and placed it on a shelf. The blue smock on the peg was much too big for him, but he buttoned it up and reached for the rolling garbage can. He crammed the Yankees cap onto his head and opened the door carefully. He stuck out his head and eyeballed the hallway. No one. The coast was clear.

He stepped back into the janitor's closet and massaged his lower back for a few seconds. The pain was still there—it felt like a constant bee sting—and he tried to ignore it as he stuffed his white smock into a plastic bag. He placed it into the rolling garbage can and then, looking up and down the tiled hallway one more time, with his heart fluttering like a hummingbird, he stepped out and closed the door behind him. Familiar voices were around the corner and he pulled the Yankees cap down over his eyes. The bill was ratty and torn. He hunched over and pushed the garbage can slowly, as if he had all the time in the world. One of the wheels squeaked and wobbled. Fluorescent lights reflected on the polished floor and he could hear a radio behind a closed office door. There was a trash can next to a drinking fountain and he went over to it, limping with pain. He took off the domed lid and started pulling out soda cans, newspapers, and sheets of carbon paper. When Keith and Azzara ran towards him, he bent further into the can, scooping up trash.

"He can't have gone far," Keith shouted.

"Johnson's checking the other rooms."

"You go upstairs. I'll check the back hallway and the other entrance. Call the office and have his badge revoked!"

Eli waited for them to grab his shoulder and push him against the wall, he waited for them to tear off his baseball cap. He reached further into the can and lifted out a three-ring binder. He pulled out an uneaten orange, and styrofoam cups, and sheets of data, and a half-eaten hot dog. It reminded him of the sausage he ate next to the crematorium at Dora. For a brief moment, he saw ash drifting and swirling on the slope.

As they ran closer he was sure they would ask him if he'd seen a mousy scientist running down the hallway. Surely this would happen. Why wouldn't they ask a janitor if he had seen something suspicious? Their shoes slapped hard against the tiles, they were only feet away from him now, and he held his breath as he reached further down into the garbage, down into all that had been discarded and forgotten. They passed him. One of them went down a hallway on the right—the other went down the left. They shouted his name.

"Eli Hessel?"

"Hessel?"

When their footfalls got softer and their voices faded into silence, he straightened up. The compressor of the water fountain rattled on, and from behind a closed door, a phone rang.

He studied the empty corridor.

Now what?

THE FLAME TRENCH

FROGS SANG FROM A NEARBY creek as he stepped out into the humid night air. A breeze made the palm trees whisper. Apollo 11 was floodlit in the distance by a bank of searchlights, which made it look like a slender steeple, a finger of white. Next to it was an orange gantry system of crossbeams that locked the rocket into place. When the engines ignited, the nine arms that pinned Apollo to the ground would snap away, and the mighty vehicle would rise.

He moved down the sidewalk with the wheeled garbage can and didn't take his eyes off Apollo 11. There was something majestic and even supernatural about it, especially at night. Clouds of cooled gas drifted past the upper stages—they twisted and curled through shafts of spotlight.

He came to the end of the sidewalk and stood there, uncertain what to do.

Although hundreds of people were in offices around him, he saw no one. He glanced at the building to his right and could see—or thought he could see—the floor where Armstrong, Aldrin, and Collins were in a private apartment. They would go to bed soon. And then, rising before the sun, they would get up, have a hearty breakfast of steak and eggs, they would put on their bulky spacesuits, and they would climb into a van that would whisk them to the launch pad. Once there, they would ride a swaying elevator to the top and climb into the capsule. The hatch would be bolted shut and the entire launch pad would be cleared. And then they would lift into the pages of history. His eyes lingered on Apollo and he felt a buoyant fluttering, a little flux of pride.

A sudden noise came from behind him—a snapping of a twig or maybe the cocking of a gun—and he wheeled around. Was someone there? Headlights twinkled in the muggy distance as spectators and well-wishers began to line the shore of the viewing area. There was already a long line of cars, and they sparkled like a string of stars.

Eli balled up the janitor's uniform and stuffed it into the garbage can. He then reached for his white smock inside the plastic bag and snapped it like a beach towel. He draped it on and fingered the buttons into place. He tossed the Yankees cap into the garbage and ran both hands through his short hair. Frogs continued their swampsong.

"Stupid, stupid, stupid," he muttered. His voice was surprisingly loud.

No going back now, Eli told himself. They'd never let him near Apollo again, especially after what he'd done in the bathroom. But even if he hadn't escaped, it was unlikely they would allow him to continue at NASA. Their questions were just accusations in disguise. It wasn't *just* about the gun or the electroshock therapy or the drinking. No, he embodied something else, something dangerous that needed to be buried. Dora had no place in this story of discovery and optimism. His suffering needed to be forgotten about.

A door slammed shut and he snapped around, scanning the night. A stocky man with wide shoulders appeared beneath one of the lamps. He carried a briefcase and had a wide beard sprouting from his cheeks. He jiggled his car keys and walked away, whistling Sinatra's "Fly Me to the Moon."

Eli didn't have a plan. He didn't know what was going to happen next. He simply needed to be out of that room and away from men that wanted to control him. He had his liberty now, but not his freedom. What to do? What to do? His car was far away, in the VAB parking lot, and he couldn't walk there—not at night—he'd be picked up for sure by security, plus there was the very real danger of alligators, so how could he get back to—?

An idea blazed to life.

He shoved the garbage can against a wall and hurried for a line of government issue white Buicks that had NASA logos on their doors. Almost anyone could use one to get around the Rocket Ranch—all you had to do was show your badge, sign a form, and you were given a key.

A clapboard wooden hut was up ahead and he hurried over. The guard inside was bald and his boots were propped on an upturned milkcrate. A portable radio hung from a nail and, as Eli stepped closer, he could hear the mumbling of a baseball game.

"It's the top of the fifth and we've got a crackerjack of a game this evening. Two balls, two strikes, Popovich on first."

He looked around and wondered if the guard knew about what had happened. Had he been ordered to keep a lookout for someone that matched his build, his accent? Had he been told a man had fled an interview? Eli shrugged. What else could he do? If he wanted a car he'd have to show his badge.

He walked up and acted as if he were deep in thought. Without looking at the guard, he said, "I need a car. We forgot some LOX readout data in the VAB."

The beefy man in his fifties uncrossed his cowboy boots and let them fall to the wooden floor—*clunk, clunk*. He cocked his head and considered this. "Identification?" he asked.

Eli held up his badge from his white smock. He stood at attention as his eyes slithered to the entrance of the administration building. Where were Keith and Azaara?

"Reason for use?"

"Like I said, we…well, *I*… forgot some readout data."

The man squinted at the badge for such a long time that Eli considered running into the cover of night. Eventually though, the burly guard with blue eyes seemed satisfied and wrote down Eli's number. His meaty hand moved for a pegboard of keys and, just as he was about to pluck one free, a phone in the hut began to ring. A red light next to the number wheel pulsed once, then twice.

"Which car can I use?" Eli asked, trying to distract the guard.

The man reached for the phone.

"Look!" Eli shouted. "We're in a hurry. See that rocket over there? That thing is supposed to lift off in less than twelve hours, and we need this data! So which car can I use?"

The guard held up a finger. "One minute." He lifted the phone and brought it to his ear. "West door," he said. The guard didn't say anything at first. He looked confused and began to jiggle the plastic prongs of the cradle. "Hello? Anyone there? Hello? This is west door."

With a shrug, he put down the phone and wiped sweat from his smooth head. His face was weather-beaten and his skin was as rough as tree bark. He wore a turquoise bolo tie and his knuckles were covered in scars.

"Which car?" Eli asked, using a sharper tone. "It's urgent."

The guard—MENENDEZ, his nametag said—reached lazily for a key. "Big ol' day tomorrow," he said happily, slapping at a mosquito. "I finish at six but I ain't leaving. No *way* I'm missing that candle being lit. You excited?"

"It's not going anywhere if I don't get that data."

The guard dropped the key into Eli's hand. "Give them boys a good ride tomorrow. The smoothest, yeah?"

"We will."

The phone rang again and the guard picked it up in one fluid motion. "West door."

As Eli hurried away, he half expected the man to shout his name and order him to come back, but these words didn't travel through the sticky air. He moved quickly and broke into a run. He focused on the white Buicks parked near a line of palm trees, and when he found car #4—the one that matched his key—he opened the creaking door. He ignited the engine, jerked the stick on the steering column down to R, and reversed out. He fumbled for the lights and pressed down on the accelerator. There was no need to draw attention to himself so he drove away, slowly. Shadows stretched on the dashboard as he moved beneath lights. The windshield had dried bug guts on it and the cigarette tray hadn't been emptied. He rolled down the window and took in the fresh, free, salty air. The ocean was near. He could almost hear it.

After he exited the parking lot, he pulled up to a stop sign. To his left was the VAB and the way home. To his right was Apollo 11, lit up in glory. The whole world was focused on it, and so few people would ever get a chance to be this close. He looked in the rearview mirror and studied clouds of red exhaust billowing up from his brake lights. It reminded him of fire, the kind of fire that would soon spill out from the F-1 engines that he had worked on. He kept looking at the hellfire clouds behind him and saw, in the distance, three men running out of the Administration Building. They looked around and shouted. One them sprinted towards the wooden hut.

Eli felt his foot rise from the brake pedal. He turned the wheel towards launch pad 39-A. It made no sense, and it almost felt like his muscles had made the decision for him. Maybe he wanted to see the rocket one last time? Maybe he wanted to prove that he wasn't a threat? Maybe he knew that nothing else would be the same ever again, so why not get closer to something that would soon be gone? The white dashes on the road were eaten by the hood of his car and the soft blue of the speedometer was calming. He imagined himself in a tiny capsule speeding away from the judgements on earth. All was quiet. He moved beneath starlight, and as he got closer to the chain link gate of the launch pad, he looked at the mighty searchlights. They bathed the Saturn V and made it glow.

He pulled over, turned off the engine, and got out. Because he had clearance he had been here many times before but now, at night, so shortly before launch and with the knowledge that he really shouldn't be here at all, he felt like a trespasser. His shoes crunched over river rock as he walked up to the barbed wire gate. Guards stood around a stubby blockhouse, and a hissing filled up the night. Clouds of super-cooled gas floated overhead and cast shadows on the ground.

He didn't plan on walking any further, he just wanted to stare up at history, but when one of the guards waved him over, he felt his legs move. The man with a large forehead and thin nose noted his badge number and turned a clipboard around for him to sign. Eli glanced down at his badge—VAB ML 119—and looked over at the official NASA car that he had just arrived in.

"Make sure you sign out when you leave," the guard said. "This whole place needs to be cleared in two hours. What's your reason for going in?" the man asked, adjusting his glasses.

Eli stared at the clipboard.

"Reason for going in?" the guard asked again.

"To, ah, visually inspect the LOX and RP-1 intake valves on two and five."

"Two and five. How long'll that take?"

"Not long. Fifteen minutes."

The guard looked at his watch and nodded. "You know the rules. No smoking."

Good one, Eli said with a pointed finger, and with that he walked past the blockhouse and hurried down a path. He thought he heard a phone ringing behind him, but he didn't look back. He kept on walking and allowed his gaze to creep up the side of the rocket—all thirty-six stories of it. He glanced back at the blockhouse and waited for guards to rush out, but they obviously hadn't been warned about him yet. His eyes drifted to the right and he stared at the opening of the flame trench.

At T-minus one second, fire would pour out from this enormous concrete tunnel as if a dam of flame had burst. The trench channeled the rocket's fearsome power and spewed it away so that shock waves wouldn't rip apart the engines. As he walked—quickly now, looking backwards over his shoulder—he ran down a low grassy hill and felt the chilly air against his face. All that super-cooled fuel, he thought, was changing the temperature around the rocket. He saw his breath. He stood before the darkened entrance of the flame trench and shivered. It was an enormous opening, a gaping black mouth.

He didn't plan on stepping inside the trench, and yet it happened anyway. Massive scorch marks were on walls and floor, and he listened to his shoes echo off the concrete. Up ahead was an enormous square of light. This was the area directly beneath the engines and, as he walked closer to it, he felt as if he were entering a sacred place, like he was walking up to the Torah ark of his youth in Neue Synagogue. The holy scrolls he was never allowed to touch were just there, just out of reach. He moved footstep after footstep closer, wanting to turn back and yet still wanting to stand beneath the mighty sleeping rocket.

When he reached that space directly below the five engines, his heart quickened. The searchlights above were so bright it was like looking up at milky dawn. Millions of pounds of hardware and freezing liquid gas were ready for ignition. The whole rocket towered above him, waiting to climb into the sky. The Saturn V seemed like a living breathing creature; it creaked and groaned and hissed from all the liquid oxygen that had been flooded into its tanks a few hours earlier. The fuel was so cold that ice sheets formed on its metal skin, and while he stood beneath it, a massive sheet of ice fell to his right. It smashed into the concrete, sending chunks the size of doors skittering towards him. The sound boomed heavily against the walls. He had a sudden and irrational fear that the engines would ignite. He placed both hands over his chest and forced himself to breath.

He walked over to a shard of ice and picked it up. It was as thick as a phonebook and he stared up from where it had fallen. A popping low growl came from the tonnage above and he dared to take in the whole height of the rocket. As he stood beneath one of its fins, clouds of cold floated by, ghostlike.

A sudden downdraft of wind made his trousers flap. A bassoon like sound came from the engines—it was a single note, deep and mournful. He had never been this close to a fully fueled Saturn V and the groans from above reminded him of a steam engine. He recalled that night, so long ago, when he first arrived at Dora. They were marched into a tunnel, given new identities, and became servants to the rockets. He looked up at the engine bells of Apollo 11 and saw bodies dangling—they walked the air—and they each had a wooden gag shoved into their mouth.

Another sheet of ice fell, and it smashed into skittering slabs to his left. There was a low booming echo in the fire chamber, and when it was quiet again he heard his name over the camp loudspeaker.

"Eli Hessel." The voice was urgent. "Eli Hessel report to security."

He looked at two steel gates where 300,000 tons of water would soon flood out. This would happen during the final seconds of countdown—water would rush into this chamber to absorb the initial shockwaves of the engines, it would keep the entire launch pad from shattering into rubble—in a matter of seconds, this huge temporary subterranean lake would be turned into steam and then it would vent out the flame trench, followed by a river of fire.

"Eli Hessel. Report to security, immediately."

How many men were needed to build a Saturn V? Five hundred? A thousand? He thought of tissue and ash, he thought about what the twentieth-century had built, he thought of tunnels, the dead, and Orpheus. Yes, he nodded. Maybe it was time to leave this place. Maybe it was time to journey above ground and look her in the face.

As he turned to leave, his shadow stretched out before him, scissoring as he moved. He took off his white smock and draped it over his shoulder. When he stepped out of the tunnel and back into the night, the moon was a smudged dark circle. Dry grass crunched beneath his shoes as he hurried away from the tunnel, making a point not to look back.

A siren approached. Flashing red lights pulsed against the night and a jeep came to a skittering stop. Three men jumped out and aimed flashlights at him. Emergency lights splashed waves of red onto the grass.

"Stay there Hessel!"

"Don't move!"

He let his smock fall to the ground, and then slowly, he raised both arms.

He surrendered.

PART III

"Sooner or later in life everyone discovers that perfect happiness is unrealizable, but there are few who stop to consider the antithesis: that perfect unhappiness is equally unattainable."

—Primo Levi, *Survival in Auschwitz*

SHADOW AND SUNLIGHT

BEAUTIFUL.

That's what he thought as he adjusted the soft blanket around his grand-daughter. She was only six weeks old and had tiny pimples around her nose. Her eyes were pinched shut and she breathed, open-mouthed, her little lungs taking in the great big world. The wall clock in the kitchen ticked and tocked as he sat in a recliner, his sock-soled feet up, and he couldn't stop staring at her. He whispered her name and made low clucking sounds. It was such a joy to hold the molecules of her being and share the same room with her, the same air. Ava. She was sunrise. She was daybreak.

His daughter, Hannah, was down the hall napping. The hard work of nursing throughout the night had completely wiped her out, so he and Lina came over to help. Lina usually baked meals that were shoved into the freezer for later while he either cut the grass or cleaned the house. Although it was physical labor, he didn't mind doing it. Not one little bit.

It still surprised him to wake up each morning in California. After what happened at the Kennedy Space Center, he and Lina packed up their sea-side bungalow—all the photographs and framed jigsaw puzzles—and drove across the country to Berkeley. Hannah had just graduated with a degree in elementary education and she was sniffing around for a posting. Her boy-friend, Kyle, non-Jewish and still wearing crazy clothes, somehow managed to land a job selling retirement funds. The striped pants were stored in a trunk but he kept his muttonchops and long hair. They got married in 1972. It was a Christian service and during the reception Eli raised a glass of wine and offered a toast. "*Mazel tov*," he said to the gathered room. He recited a prayer in Hebrew and wished the couple a long, happy life.

Hannah got a job teaching first grade and she often came home with fin-ger paint on her arms or Bugs Bunny stickers on her dress. Kyle began to use words like *fiduciary*, *amortized*, and *limited liability investment*. The words didn't interest Eli in the least but, he had to remind himself, the language he used in his own job would be equally foreign to the young man who was now his son-in-law. Eli spoke the language of rocketry at the University of California, Berkeley. What had started off as a temporary adjunct position turned into something more permanent. The physics department was deeply impressed that he had worked at NASA and he was often asked questions about his father working alongside Max Planck and Albert Einstein. For his own part, he enjoyed walking into a classroom where he scribbled equations onto a chalkboard. Although his students slouched in their desks and often looked bored, they sometimes surprised him with excellent questions—questions that made him hopeful about the future.

Teaching was in his blood. After all, his father had stood before classes in Berlin, and now he was doing the same thing. So was Hannah. They sometimes compared notes and laughed at how similar their students could be in spite of their age difference. They both had classes full of learners who were sleepy, over-excited, and eager to please. "Your freshman sound like my first graders," she once laughed.

Now that it was summer, they were both on break. It was perfect timing, he thought. Ava was born on May 15 and this meant he could be with her for three glorious uninterrupted months.

She stirred in the blanket and this made him refocus his attention. She opened her mouth in a silent cry—the snail of her tongue curled—and she drifted back to sleep.

"Oh little one, who will you become?"

He wondered if she would ask questions about Germany. His students didn't know or seem to care about the Holocaust. He told himself that maybe they were just being polite and didn't want to cause him pain by bringing it up. As for Apollo, he assumed they would be curious about what had happened at the Rocket Ranch, but in fact they weren't. By December 1972, Apollo was scrubbed. Finished. Moth balled. The purse strings needed to fund the great lunar adventure had been cinched shut by President Nixon, and when this happened some of his students said things like, "Good. Waste of money." One young woman got very annoyed and said, "We could've fed people in Chicago for *years* on that kind of dough." Another one added, "Think of what we could do for schools."

When Eli heard all of this, he told his students that during the same period of time that Apollo operated, more money was spent by Americans on soft drinks. "Apollo gave us new technology," he said. "Computers are already better and faster because of it. Apollo helped us dream, and now that it's over we won't return to the moon for years. Maybe decades. Your children will wonder why we stopped going."

At night, when he graded papers and drank raspberry ice tea, such things frustrated him. To think that we knew everything worth knowing about the moon just because twelve men had bounced upon its surface made him shake his head. It was preposterous. It was stupid and arrogant. The moon is a quarter of the size of the earth, it is a vast desert pocked by immense craters, and to think we know enough about it simply because boot prints have been placed onto it? Eli shook his head. A lead weight filled up his chest whenever he thought about the machinery of Apollo being pulled down. What had once been the future was dismantled.

Of course, there was also what happened after the flame trench. That too was a type of dismantling.

Keith Doyle, Mike Azzara, and Franklin Johnson took him into custody and they weren't gentle about it. They handcuffed him and threw him in the back of the jeep. One of them—Johnson?—punched him in the kidney. When they returned to the little windowless room, more suits showed up, as well as two burly soldiers with machine guns. Eli was chained to the table and peppered with questions about why he ran away and what the hell he was doing beneath Apollo 11.

"Are you nuts?" Azzara demanded. "Have you gone totally fucking nuts? What were you *thinking*?"

Video footage was studied and it was determined that he hadn't done anything more than just stand beneath the engines. The three cameras in the flame trench were behind special glass and they all showed his ghostly image looking up at the rocket. The black and white footage made everything seem otherworldly and, when they showed it to Eli, he couldn't help but think it looked like footage from World War II. It was decided that he hadn't done anything to the launch system or the vehicle (several engineers were brought in to confirm this) and the idea of scrubbing the mission for a minor security breach was out of the question. It was decided that Eli had simply lost his grip on reality and wandered into an area that he shouldn't have gone. A report was written up and marked CONFIDENTIAL.

"We're still go," it was decided.

He was handcuffed to the heavy table, his ankles were shackled, and he was kept in Room 2B as the countdown continued. He had to sit there while the rest of the world watched the T-minus clock tick down to ignition. Rumbling thunder swallowed the building, and he watched the ceiling tiles quiver overhead. A change in air pressure made the door shake, and when the crackle of the engines gave way to silence, he heard cheers in the hallway. He felt the corners of his mouth lift into a watery smile. Good, he thought. They had a smooth ride.

After two days of interrogation, it was determined that he wasn't a threat nor was he working with the Soviets. They labelled him "Psychologically Unfit" and terminated his service with NASA. Armed guards marched him to a car and, as he was driven away, he watched the towering edifice of the VAB sink behind him.

As he tried to figure out what to do next with his life, it occurred to him that he was unemployed while von Braun, Rudolph, Debus, Dornberger, and Strughold were all still getting a paycheck and receiving medals. He wanted to climb into a bottle of whiskey but, instead, he drove to Winter Park and talked to a counselor. He walked around a lake with Lina and they mapped out the future, together. He went back to doing jigsaw puzzles and tried to ignore the memories that clawed at the inside of his skull. Climbing out of the wreckage of Dora had been so much harder than he expected. But yet here he was. Sober and satisfied.

Ava stirred in his arms.

"All is well." He bounced her and used the words of his mother. "*Alles ist gut, mein schönes Kind.*"

Her eyes fluttered open—such deep blue, like the sea—and she nuzzled back to sleep.

Lina was down the hall in the laundry room. The rhythmic whirring and thumping of the dryer started. He looked out the window and watched a bicentennial flag on the neighbor's house flutter and flap. In a few weeks it would be the birthday of his new country. Two hundred years. Such a young nation.

He liked California because it was a place where history didn't seem to exist. It was a type of dream factory. Hollywood was a few hours away, so was Disneyland and William Randolph Hearst's fantasy palace of San Simeon. In California, reality was distorted and made better. The bad bits were buffed away and the goodness was brought to a higher shine. Just a few weeks ago, while he was at a local museum, he learned that the name "California" came from an imaginary island that was created by a sixteenth-century writer named Garcí Ordoñez de Montalvo.

"A land of sweet dreams," he whispered to his granddaughter.

He studied her face, and in a certain light, it had to be admitted that she looked a little bit like her great-grandmother. She had the same eyes and nose. It was strange seeing the architecture of a face that had been murdered long ago. His mother, yes, he nodded, she would have loved her. She would have spoiled her rotten. She would have carried Ava around the garden, kissing her forehead and whispering goodness in German.

"*Alles ist gut, mein schönes Kind,*" he hushed, imagining his mother saying it.

Ava rested on the tattoo that had been stitched into his skin at Auschwitz. Although she covered up the blue ink of the numbers, it was still there. *142757.* When she was older, she might ask questions about it and, if she did, he would explain how her family had been taken from their flat, how they had been separated in the camp, how they were sent up the chimney, and how he had been sent to Dora. He would tell her how hard it was to climb out of the tunnels and into the brightness of a new life. He would tell her there was no moving beyond what had been done to him. The Holocaust was an open wound that he had to live with for the rest of his life. It was like chronic pain. It was never going away, and it would never heal.

People sometimes asked Eli what he had learned from the Holocaust, and whenever this happened, he stared at them uncomprehendingly. The question made no sense. There is no lesson, he wanted to say. There is only a void, and the lost lives that had been shoved into that void. To look for a lesson was to look for a candle in the night when, really, it was the overwhelming darkness that needed to be viewed. A lesson? A moral? From the Holocaust? Such thoughts made him dizzy. There was only a tunnel and a ravine full of human ash. His survival did not mean there was a happy ending. And, as he looked down upon his granddaughter, he wondered how he could possibly explain such things to her.

When Lina came down the hallway he watched her move into the kitchen.

She was slender, her hair was pulled back into a messy ponytail, and she padded on bare feet. In that moment he so badly wanted to take her to Clärchens Ballhaus—did that place still exist? Had it been bombed out? Maybe they could take dancing lessons somewhere in California? Yes, it wasn't too late. He would ask for her hand and show her why his friends once called him Fish Bones.

A squeaky cupboard opened, the gas stove clicked on, and a kettle was filled with rumbling water. He sat there, listening to the ordinary music of the world. Several minutes later the floor creaked as Lina walked towards him with a baby bottle. She flicked milk onto her wrist and rested it on a wooden table. She pointed to the bottle and whispered, "When she's awake."

He thought about Orpheus and Eurydice, and about how one couldn't look upon the other as they left the underworld for the world of the living. He looked at his wife, really looked at her, and when she smiled, wrinkles pinched the corners of her eyes. She tucked wispy blonde-grey hair behind an ear and played with a gold earring that was shaped like a butterfly. She spun it around and around. Her eyes were warm chips of green and Eli remembered the first time he saw her back in 1946. She was even more beautiful to him now.

When she spoke, her New York accent was still there.

"There's an eclipse tomorrow afternoon." She pointed at her wrist even though there wasn't a watch. "Let's drive someplace peaceful and see it."

Eli nodded and gave a thumbs-up with his free hand.

She glanced out the bay window and said, "How strange to think the moon will cover us in darkness soon."

He thought about Nazis parading through Berlin and swastika banners dripping like blood down buildings. Darkness fell so quickly across Europe when he was a child. And to think some people in America didn't believe the Holocaust had happened. There were also some people who didn't think we had landed on the moon. As far as these people were concerned, both events were hoaxes—the Holocaust—Apollo—they were both designed to hoodwink, to deceive, to create false realities that hadn't existed. Eli had no idea what to say to people who believed such things. This much he knew: the greatest crime of the twentieth-century was directly linked to its greatest achievement, and he had seen both. Rockets rolled out of the tunnels of Dora and moved onto the launch pads of the Kennedy Space Center. We are capable of doing such awful things to each other, he thought, and yet we can accomplish so very much when we work *with* each other. He had witnessed the worst and best of what it means to be human. To some people, the Holocaust and walking on the moon both seem impossible. It was easier to trust that human beings are not capable of such raw evil and such brave ingenuity. These people use the word "hoax". They create elaborate reasons to undermine reality. It is no accident that some people want to believe that the two most profound events of the twentieth-century never happened. But they did happen. They both happened.

He concentrated on the air moving in and out of the fleshy bellows of his lungs. He was alive. He was here. He was holding his grandchild. Breathe in. Breathe out. Feel her weight.

There was at least one thing he had learned over the decades, he thought with a nod. The sun rises every second on the great big spinning Earth. All you needed to do was imagine it coming up. Sunrise was as perpetual as sunset. Both were constant. It was just a matter of where you stood and where you looked.

Lina kissed his cheek. He hadn't shaved for a few days and he knew his stubble would be rough on her lips. She moved for his ear and gave it a nibble. When she spoke, her breath was a warm whisper. "Where should we watch this eclipse?"

"A state park?" His voice was louder than he expected, and this startled Ava. He tried jiggling her back to sleep.

Lina reached for the baby bottle. "Let's bring a picnic."

As Ava opened her mouth to cry, he thought about the ghostly gravity that ruled space. Soon, one heavenly body would block the view of another. The sun and moon would hang together, affecting what life looked like on earth below. An eclipse, he thought. Shadow and sunlight. What remained of Dora was in shadow now. At this very moment, rusting parts of V-2s were hiding in the tunnels. Nothing was left but waste and ruin and twisted metal. Also at this very moment, in the Sea of Tranquility, there were undisturbed boot prints on the surface of the moon. They were up there, dusty, powdery, and bathed in permanent sunlight. In a few years, the American flag that had been planted on the moon would be bleached white from the never-ending glare of the sun.

"So it's a plan?" Lina asked stroking his un-tattooed forearm. "We'll see the eclipse? You can make some sandwiches and I'll bring some raspberry ice tea."

He looked at her and nodded. His whole life and been shadow and sunlight, the poles of the human condition, and no matter what anyone else said or believed, he had seen it all, the bodies dropping and the rockets rising. He knew the truth, and he would tell about it.

His granddaughter stirred. Her mouth opened in a yawn and she made a noise that was not loud. She woke up, softly, and looked into his clear eyes.

"Hello little one," he said, kissing her forehead. "Welcome."

AUTHOR'S NOTE

AFTER I FINISHED WRITING *The Commandant of Lubizec*, which is also about the Holocaust, I needed to turn away from the industrialized genocide that swallowed up Europe and focus on something life affirming. I've always been fascinated by America's space program so I found myself reading more books about the Mercury, Gemini, and Apollo missions. As I did more research, it slowly occurred to me that the two most defining events of the twentieth-century— the Holocaust and the moon shot—aren't entirely without their connections. And as I started to think more seriously about the V-2, something flared in my imagination, and the narrative for this novel was ignited. I could see Eli in the tunnels and I could see him working at the Kennedy Space Center. To be sure, these are two very different places, but many prominent personalities from the Third Reich were in charge of both. Although we may not want to acknowledge it, the men who were responsible for the V-2 were also responsible for the Saturn V. Technology, like everything else, has a buried history.

I'm therefore indebted to the following books because they helped me to understand Dora-Mittelbau and NASA all the better: Gretchen Schafft and Gerhard Zeidler's *Commemorating Hell: The Public Memory of Mittelbau-Dora*, Annie Jacobsen's *Operation Paperclip*, Eric Lichtblau's *The Nazis Next Door*, Wayne Biddle's *Dark Side of the Moon*, Michael J. Neufeld's *Von Braun: Dreamer of Space, Engineer of War*, and Jonathan H. Ward's *Rocket Ranch*. I am particularly grateful to André Sellier for his detailed and emotionally powerful book, *A History of the Dora Camp*. Not only does Dr. Sellier offer a precise historical account of what happened at Dora, but he was a survivor of the camp—an eyewitness.

The scenes involving Eli are of course fictitious but the scientists mentioned in the narrative really did have a direct hand in the development of the V-2, as well as its deadly production at Dora-Mittelbau. Many of these men went on to hold high ranking positions with NASA, the Marshall Space Flight Center, and the United States Air Force. In an effort to help the reader understand what some of these men did after the war, what follows is a list of some of the more prominent personalities that shaped America's space program. Walter Dornberger was originally captured by the British and, while preparations were underway to try him for his role in the V-2 attacks on London, he was sent to America via Operation Paperclip. He went on to work for the Air Force where he developed guided missiles and high-performance aircraft. In fact, his expertise helped create some of the early designs for the Space Shuttle. He retired to Germany and died in 1980. Arthur Rudolf, who was the operations director at Mittelwerk and oversaw concentration camp labor, later became known as "Mr. Saturn" for his production of that mighty rocket. He retired in 1968 and was later questioned by the U.S. Department of Justice for his role at Dora. In order to avoid deportation hearings, he reluctantly agreed to return to Germany if he was allowed to keep his pension. This wish was granted under the provision that he give up his American citizenship. He died in Hamburg in 1996. Wernher von Braun continues to be a polarizing figure for both his genius in creating weapons of mass murder and also for creating rockets that carried lives into space. He was head of the Dora-Mittelbau Planning Office and a member of the SS. As the war came to an end, he gathered up his specialists, negotiated with the Americans, and settled in the United States where he would eventually take charge of the Marshall Space Flight Center in Huntsville, Alabama. He was the architect of the Saturn V and remained an enthusiastic spokesperson of space exploration long after his retirement. He died in 1977, in Virginia, and remains the most celebrated rocket scientist of all time. Rusted out parts of his V-2s are still in the tunnels of Dora-Mittelbau and an entire Saturn V is on pristine display at the Kennedy Space Center. He is responsible for both.

The guards mentioned in this novel were a genuine terror to prisoners. Erwin "Horse Head" Busta was feared the most. He escaped punishment and died at home, in Germany, in 1982. Other guards and kapos at Dora were given either light prison sentences or they were acquitted. Most of them were not put on trial and they returned home to begin new lives. Otto Förschner and Hans Möser were not as lucky as their colleagues—they were both hanged in 1946 and 1948, respectively.

I want to offer my thanks to the staff at Dora-Mittelbau who were helpful beyond measure. It was a powerful experience to walk around the ruined camp and I'm grateful to have gotten into the tunnels on several occasions. Inside, they are dark, cold, and littered with rusty debris. Although the water table has risen and flooded several areas, it's still possible to see painted numbers on the tunnel walls. Several desks, smashed toilets, and engine nozzles can be seen in the cone of a flashlight.

I'd also like to thank the staff at the Kennedy Space Center, the Marshall Space Flight Center, and the Johnson Space Center for helping me to understand Apollo all the better. For someone like me who is fascinated with space exploration, it was astounding to stand where history took place. I'm also deeply grateful to the following institutions for funding my research: the Loft Literary Center, the Madeline Island School for the Arts, two ARAF grants, and the South Dakota Arts Council. Without their help, this book would not exist. They gave me time to write, time to think, and time to travel. You are holding this book because of people who believe in the arts.

And lastly, I'm grateful to those who offered advice, encouragement, wisdom, forward momentum, and friendship. Writing a book may seem like a solo act, but it never is. If you're very lucky, good people are behind the scenes helping you out. This includes the English & Journalism Department at Augustana University, Lynne Hicks, Jim Hicks, Sean Hicks, Sheila Risacher, Erin Crowder, Jayson Funke, Stephen Gais, Nick Hayes, Will Swart, David O'Hara, Murray Haar, Margaret Preston, Jeff Johnson, Steven Wingate, Christine Stewart, Jim Reese, Maria Mazziotti Gillan, Jon Lauck, David McMahon, Brian Turner, Tim O'Brien, Larry Heinemann, Lori Walsh, Andrew Erickson, Nicola Sadie, Jim Fairhall, Jessie Lendennie, Kendra Wickre, Jennifer Widman, Sherry DeBoer, and everyone at the South Dakota Humanities Council. Thanks, my friends, for your support and cheerleading. I'm also deeply grateful to Andria Williams, Max Cea, Eryn Loeb, and Neel Dhanesha for offering editorial advice and for publishing earlier versions of this novel in *The Wrath-Bearing Tree* and *Guernica*. My ongoing thanks to these forces of light: CSB/SJU and AU. I also want to thank Neil Peart—you are missed by so many.

You wouldn't be holding this book if it weren't for Kimberly Verhines and Sara Henning at Stephen F. Austin State University Press. Thank you, Kim, for your editorial feedback, your steady hand in mission control, and for taking a chance on this story. You're a lucky author indeed when a book you've labored on for years finds the right home.

And lastly, I offer thanks to my amazing, lovely, patient, whip smart, and endlessly supportive wife, Tania. When I had doubts about this book, you never did. Not once.

PATRICK HICKS is the author of *The Collector of Names*, *Adoptable*, and *This London*—he also wrote the critically and popularly acclaimed novel, *The Commandant of Lubizec*. He has been published widely in some of the most vital literary journals in North America and his poetry has appeared on NPR, *The PBS NewsHour*, and *American Life in Poetry*. He has been a finalist for an Emmy and he has received grants and fellowships from the Bush Artist Foundation, the Loft Literary Center, and the National Endowment for the Humanities, among others. A dual-citizen of Ireland and America, he is the Writer-in-Residence at Augustana University as well as a faculty member at the MFA program at Sierra Nevada University. When not writing and teaching, he is the host of the radio show, *Poetry from Studio 47*.

CPSIA information can be obtained
at www.ICGtesting.com
Printed in the USA
LVHW022351160920
666238LV00002B/2